Alberto Bevilacqua

CALIFFA

Translated from the italian by
Harvey Fergusson II

GREMESE

Original title:
La Califfa
Copyright © 2001 by Alberto Bevilacqua

Cover:
apostoli & maggi

On cover:
Romy Schneider in a scene from the film *Califfa*

Photocomposition:
Graphic Art 6 s.r.l. – Rome

Printed and bound by:
La Moderna – Rome

Copyright GREMESE
2001 © E.G.E. s.r.l. – Rome

ISBN 88-7301-436-4

PART I

CHAPTER ONE

It doesn't take them long to call you a whore, a woman from the gutter. They brand you, then they turn their backs. In other words, you can't live it down, because who has the honesty to go the bottom of anything in this thieving country where people hide their own sins like smuggled goods, just so they can point their finger at what other people are doing? This is the only Christian charity or brotherly love I've ever seen...

But I've never been one of those who put up a good front and do what they like in the dark. My name is Irene Corsini and they call me Califfa. What shows on my face is what's inside me, and to hell with the rest!

And so anybody I met in those days couldn't even stand to look at me, because he could see all my troubles right there.

"Califfa," I was saying to myself, "things can't get any worse unless you go to jail or die." But just think what I still had to go through!

I was thinking of that baby who had died only a few months before, and that husband who'd been kicked around so much – and I was avoiding even people who might have comforted me. "Califfa, where're you going? You're always on the go like a tramp!" Viola was yelling at me. She lived at the edge of town then, where the open flat fields began. She shook her big red head as soon as she saw me walking up the path in a sweat and hurrying as if someone was expecting me.

But there wasn't anyone waiting for me and I wasn't really going anywhere. I was just wandering around under all that sky over the countryside, which was red with poppies.

"Go on home," she yelled at me. "Things are tough all over anyway!"

But I didn't. I shrugged my shoulders at her and didn't even turn around. I thought the only place I could breathe was out there where there were lots of cicadas and trees and there wasn't another soul. I just sat on the ground looking up at the sky like I was crazy.

I was like the cats are when they have to do it: they don't like it if someone is watching them. At least there in the grass I could let myself go a little and cry, couldn't I? What would I have done at my house? That bureau, those beat-up chairs and that bed with no legs propped up on bricks – if I put my head on the pillow, I could think I could still smell that baby who died there.

And on the table there was half a glass of wine and just enough bread to keep us from dying for another day. It would have been better to end it all right away.

"Califfa! Califfa!" called Viola, looking for me in the fields. I just sat there without saying a word and watched the sun go down: silent and stiff like some evil apparition.

But they say that good luck is like good weather: it can't help but come. And so, in our neighborhood, posters and rumors began saying that we'd all be working. Farinacci's, a factory from the new part of town, was going to open a branch by us in the old neighborhood. Anyone who lives there is accused of communism even though it's not true, because that's always been a red neighborhood. And with this excuse they often forget that you have two hands and a brain. And for that reason I always say: when wrong ideas are convenient, no one dares to change them.

But not now. Now they seem to have become saints. They go around with halos on their heads and they swear there won't be any more political favoritism and that we'll be considered like the rest, starting with Farinacci, who was about to launch a new product and needed strong arms, no matter what political flags they may have waved.

And so I took hope and said to myself: if they'll take even you, Califfa, you'll earn some money and you'll feel better and maybe you'll even find peace. Oh God, if it was only true, for me and my people, who only want something real and worthwhile to work hard on!

II

"Am-more, am-more, am-more, am-more mio...," sang Califfa with joyous enthusiasm, pulling up the blinds with one fell swoop, as Farinacci's machines began their procession like so many tanks through those narrow streets where they could hardly pass, bouncing and clanking about on the loose pavement.

This farce had been dreamed up by Ubaldo Farinacci in agreement with the Mayor, since the local elections were barely a month away and something had to be done to shake up the subversive apathy of the old part of town.

"Everything is to be agreed upon," proposed Farinacci.

"And how?" asked the Mayor.

"One hand washes the other... You decide on certain confidential subsidies in favor of my company, and I'll promise to hire anyone who's important to you."

"Confidential, confidential," murmured the Mayor, not very convinced.

"There are some machines we need. You buy them for us and we'll expand the factory. It'll be worth the expense."

"And suppose they act up even when there's work for them?"

Farinacci smiled with pity. "Excuse me, but you're showing that you have the wrong idea of the people in 1960... It's simple; we'll start off with a fine procession!"

"A procession?" exclaimed the Mayor.

"Oh, not with Saints or Madonnas, but a procession in a Marxist sense!"

Every machine was shined and every machine had more tassels on it than a prize dog. Pulled by tractors, they passed through the wash on the line and the crowds of people who had jumped out of bed and run to the balconies. And every tractor carried a prominent citizen seated in majesty next to the driver, showing by his suspicious smile and the comradely wave of his hand that he distrusted the maneuver in which he had become involved.

There was also Ubaldo Farinacci like a little emperor with his shiny bald pate under which a snub nose and two beady eyes were deformed by a smile of benevolent triumph (but Califfa, from above, could see only the shining ball turning to the left and the right among the flapping of the flags), and Martinolli, the Auxiliary Bishop, on the following tractor, with his fingers unfurled in blessing.

Farinacci had been explicit with him too: "They're straight out of the sewer. They're thieves and murderers, but they have the psychology of children, that's the point, do you understand, Reverend? That's where their poetry is, but that's also their fatal inexcusable weakness. They can be played upon with some trinket as long as it shines, Reverend, as long as it shines! You'll see how effective it is."

And, unfortunately, there was an effect. "Made in Germany," the new machines of Farinacci's company, spreading the stupid thing which hope is, had heated the blood of that swarm and given it the will to live. And while the mysterious iron forms were clamoring over the bridge, under eyes at first doubtful and then smiling, swaying over crowded embankments as if hanging in the air to show how shiny their shapes were, Gianvito Alibrandi leaned over his balcony, shouting, "Hurrah for dieting! I told you so myself! "

Mazza, who was called "Justice and Liberty" since he had belonged to that Resistance group, was also trying to see out of his crooked window. He raised his head and said: "But what did you say?"

And Alibrandi: "They're trying to take advantage of the great truth that people with money eat too much."

"It's a truth lots of people have taken advantage of, Vito!" Mazza said to him.

"They'll produce a dietetic product... di-e-te-tic," Alibrandi scanned. "That should mean that the rich will eat a kind of pap which is the same thing as salami, chicken, soup first, then a second course, and fruit!"

Mazza twisted his mouth: "Salami, chicken… it's the usual stuff. And that's just the kind of work for us, hungry as we are."

But Alibrandi didn't care about telling Mazza what a dietetic product was. And if he was standing there in his undershirt, leaning against the window of his balcony, with that smile, and with his skin shining in the sun, it was because Califfa, her elbows on the windowsill, was letting her bathrobe slip toward her naked breasts.

Ah, Gianvito! As the flags and the shouts faded away by the trees on the main road, Califfa turned back from the window and closed it, stopping a minute to look out with a smile. Then she turned her back on him in an impudent way. But she felt like singing again.

Alibrandi was always there, lying in wait on his balcony to spy on her, to seek her out in the shadowy secret of her bedroom as far as the dirty glass of the window or the slats of the shutters would allow, to seize upon every bit of her wretched life, as she undressed around the bitter exile of that bed.

III

Irene Corsini was chosen and went to work. She got up at six in the morning with her head so full of sleep that she hardly knew she was walking as she proceeded across the bridge, let alone that she was hurrying so as not to be late.

She really woke up only when the time clock punched her card with a great noise of the bell – the bell which livened her blood – and she found the plastic safety hat on her head, which the foreman put resolutely in place.

The hours of work were long and severe, but this was what the job did for Califfa:

…Many of us had found work. One of the few who were too stubborn to take up the offer was Guido, my husband. He had even refused to discuss working at Farinacci's. He said Farinacci's was a bunch of robbers, and he had been very bitter when the people from City Hall came to see him, not

11

imagining that they would find him in bed at noon, dead to the world with sleep.

"You don't wake a man up even to tell him he's been elected Pope!" he shouted, sitting on the edge of the bed, while they stopped in the middle of the stairway which led to the bedroom from the kitchen, with their heads coming out of the trapdoor, frightened and amazed. "And certainly not to offer him a handout!" and he swore at them all the more because they'd waked him up.

Imagine those pious faces! They disappeared under the trapdoor as if they'd breathed a breath of hell, and Guido was still shouting: "Mr. Guido Corsini has his dignity and knows how to look for work by himself if he wants! He doesn't need churchmice, get it? And he never takes a handout from anyone!"

Just think: dignity. Drinking all night and staying in bed all day – that was what he called dignity. So I was the only one to go to work. But I managed to earn enough money.

The factory was awful; it was hot as hell, because the mouths of the ovens were up there by the ceiling. And the sweat ran so much under our aprons that at the end of the day they were like another skin on us, not cloth, and we had to tear them off our backs.

But at work the hours went by fast, watching the little bags go by on the moving belt, on their way from our hands to the sales we needed. And we would laugh because hope, when there's an epidemic of it, stirs up the stupid joys of childhood. What we laughed at the most was Ubaldo Farinacci, the owner. Referring to an old saying of ours, many of us said that he had his underwear on backward – which meant that he couldn't stand women, that he couldn't even bear to look at them, since he was distracted by certain things in this line which I frankly never could understand.

"Ubaldo, you've been a little boy long enough; it's time you got married," his parents would say to him. "Get married, because you're the last of the Farinaccis and if you don't have any sons, watch out, because our cousins will take the company away from us! That's what the will says. And every year that passes without your getting married makes them all the happier!"

And he answered that yes, yes, he'd try, and even with all the good will he was capable of. He let them choose a wife for him and then, after he'd used up all his excuses, when it came time for the engagement party with all the guests invited, a cold buffet, and a ring with a big diamond, he suddenly remembered he had to catch a train. So he packed his bags for a change of air. And he wasn't just kidding. No: he really took off. And they had to come get him and haul him back to the office from his strange vacation and begin all over again.

And so the time went by, until the moving belt stopped in front of our eyes and the electric wheel stopped humming and we crossed the yard of the factory toward the locker rooms, lined up like a group of nuns.

When the shift was over, Vito Alibrandi was waiting for me at the gate with his motorcycle. He worked at Farinacci's too, in the shipping department. I pretended not to see him and started to walk away. But he kept singing his usual song: "Why not get on? You'll save yourself all that walking."

He had eyes of such a pretty color, and his face was so handsome that my heart sang to see him. But that wasn't why I got on. One night after work I was so tired that I said to myself: "Yeah, why not get on?" But if I'd known that they'd start talking about me then, and that I'd get into all that trouble afterward... But let's not go into that now.

I would go home and get on my knees to pray to Saint Anthony, with the light burning under his image, the way it had ever since my son died. "Pretty little one," I was praying, "it would be so good if the gentlemen could eat less, so we could eat more; and if they could have just a little trouble, not too much, just a little pain in the tummy, since our product is for little pains in the tummy..."

And there I was, with my head in my hands, and I thought someone was by me keeping me company. A feeling of happiness went through me: "Pretty little one, please..." and I would send him a kiss.

Those were days when I no more wanted to act like a whore than I wanted to kill someone, because when I'm happy I don't do anything wrong, let's get that straight. But there was only a month of that happiness and then another bombshell. And it was all because of the bellies of the gentlemen, which I just can't stand to look at now, for some reason or other.

IV

Ubaldo Farinacci's dietetic product, which was created for both commercial and political reasons, was not a success. The various stomachs involved continued to be filled with various kinds of salami. And after the elections, the financial assistance was of course no longer forthcoming.

Knowing that something was up, Califfa and her friends did not laugh any more. With lumps in their throats, they put the pap in the cellophane envelopes without raising their eyes from their workbenches. The lights of their tenements, of the seedy rooms into which life had come in those last few days and where the sad comedy they had learned in too many years would soon return, all passed through their minds in an instant. They would laugh on the outside and cry on the inside, so as not to give any satisfaction to their cruel fate.

"What an idea, to think people could eat less in Italy," murmured Califfa, putting her work clothes in the laundry basket. "Dopes!"

They began by sending the women home first. One morning Califfa found the main gate of the Farinacci factory closed in her face. The others were crowded together below, beating their heads on the iron plate, but, finally worn out by humiliation, they went back with bent heads to the poor slums they had come from.

But not Califfa. With her hands on her hips, she began screaming in an outburst of rebellion: "Bring out Farinacci, you dirty pigs! I'll spit in his face! I'm not afraid of him, or any of his goons!"

"Califfa! Califfa!" they were shouting at her. "What are you yelling about? It's no use! They've got us all by the short hairs!"

But Califfa did not pay any attention to them. She stood there like a Swiss Guard, alone in the square in front of the factory while the others stood quietly outside.

"Come on out, Ubaldo Farinacci! Come on out and talk to me!"

But it wasn't Farinacci who came out the gate. The policeman on duty came instead. He went up to Califfa as if his ugly face and his hand on his Sam Browne belt were enough to calm her down. They looked each other over, but she was not at all intimidated. She pushed back her hair in a challenging way as if she didn't give a damn, the way she always did when she felt like protesting.

"Go on home! That's enough now!"

Nothing happened. Califfa, with a poisonous little smile, cocked her head to look at him from another angle: "You'd be cute if you weren't a cop!"

The rest of the women were beginning to get restless and the policeman stopped for a moment undecided, because there was quite a crowd of them and Califfa's performance was drawing them closer to the factory. There was an instant when the women were about to rush him, to rediscover a violence which was tempered less by fear than by the certainty that everything was useless. But the policeman seized Califfa by one arm in time and dragged her toward the gate. She fell to her knees and hung on to his uniform by sheer force.

They began to fight and Califfa rolled on the ground, bit, kicked, tore her red skirt on the stones, and bumped her head, while other policemen came from inside.

And Califfa wound up in jail.

She was there for a day and when she came out the sun was setting over the houses of the city. The bells on the Apennine hills were chiming among the fading shadows of the woods, under the new moon, and the sun had already faded from the walls. All that was left was that heat of the dog days where Califfa, keeping close to the wall like a thief, was walking sadly along with downcast eyes.

She walked out of the city. And her cry burned like embers on a fire. "Califfa, why don't you end it all? Why don't you kill yourself, Califfa? It'd be better for everybody!" And as she walked up the hill, her breath stabbed her like a knife.

Viola was always there, lolling around the house, with her children sitting around her, mute, pale, and thin as shadows, worse off even than Califfa was. They didn't even look at each other, those two women. They were fond of each other because they did not need words for understanding. They treasured their friendship and they were afraid that a word or a gesture could hurt it.

Califfa walked through a poppy field and some grass, went up the little road where the lights had been lit in the red of early evening, and only when her fingers were pressed on the rusty gate did she realize where her desperation had taken her.

The white wall along the trees and the silence made Califfa afraid to push the gate open and go in. She leaned her forehead on the bars; perhaps it was the wind, and perhaps it was the knowledge that her son's gravestone was the one she could see in the corner by the pine tree, which gave her a little peace.

Then she realized that someone had come and was looking over her shoulder.

V

"I see you there in back of me, Alibrandi, with a face like a saint in church."

"You know," he said, "it's because I love you. Let's face it, you probably don't know what love is, what with that husband of yours who doesn't even look at you. I'm sorry for you. Believe me, Califfa, I'm not just saying this to take advantage of you, that would be blasphemy. I swear to you in the name of that poor kid over there!"

16

And so I cried on his shoulder and he took me in his arms and stroked my hair and said to me: "I was behind you on the road all the way and I just about went crazy looking at you…"

And I could feel him shaking with desire. If I'd acted like a dog the way the others did, he would have taken me right away and that would have been that. But he stayed there by the tree with his eyes looking up, not looking at me, so he wouldn't lose control. And he was talking to me tenderly, not like a lover, but a brother.

His eyes and his mouth gave me a feeling no one had ever given me before. I fell down, holding his knees and then on the grass, and then I told him between my teeth, yes, yes, because I didn't want to think any more, because I liked it, and because there was no one else beside me, just him.

But he was so nice, so good-looking, I swear it, that if what I did that night was wrong, then even the saints are wrong. And as long as it lasted, it wasn't like the other times.

When we went away, the whole countryside was dark and my head was light and empty, as if I were way up in the air, among the galloping clouds, and my eyes were shining.

He was singing as he drove his motorcycle through the dust, drunk with happiness. And I didn't care that they could all see me holding on to him, since that meant spitting in the face of my dirty life, and at the people around me, at the misery we were coming back to, at my neighborhood, at my little street, and at my building.

Alibrandi stopped in front of it. He was puffed up with satisfaction and youth. Lucky him. But I ran off without saying good night and put my hand on the door, and when I did death came back.

And that was how I went wrong the first time.

17

CHAPTER TWO

What fun those years were, and how they wanted to live! She was crazy, or maybe they both were, not to have enjoyed it enough, whenever they could, without thoughts, without fears or obligations. Then at least, when they looked back on them later, they could have said that they'd had their fun like other people, and not that they were happy for all too short a time.

But they didn't think of tomorrow, or of trying to build something with their own hands, something for the children which were to come, relying on honesty and youth. What madness it was! If only he hadn't beaten his head against a blank wall later and ruined everything by giving up so easily.

Because that husband of Califfa's, who later became a wreck of a man who didn't amount to anything, felt young and secure to her then, and was so warm with hope that he announced it to everyone from morning to night.

He was the one who got up first and threw off the covers. The day would begin with his happy voice calling her:

"Get up, Califfa. If we get there first, it'll be all the better for us!"

They would leave the house when the sun was barely over the hills, giddy with too little sleep, with having enjoyed each other at night with the violence of those who don't expect anything more and haven't the courage to say so. And every day it was the same *via crucis*: shop after shop, street after street, offering themselves.

"We have two arms and we want to work! Isn't that enough?"

Califfa's tongue was bitter in her mouth, and her belly was cold. The only place there was any fire was in her womb. But when he held her by the arm on the bridge and showed her the houses of the new city beyond the river's dirty waters – white, clean houses in the first light of the day – then her head felt a bit of warmth, and the serene sky and the light plain under the paling stars conquered her eyes again.

He was saying: "We'll go live up there, you'll see. One day we'll be able to manage," and walking along in front of her with his hands in his pockets, he added: "And we'll take our children up in elevators, and each one will have a room of his own, and there'll always be enough to eat."

Those were days to remember, Califfa was thinking, when it took so little to change hope into contentment and contentment into desire, so that they kissed there, under the eyes of the police, who were snoozing by the corner of the bridge, closed up in their little sentry boxes like angels in church.

Then they went to walk the streets. But she kept behind him for a little while longer, looking at him some more, from the corner of the last house, that border of clean apartment buildings with flowers and curtains on the balconies.

She was figuring out the future, as he would say, or better, she was trying to because she couldn't originate anything in her mind, and she couldn't really imagine what life up there would be like, beyond that river which was like a frontier dividing the factories from the shops, the apartment houses from the tenements, and the sun from the dark little streets from which he was calling her:

"Califfa, Califfa…"

She ran up to him on the stones. And that uninhibited sound of her heels on the stones and that repeated call "Califfa!" "Guido!" woke up the neighborhood even before the shutters came down and before the factories on the other side of the river blew their whistles.

II

…But one day I found her there. That old woman with a face like death warmed over was right in front of me. She was

19

pale and her eyes were swollen. Around her neck and head she had a black veil. She didn't want to say what she'd come for. I said sit down, but she wouldn't. She leaned on the mantelpiece and looked like a funeral. With what I know now, I could have told anyone what she wanted, because you never know where you get ideas like that, since those people are all worse than you are, but then, when I was much younger…

I squinted at her and moved about; she looked at my girlish things with a smile on her hairy mouth.

At times, it looked as if she were grinning, as if she had something up her sleeve, as if she were studying the house to impress it on her mind.

She had asked if I was Corsini's wife. I said yes. She said:

"Well, it's your husband I'm looking for."

I could tell there was something wrong and I wasn't very nice to her. "Before he gets back, it'll be —"

But she was hard. "I don't care. There's plenty of time before we're all dead."

I puttered about the kitchen, I walked around her, I pretended to straighten things up, but I was scared. Now as I say, if it'd been today that she'd come, I would have thrown her down the stairs. But then what good would that have done? Because sooner or later… In other words, I tried to make it look as if I didn't see that old girl leaning against the mantelpiece, who looked like she belonged in a coffin, even though I could hardly keep my eyes off her, dressed as she was in black stockings and black veil. I could hardly look any place else.

She talked in fits and starts and she made me shiver whether she was talking or not.

She said: "I came from Udine and spent the whole night on the train!"

I asked myself what she could want with my husband.

"But are you sure? Guido Corsini?"

"I'm sure!"

Then she took out a picture and showed it to me. There were two nice-looking boys in uniform with blond hair and blue eyes.

"Two brothers!" she said with her hard voice. "My sons! Both of them!"

"They're good-looking boys," I said, puttering around in the kitchen.

"They were Fascists," said the woman, and she stared at me to see how I'd react. "Fascists!" she repeated. "And they killed them just for that! They murdered them! They were just nineteen and twenty and they lined them up against the wall, just because somebody made them wear a uniform!"

She came closer to me. Her eyes had tears in them, but she wasn't exactly crying, and her breath had an awful smell.

"All the way from Udine," she repeated, "just for this." But Guido whistled from the staircase. I felt so strange when he came in that I went off to one side as if I didn't belong there.

So it was just the two of them to size each other up. And the old woman was paler and more nervous. It looked as if her eyes had shrunk and were almost swallowed up by the watery sockets. And she took out that picture again, showing it to him as if it were a sentence against him.

For a minute Guido studied those faces, those blond heads of hair and those blue eyes, and the insignia on the uniforms.

"They were both my sons. I brought them up, day by day… Do you know them?"

My husband hesitated and I didn't 't understand. He looked at me and then he looked at the old woman and his words choked in his throat. He didn't know what to do and I couldn't figure out what was happening. So it was she, the bitch, who practically jumped on him:

"I came for you, to spit in your face, you murderer!"

When he finally shook her off, he looked old, tired, and humiliated, with the spit dripping from his nose onto his mouth. He, my man, my Guido, who couldn't even wipe it off his face.

The old woman looked at me for the last time and went away. And I was so mad I wanted to run after her, throw open the window and scream at her while she went down the stairs. God, I was mad…

So the first stone had been cast, and it's easy to throw

stones at a man who just wasn't born to defend himself, no matter whether he's innocent or guilty; it's easy to tell him that it was a partisan action, to accuse him of taking advantage of the situation to settle his own accounts, going as far as crimes, including cruelly killing the innocent.

Two months later there was the trial. Guido, with his head down, was there with some of his friends in the midst of some policemen. And I still didn't know whether he was a criminal or a victim. I didn't know if he was faking or if the others were. I hardly knew him when I went to see him during visiting hours. He was so humiliated and so thin. Holding his hands, I begged him on my knees to help me to understand, just to tell me whatever he'd done, because I would have forgiven him all the same.

But he hung his head and wouldn't answer me. I sat opposite him and I wanted to yell or to cry, but I held myself back so I wouldn't make it worse. I was his woman, the one he wanted next to him for all his life. But I felt he didn't trust me, that he was afraid of me the way he was afraid of the others.

And before he'd said a word to me, the guards took me away to the anteroom and I thought of him with his head down, on the stairs, not even turning around, leaving me like that without so much as a smile.

In the courtyard of the prison, Viola, who went with me, was looking up with me at the wall where some lights were to be seen behind the cell doors, and I asked:

"Which one's his, Viola? Which one's his? Where is he?" The lights looked as if they were way up in the sky, with the guards walking along the walls. And Viola was dragging me away without saying a word.

She was dragging me away, amid the people looking at us. And she kept staring at me, as if it were my fault.

"But when did you meet him?" people would ask me. "Didn't you know? How could you marry somebody without knowing who you were marrying?"

I said no, I hadn't known anything. But even if I had, I would have married him all the same, because all I look for

22

in a man is whether I like him or not and whether he looks honest.

But they all said to me: "He's a loser. If they gave him three years, he deserved it. You've been sleeping with a murderer! Because if you torture and shoot some poor boys on account of the color of their shirt, just for the fun of shooting, it means you're a murderer with blood on your hands, even if you are a partisan."

I slammed the door in their faces, those bitches. They'll always need someone to crucify and the stupider he looked the better it was. But when, later, he passed by in handcuffs he said to me: "Forgive me… It had to happen now, Califfa, just when things were beginning to get better!" And then he cried like a weakling, as if he were my son and not my man.

And I needed so much for him to be strong! "Yes, I forgive you," I called after him, "but you don't need that, Guido!"

When I tried to run after him, desperate as I was, before he disappeared at the end of the corridor behind the grate, I understood for the first time how good it was to shout "Son of a bitch!" at a cop when he put his hands on me. They slapped me till I was quiet, and sent me home.

And I thought that for three years – just when that creature was beginning to grow inside me – I'd have to go looking for work, saying, "Here I am, take pity on me, not because I know how to work too, but just take pity on me!"

And three years went by. When Guido came out he was a different man. Keep on hoping in a man, even if he's made a mistake. After all, who hasn't made at least one mistake in life? And then when you see him again face to face, when he comes back home to that house you've been keeping up by taking years off your life, he looks at you as if you'd done wrong to wait for him; because, according to him, you should have let him die in his gutter.

He doesn't smile at you, and barely says hello. He looks at his son as if he were someone else's. And you understand right away that he has so much hatred he wants to spit out, but so much weakness to fall back into as well that you'd be better off just letting him go, kicking him out of the house as well. But instead of kicking him out, you're stupid like all the other women. You pet him and take him to bed:

"Just like it was before, Guido, just like before…"

And he thanks you for it by living off you, picking fights with you and your son and throwing away the money you give him for some decent clothes and some medicine for that cough which wakes you up at night, the one he caught in jail, that hurts you just to hear it.

And your son can't understand that that's his father you've described to him. And gradually you don't believe there're even any decent thoughts – never mind dignity – in that bum who hasn't shaved.

And having gotten that far, you don't love him any more and you can hardly stand him…

III

And then there was this Vito Alibrandi. He was strong and good-looking and he had a lock of hair combed down in front just to attract cheating wives and innocent girls, and he had shrewd eyes like a cat's. He knew how to use them with women, from the wrong side of the river or the better part of town, raising them in a wicked sort of way, or keeping them modestly down under his lock of hair, with the wicked humility of a bedroom casuist.

"Go on, Vito, show them!" they yelled at him from the stands. And Vito strode up and down the field in the savage way he had in bed. To hear people talk, you would think he was the only one who deserved to wear the uniform of the local soccer team.

"He'll end up in the big leagues. He can kick like Meazza, he can. I never saw anyone who can kick like that!"

And Vito took the ball and came forward with a smile, shaking his shoulders in an undecided but self-confident way, and moving as fast as lightning when he had to, or when it was least expected.

It was just the way he was when he came from the wall to

meet her, thought Califfa, during their clandestine meetings. He looked half dead with sleep; and then he would take her without giving her a chance to catch her breath or get free. And she would imagine the violence of his body, which she knew so well, while he knocked over his adversaries on the soccer field amid the shouting and cursing, savage and noble at the same time.

And when Vito disappeared into a pile-up, he was like a bull at the end of a bullfight, hitting the matador with the last blow of his horns. And the ball would slip into the net with a roar of exultation from the stands, which was as intoxicating as the sigh he sometimes extracted from her, who was waiting at the edge of the field to receive her part of his mocking and violent youth.

"That one'll end up in the national leagues! You can tell it a mile away, you can!"

"What do you mean, the national leagues? Maybe if he can last through to the finals... But with that head of his and his whoring around..."

No one paid any attention to her and no one knew who that girl was, hiding in a man's overcoat, who had sneaked in through a hole in the fence and who was shouting without restraint, trying to inspect the people assembled on the stands in a sea of handkerchiefs and newspapers, asking herself, "How many of us are there?"

But hers was the honor to ride first on Vito's new motorbike. A fine honor that was... She was waiting for him behind the pillars by the entrance to the stadium, leaning against the wall until the people had gone away, with their flags under their arms, and the noise of the motorcycles and automobiles invaded the square. The stands were empty except for the wastepaper blown about by the wind. And then Vito appeared with his bag in one hand and the other in his pocket, negligent and attentive at the same time, like a mistrustful beast.

"Get on..." and Califfa held on to him, overcome by that smell of healthy sweat, massage oil, and that odor of rotting hay, and she squeezed those shoulders warm with fatigue and applause.

An embrace which was not love, or, better, was a different passion – a dedication to her bitterness, a bitter and inebriated egoism, but an even greater fear of solitude; for which, pale, and with her hand hanging on to Vito's jacket, she let herself be taken to the escarpment by the railway, in the fog, where there was only the pale reflection of the shining rails.

And she was thinking: "That's enough. This is the last time! It has to be the last time!"

Then the darkness fell on their united heads, on her face which had no more lipstick, marked by the soaking grass; and the wind arose in that darkness, moving freely over the countryside among the tops of the trees. Her back was against the ground and she was watching the clouds in the dark, as if they were going to fall on her.

Or she was there, under Vito, just to keep warm. And if she was trembling, it was for the cold, not because she was happy making love. But it was right that Vito should be like that and that everything he did was a slap in the face for her, even when he wanted to be gentle. And sometimes he was, like that day when they had begun. She knew what Vito would say about women: "Women are like motors, you have to judge them by how they start. With women you have to get in gear right away, just one push and away! If you don't, you spoil everything."

And that was right too. Just as it was that she felt him leaving her – and she could barely see him in the fog. He was abandoning her, worn out on the makeshift bed of his jacket, like some animal from which he had taken the will to live, just a thing to be found the next day at the same place, in the clearing behind the pine trees.

Guido was gentle, at least afterward. But Vito wasn't. Califfa had to look for him in the fog and guess where his shadow was, bouncing dexterously along on its way to the street, while she groped along behind him and could have cried because there seemed to be no end to the escarpment.

"Vito! Is that any way to act? Vito!"

"Oh, be quiet! I'm here!"

"Vito! Wait a minute! I'm scared! There are thorns here!"

"Come on! It's late!" He took her by the hand and forced her to run along with him, because he had left his motorcycle on the road and could not wait any longer, that is, either he couldn't or some other slut couldn't, whoever she might be. He let her off at the first corner and the motorcycle went away, belching exhaust into her face. "Sorry! But I have to get going. And then I'm doing it for you too. They shouldn't see us together, at least on the street...because, for better or worse, Califfa, you've got a husband." He smiled as he warmed up the motor. "I'll be seeing you!"

She stood there for a while, thinking about Viola and what Viola had told her, trying to reason with her:

"But is that love? To be treated like that; to be degraded just to make up for what they've done to you?"

"But what do you understand about that?"

"Listen to me, Califfa, give him up. I know why you're doing it; I know you too well!"

"At least this way I can't make any odious comparisons," rebutted Califfa. "At least this way I don't have any more right to judge someone else's life, my husband's or anyone else's."

"You're just stupid! Stupid!" And Viola took her in her arms like a child.

But it was no use. Califfa stuck to her guns and repeated: "It's better this way, Viola, much better. Because when someone's honest, he suffers from it, because he understands, because he feels himself judged."

Viola opened up her arms, and desisted. "All right, go ahead, Califfa, go ahead. Wallow in the mud and thank him for it. But if that's the way you think and if you have so little respect for yourself, you're better off on the street, waiting for the first man who passes by. At least you'll make some money that way!"

"Now we're all on a ship and there's not much left to save..." And Califfa went to shut herself up in her house. She sat down on the chair by the window. The only thing she regretted was bringing the smell of Vito to that room where she had seen her son laughing, where she had tried to bring him up properly, like a gentleman. And she thought of that affair which had begun in that hopeless melancholy way with his long handsome eyelashes. The melancholy was something she could not overcome when there was still time.

Califfa eased her foot from her shoe and passed it naked over the bare bricks, feeling their rough surface, with the same gentle care she had seen her son take in doing the same thing, when, in afternoons like the one now ending, he would listen to her talking and raise his serene eyes to her, mute, pallid, and attentive.

Califfa's foot, white and defenseless like that of a saint, rested on the cold bricks, and the sharp heat of life which had gone out of her flowed back into the slender veins which beat under the delicate skin. She pulled it back with a sigh. Then she raised her eyes and stared at the windows.

And now the young grass was beginning to burst through the wall in front. The milder weather to come was announced by the clouds gathered over the fields outside town. And in the older part of the city, the sun for some days had been lingering longer by the wide-open doors and the gaping windows under the eaves.

The dialogue went on in her head and she was saying to herself: "Just ask him, 'Is it good that way, Vito?' and then ask him: 'Do you like it that way, Vito?' " as he looked at her like a gentleman, dignified and handsome as a pope and an egoist in every pore of his body. But afterward, Califfa, afterward, when you take your head in your hands and feel it empty, and you have to beg God for enough strength to get up and go home...

And if she were to open the window and look down toward the plain, she would see her friends taking the laundry from the hotel to be washed in the canal. She knew what it meant to wash in the canal on days like that when the winter was not yet over, with frozen fingers and a fever to cope with, on your knees with bent back as if it were a sin, breaking the ice with bare hands. They got only a few lire for each sheet and the sheets were all dirty with lipstick, love-making, and other signs of the good life. And it was humiliating as well as exhausting to rub out certain shameful things. But then, too, it was a blessing and when Califfa was offered some of this piecework like the others, she accepted it without any chatter.

IV

She felt that urge then too. She turned on her chair and looked at herself in her mirror, twisting her hair in her hands in back of her neck like a sheaf of wheat. And she saw what color eyes and mouth she had, and how narrow was her waist and full her breast, and what white skin she had...

You still have so much life left, she was saying to herself. Tell 'em all to go to hell with their vices, miseries and sins. You have just one sin – that you didn't realize soon enough how much you could enjoy life.

Wouldn't that be just fine, to end up like your mother, bent over a sewing machine, trying to raise ten children, not to see the sun except on Sunday in a hurry on your way to mass, to die squeezed out like a lemon and not even to have the consolation of being at peace when you're dead, not having the money for a tomb where the grass grows, and ending up in a municipal graveyard? And no one'll come to see you for all eternity.

Is it worth it? Because that's what you're headed for and you know it. You're in the sewer up to your neck. Before you drown in it, think a bit. There aren't any women like you in this neighborhood. Want to go to the square to bet on it? Let's raise up those skirts and see who comes forward!

Come on! Have another glass of wine and do what you have to! Start tonight, right away! *"Am-more, am-more, am-more, am-more mio...,"* she sang. Let's go, Califfa, open the window and sing so they can hear you on the other side of the river, up by those new houses, there where you wanted to go and live, where you can still hope to go later, because you never know what's going to happen to you in this life, because you, with your hands...

But when she opened the window, she could see that it was night already. Night had made a red highway of the street and there were only the stars above the houses. There was no light to be seen, no one passing by, only a train coming into the station with that funereal sound, as if the whole world were being carried away in a freight car, and as if everyone around her were dead and nothing was worth doing any more.

Her urge passed and she went back to her chair. Guido came in, slamming the door and bringing the cold from outside into the kitchen where the fire had gone out and there was no more wood.

"'lo…"

"Hello!"

He didn't even look her in the eye. He went to the upper room and she could hear him walking back and forth like a soul in hell.

CHAPTER THREE

In those evenings full of warm spring breezes, when even at night the sky was shining with the wind and the nearby hills seemed so much closer, Califfa felt a new presence in that house unblessed by hope, like an abandoned hut in an abandoned place. And she was thinking that the best way for her to destroy her life, or to let her life destroy itself, was to continue as she and Guido were doing. Guido had not an ounce of feeling to prevent him from abandoning the struggle against his self-pitying satisfaction at feeling himself beaten and accepting their defeat.

Emotion was involved and love as well. But pity passed too soon into an abyss of bitterness to allow what little positive and fertile qualities there were in their desperate encounters to save them or free them.

But so little would have been enough, if they hadn't turned their backs on each other in that great walnut bed whose creakings had registered too many lives, too much love-making, and too much death.

It would have been enough if one of them had had the courage and the humility to renounce his own pretensions and the conflicting feelings which were summed up in one pity: the courage to extend a hand or a foot, to touch the other, even for a fleeting instant. To caress the other's naked side, and after months of absurd hostility to feel the bare skin of the other running under the fingers.

How easy it would have been then for pity to change to desire, and that could have been the fire capable of burning off their enmity. Suddenly to feel again the revelation of life beginning anew, of the well-being which seizes one in the swollen lucidity of sex; to say once again:

"Guido, are you asleep?"

"No. I can't sleep!"

"I was scared today!"

"What of, Califfa?"

"That, sooner or later, it'll be the end. That one day I won't like to touch you any more, that I won't feel like touching you."

"Well, that'll mean you're getting old."

"And when will that be, Guido?"

"And how should I know?"

"At forty, Guido, at fifty?"

"I don't think old age comes at any particular time, Califfa. You're as old as you feel."

Now the fear she had experienced that day, squeezing the pillow and trying not to think of it in the solitude which was taking on enormous proportions within her, opening up vast spaces in her mind, was that she was slipping into old age. Maybe it was because of what had happened, or just fate – in any event, the hand which was holding her stomach, which had a grip on her at the other side of the bed, gave her the cold shiver announcing the departure of youth as she saw it and the coming of old age.

But how to come out of that state of mind? How to feel the face warm and the blood running with emotion, any sort of emotion, and the heat flare up especially there, cheerfully contaminating her with the folly growing inside her, but pushed down and on the point of suffocating.

With Vito it had been nice only the first time, out there in the fields. But this was not because she got some momentary pleasure from what they did. It was due, rather, to the deliberate enthusiasm she put into an act, which came to seem almost banal to her when she thought back on it later. And the pleasure Vito had experienced, his happiness in possessing her, in giving her self-confidence, in satisfying her urgent desires, had perhaps all been figments of her imagination.

If this was not true, the other times would have been different. There would at least have been a bit more tenderness, insincere perhaps, but at least consoling.

II

Behind the windows, the wall by the main road was already swollen with foliage, and even the road through the suburbs – leading straight to a lonely inn from which the sound of drunken singing could be heard if the wind was coming from the right direction – was loaded down with grass. Its smell, which reminded one of things deep in the earth, filled up the narrow streets in the old part of town and insinuated itself into the alienation contained in their wide, empty bed, with its cold and rigid sheet, above which hands did not dare to venture for fear of an encounter which could decide everything, either salvation or the most rapid destruction of them both...

"Califfa, if I have to wait any longer, my head's going to burst."

"But we can't do it here, right by the road!"

"And who's going to see us in the dark?"

Wasted words, they seemed absurd then. In those days they used to walk for miles to find a darker bit of darkness, until there were no more headlights around them, and all that remained was a great sky, an immense black wing, shining with the happiness which fell on her when Guido took her and threw her on the grass, the freshly mowed grass in the fields along the canals, either piled up or still lying where it was cut and so strong that when you put your foot in it, you felt something so springy and resistant it almost seemed alive.

The more road they covered with their anxious feet, the more energy was renewed in their moist and humid bodies. And that was the moment they had been waiting for all day, a moment gained at the expense of endless walking, abandoned scruples and lies told to her mother, when they threw themselves, drunken and savage, into the grass without thinking any more, throwing off whatever was in their way.

33

And when Guido had undone her bra and her breast became stiff in his hand, there was life in those hands, in his words, and even in the stars which were the only things looking down at them beyond the pile of grass above them.

The grass was the boundary. Beyond it were the shops where piecework was given out, where there were strikes and struggles, and the large buildings of the new part of town, and the bread earned by the sweat of the brow.

And that was how her true soul, her real awareness, came out from under the confines of a life of thieving, tolerance and humiliation. Charity, the love of God, the condemnation of any other wrong-doing, the desire to live a clean life – all derived from that moment; from that opening out when first his fingers and then Guido himself penetrated within her, and Califfa closed her eyes and abandoned herself to it, in that countryside made melancholy by the sound of far-off trains from who knows where.

This was her Gospel and her religion. She did not believe in anything else, only that. This was her only wealth and her only pride, and only because she could hold it close to herself and keep it warm in her hands; because she felt it being continuously caressed, kissed, and profaned when she walked by on the street (all she had to do was show herself with her walk in which the curve of her leg beat against her dress and her behind appeared and disappeared, with instinctive, astute and ingenuous knowledge). And she felt this wealth wasted and denigrated and she wanted to cry in those nights when sleep was defeated by her unquiet state of mind.

She would bite the sheet, so that he wouldn't realize what was going on. He was sleeping with his mouth wide open and his breath loaded with wine and anxiety. But tears were swelling in her eyes and went slowly down her cheeks, lazily, as lazily as his habit of letting everything go, with no more certainty of success beyond turning out the light when everything was destroyed.

And her religion was also the vital need for what experience had denied her, to cleave to something or someone, to love without egoism but only with dedication.

And without her religion she could not go on living. But how could she start all over again? With whom could she reestablish within herself those fragments of a vitality which had been kicked about and destroyed by hard luck? She had left her energy and her will to live on the walls and along the dark and dusty corridors of the courts, on the benches in the waiting room, on the gravel of the paths in the cemetery, and on the rusty bars of the iron gate where she had so often leaned her forehead.

She had tried with Guido and all she had left was that body which was now lying by her side, defeated, enervated, and dragged along like some bit of refuse by the succeeding days, a body which had once represented hope and faith to her, which she herself had chosen because she had seen that instinct of profiting from life which no one had been able to transmit to her, neither her father, nor her mother, nor the people with whom she had grown up, all of whom had in common the fact that they lived for someone else's gain.

And now Guido was only an excuse for thinking about how the past might have been. He was worth nothing but the four bones on which his flesh was wasting away day by day, and those eyes which continued to founder in the threatening of their red sockets, consumed by a confused mind.

Guido, sitting in the bars, sunk in smoke and curses, fired, driven away from work for arrogance or incompetence, avoided by his former workmates, a man who had hastened his old age and who was now hastening his death, only because other people had not had enough of the understanding necessary to change him, attributing wrongs to him which he had probably not committed, and responsibilities which had been grossly exaggerated in the minds of others by his attitude of resignation.

Uselessness; nothing else. And this was accompanied by the dried-up feeling which overcame her with the death of her son, that feeling which originated in her betrayed womb and spread irresistibly like a poison, so that she felt it in her flesh as if it were a physical malady.

Her son had been her second attempt to reach Guido. It was more subtle and honest, and its failure was that much more cruel.

How peaceful it was over the heads of those poor houses, in the outskirts of the city which she could glimpse beyond the windows and the frame of the bed. The wind was not rustling clean curtains such as she had seen in the windows of the apartment houses in the new city, but only old newspapers and cardboard stuck into the holes in the glass, but it was beautiful all the same, as was the smell of that earth which she considered inebriating when she was making love, because the real land was right under the walls of her house.

The odor which later came to the whole city first came to her house; Irene Corsini, called Califfa, had no other privilege...

And if her son had been alive at that moment, he would have been about the age of that group of boys who had been running around in the street for a long time. How she enjoyed their laughing and how savage was the sweetness of their singing, intimidated and excited by the night and by their complicity.

"Our son's interested in women already," she might have said to her husband, maybe coming closer to him and enjoying this discovery which would have brought them peace.

"Don't forget that I've loved you so... don't forget, don't forget..."

What peace there was in that song, while the light from Farinacci's chimney was lit and went out, lost in the sky already swollen up with summer. But her son's voice was not among those of the other boys who had been born when he was, and who had shared his misery, and who had called his name during their games and little adventures.

They were calling to themselves under Farinacci's wall: "Mario... Nicola... Luca..."

But no one was calling "Attilio" with the complicity with

which the others were calling, urged on perhaps by their first drunk, or their first desire to make love.

Califfa was imagining their smooth white bodies, their tender skin, the shiny muscles of their restless legs, and their bent backs which had already known fatigue. And she was suddenly terrified by a feeling of disgust and hence of unworthiness, as she saw in her mind's eye that small fragile body which she had arranged with her own hands in that bed she was in at that very moment, curled up and trembling like a leaf.

Again she saw the bones in his thin legs, and they looked even bigger because of his illness, his penis, like a drop of dried-up flesh, hanging from his defenseless body, his side like a wooden Christ figure, and the pale skin under his armpits.

And that was the very cushion on which Califfa had put the mass of her hair and on which she had seen her son's head that day for the last time, lolling a bit, with the eyes looking upward and the mouth half open, showing his little teeth which she had awaited happily for so many months.

The crowd of boys was still singing in the night, leaving the buildings, and their song faded into the distance toward the country; but because of the still intact happiness of those who had played with her Attilio on the stony streets of the old part of town, who had learned to talk and laugh with him – his face, like that of a small crucifix, came back to her and expanded within her until it took her breath away.

"Why, Attilio, why?... I was the one who covered your face with a sheet, I was the one who closed your eyes forever with my hands... Forgive me, Attilio."

The boys could still be heard, and the night was retiring with their proud song of unconscious revolt, the revolt of their blood, of their people, revealed in the commotion of adolescents excited by the darkness and the thought of manly risks.

Califfa could not stand being in bed any more, so she slid onto the floor and looked for her clothes on the back of the chair, but then she changed her mind and just put a shawl over her shoulders and went down in her nightgown, so as not to make any noise.

The wind was cleansing the air, and it seemed almost like day, a strange dawn with a timeless light, the glimmer that clouds have just before a summer thunderstorm, when she opened the door of the house and sat on the rocks on the ground.

The lights on the Via Emilia stood out clearly. That main artery was obscured by the buildings of the city, and here and there it would surface and then lead straight to the horizon. In the tenement quarter, all the windows were open. Behind the clothes on the line, Califfa could hear the people inside, some snoring and others complaining. These sounds were the only ones that could rise from that confused mass of unhappy bodies, and they were giving a happy and grotesque music, which made people smile, to that fugue of white façades.

"Justice and Liberty" was snoring by fits and starts just the way he talked, and perhaps those syllables were giving bent to his fevered brain's habitual ideas: justice among men, which had been stingy to him all his life; the changing of the guard among the rich and the poor, and among the intelligent and the ignorant; and finally the names of his enemies, pushed out through clenched teeth, like the butts of his cheap cigars.

Califfa looked at that window, and she could have painted the scene within: Mazza's head the way it was at that moment, so precisely did she imagine it, leaning way back, with the mouth thrown open and trembling as his snores reached a high pitch, and where there shone the old man's only wealth, that golden tooth which he did not want to use in eating since he was afraid of wearing it out. And she could see the poor man's hands holding his Syrian cat outside the covers with the rapt bitterness of a saint holding onto his crucifix:

"What a hell of a note! We've fought and struggled for fifty years. We've been exiled and imprisoned: fifty years of lice and beatings, anger and humiliation, just so we don't have to tip our hat to I don't know who, and now look at us, naked as jaybirds, look at our hands... It's easy to say fifty years, but that's half a century, you know..."

Pulling the shawl more tightly around her, Califfa continued to look over the windows, the roofs, and the balconies seen in the white perspective of sheets hanging to dry and in the black one of the drains, where neither the dividing walls nor the differing family names accounted for much. What was important was the fact that ties of blood, adultery, incest and fornication over the years had made them all more or less related; and the fact that they had in common the same pain, and a mood restless for rebellion and yearning for hope.

And suddenly she started and began listening, when her glance fell on the grating of a balcony where hung the shirts, undershirts, and underpants with whose contents she had already become familiar in the intimacy of love-making. The windows were open, but no noise was coming out of them, even the birds were sleeping in the cage hanging on the shutters. She imagined the room empty, the basin in a corner, the walnut bureau against the wall and that single bed, always unmade and the bedclothes rumpled, where Vito had held her, trying to restrain her with the force of his knees, that bed where everything was so hard because with just one extra move you would slide onto the floor.

Was he there? Califfa was sure he wasn't, but this certainty, if it increased her solitude, did not make her angry.

"Vito," Viola would say, "uses up twenty miles of gas to go make this guy's daughter. The guy used to be a cowherd, but now he's a landowner. Vito makes her and enjoys her, because she's cute and plump as a sack of flour, and he knows that as he mounts, the ham, the grain, and the oil are in the next room and sooner or later some of them'll be in his hands. Because Vito doesn't spend that gas just for the sake of that slut's body."

Califfa shook her head. Let Viola and the others talk. She didn't care. Vito could cheat on her and make all the cowherds' daughters from Piacenza to Bologna and he planning on acquiring more land than Farinacci, since it didn't make any difference. There was no human logic between serving Vito and the feelings nourished by the truest part of her femininity; and without logic there could be no suffering or true anger. As with Guido and her son, so with Vito, with his unyielding stubbornness and his handsome, impudent as well as wasted life, it had been only a pretext.

He was a youth who seemed made just to lie there in his habitual pose, sculpted like a statue, with his elbow against the pillow and his tan body draped over the whiteness of the sheets, while he enjoyed her with his eyes. And she was stretched out on the foot of the bed, excited by the humiliation and by that silent animation given her by her wordless enjoyment of that too long inhibited gratification.

"Take it off, Califfa, that's right... take it all off," he would say to her. "What a body! What legs!" and she continued to move in the sun which came in from the windows, with no shame any more, rocking her stiffened breasts like tongues. And she could feel a blush coming to her cheeks when, hearing the voices and the happy singing of her people in their tenements who were waking up in their respectable beds, she became aware of her defenseless body, outraged by his excited stare.

But she needed that shame. Maturity, true pride, she was thinking, consisted perhaps in not needing other people, in being so sure of one's own feelings that one no longer feared uncertainty. But she always needed to lean on someone: a husband or a son, to attempt to feel at one with honest and happy people – or else a lover who wanted only to go to bed, in order to fall into that more numerous group of those who had to struggle with their consciences.

In good and evil times, Califfa wanted to feel her body burning with sincere passion and to have a clear reason for her ups and downs. But the real fear she was desperately trying to evade came from the awareness of unexplained suffering. She feared death when it did not respect youth, and condemnation by men for unknown reasons, and poverty imposed by arbitrary rules.

To be able to say "God forgive me!" or "Thank God!" when you know why you're saying it – this was what Califfa accepted from life. This was what she understood.

And now from the countryside a light came shimmering from the horizon full of clouds on their way across the mountains, announcing a new day; and a fresh wind came, with something of the smell of the sea in it. It raised her hair and her nightgown as Califfa leaned her head on the doorpost and fell asleep there, seated on the threshold.

CHAPTER FOUR

Monsignor Martinolli, the Auxiliary Bishop, who had *"potestatem ordinariam, sed vicariam"* over the city, went down into its older quarters once a year – at least, only once on an official visit – and that was the Sunday before Easter. For this reason Califfa and her friends got the idea that he was progressively decaying, and especially when they thought of what he had done and not done for the city. Each year his hair was a little whiter, his skin a little more flabby, and his eyes more uncertain, in that glance which was difficult to understand. And all of this, together with other dubious indications, contributed to give a bad account of the man.

But when they discussed him, Califfa was inclined not to be too severe. They talked about him a lot, because religious observances, even though they are often irregular where life has few rules beyond bitterness, were perhaps more keenly felt in Califfa's neighborhood than on the other side of the river.

"As far as I'm concerned," she would say, "he's no worse than the others, and whoever says he's a shyster is exaggerating. He's just a priest who can't make up his mind and who can't make his religion appealing. And he's neither patient nor shrewd, he tries to pretend without succeeding. What I mean is that if someone makes his living selling hope, he shouldn't boycott the product, but he should play the game even if he doesn't believe in it. But he…"

He was quite a sight, Martinolli was (and people called him just that, without any title, following a local custom long used with respect to clergy of much greater rank), when he decided to cross the bridge and leave behind him the tranquil habits of his episcopal residence to throw himself into the midst of that neighborhood where the least cordial of doubts were more to be seen than sin. He would torment himself for days over the idea; he would receive the advice of his collaborators and then, driven more by certain timely proddings from Rome than by his own conscience, would allow himself to be dragged into the affair, bringing along a group of fanatical young priests and municipal policemen.

The policemen served to keep the people back, against the walls and in the doorways, so that Mazza, when he had to climb onto the curb, protested that it was more a raid than a pastoral visit. But meanwhile, in the sparse sunlight that penetrated into that neighborhood, he appeared in his car, like a wooden saint, towering over the policemen's helmets. And his handsome tapered hand, passing by as he stood and extending beyond his protective cordon, fled like a butterfly from under the nose of those poor people.

"Not even time enough to kiss his ring," said Viola. "And he didn't even look us in the face!" In fact, he would just come and go, perhaps because all he needed was to be able to say to himself: "At least I've been there." Even the mass which was celebrated in what Farinacci had defined as the most Godforsaken parish in Italy, was gone through at a run. But His Excellency was careful not to sing off key and to climb up on those high notes which rose from his stomach until he was out of breath, so as to save face, at least among those people who had the opera in their blood and could be offended at a false note.

Martinolli was like that, but he was neither inept nor possessed of a blind faith. He understood the solitude and the pain which spread around him from the moment of the *introibo*, even if he had not the strength to overcome them, and he was well aware of what was happening in the minds of those men, women and children who followed him with suspicious glances as he busied himself around the altar.

He knew that while he prayed to Christ in their name, that while he implored Him for pity on them, and that while he raised the Host above his head with its well-cared-for head of hair, they were thinking that he detested them, that he was saying *ora pro nobis* and wishing them the worst. And he found this humiliating. This humiliation remained with him and wounded him deeply, because it was not true, because only his resigned and bitter conviction that a different kind of encounter would have been as useless as it would have been difficult led him to act like that.

The uselessness of everything he did, of all his words, sermons, and smiles, prevented any relief of his guilt, whose origins were to be sought in remote years, and which did not differ much from the attitude of those crowded together on the benches, who had come there more to open up a mutual conversation with Martinolli than to attend mass.

And was it the people's fault if Martinolli was still only an Auxiliary Bishop, if Rome found him wanting and brought more or less direct pressures on him and sent him warnings? Tedious complications which, just as they had wasted his maturity, were now wasting his old age, which Martinolli would have wanted to enjoy in peace, perhaps in that country house he had on the Po which was filled with the odor of cows and smoked ham.

He would have liked to end his days down there where he had been born and where his father and mother were buried, along that little country path where as a young priest he had taken the way to he knew not where. And instead he had stopped at the first station, only a few miles further on.

With minor gluttony to indulge in, and amid favors exchanged with the small manufacturers who formed part of his court, he would have been able to live out the rest of his life pleasanty enough, if it were not for that other Monsignor from Rome, persistent and pedantic as certain bureaucratic priests can be, who refrained from taking the express when he went to Milan just so he could stop in Emilia and chat with Martinolli.

There was the usual walk in the square before going off to eat, the cordial reminders of so many official duties which a faithful man of God must always keep before him when he is in difficult territory. The Monsignor from Rome went through a fast selection of some of these duties and allowed himself some cautious allusions, as if it had been just a few days, not many years, since Martinolli had been invited to take a position "with charity but firmness" about those "thorny flowers which could be made into lilies," as the other Monsignor so pompously put it.

"And now, my friend," asked the Monsignor from Rome, half joking, "when are we going to clear up this thicket, eh? When are we going to clear it up?"

For all those years Martinolli had limited himself to stretching out his arms and playing his part, which was to answer with some *I'll try's* and some *We'll see's* of which he was none too convinced, filling out the argument with such assurances as:

"I've tried everything, believe me, and I don't have to tell you... you know full well, you're familiar with the good and the bad side of things... And I love them, I give you my word that I love them, but I'm in a dark tunnel where I can't yet see a ray of light. You should come here for a while and see for yourself."

"I can imagine."

"When I put my foot in, something blocks it here; you see, that hurts me, and I feel as if I had a wall in front of me, a wall against which my pity seems fragile, very fragile!"

And the other man would answer: "Don't see insults where there aren't any! This happens to everyone... I mean, to everyone who has responsibilities like yours. But if this can be of some comfort to you, I'll tell you that in Rome, strictly speaking... I mean that we know, and we're sure that if not today, then tomorrow..."

But the last time they had gone down into the square toward the restaurant, Martinolli had had no desire to play the usual game and the Monsignor from Rome noticed that his face, usually colored by his taste for food and conversation, had a tired pallor, like the coloration of some disease which is about to strike, or has just finished its course.

"Don't talk about thickets again," objected Martinolli with a smile, and after some hesitation he said with his eyes to the ground, "and certainly we're right... but... maybe because I'm old, and years mean a lot in these things, yes, a lot... it's not a doubt, but..."

"Tell me," urged the other man, who was so used to putting himself instantly on his guard.

Martinolli swallowed as he raised his eyes in search of the right phrase. "It's as if I were beginning to see a rather unusual difference between a rose bush and your thicket."

"Oh, no, don Martinolli... either you explain yourself or I'm going!"

"All right," and Martinolli took his colleague by the arm. "I wonder what we're going to do about these people! It's right for things to change this far – I mean, it's right that bars be replaced, if not by our churches, then at least by the headquarters of our youth associations. But just think what's been happening for some time, when I'm among them and I look at them and their children, shaking their hands – "

"What?" interrupted the other Monsignor.

"Every once in a while I think we're on the wrong side of the stage."

Now, that's enough!" said the other man, getting nervous. "Don't be like one of them, don Martinolli. Don't you bore me with verbose excuses too! Put the pressure on 'em! In other words, if I've understood you right, we're to leave those people to rot in the hands of those four vultures who fill their heads with all sorts of nonsense!... Tell me if that's what you're thinking! If it is, we'll just conclude this conversation and I'll say good-bye to you!"

"That's not what I mean," continued Martinolli, taking up the cordial walk once again. "And don't be angry... Because I'm telling you these things as I might tell you that I had a stomach ache last night, without presuming anything. These are things we can say among friends on the way to lunch, aren't they? It's about their state of mind – "

"Yes, yes," said the other, but without his former cordiality. "Don't let that state of mind take root! Uproot it! Uproot it!"

"What I meant was that if there is a way of coming to God

through suffering, even the blindest, most ignorant suffering – and there is such a way, and we know there is – it can be that suffering has already made these people ready, has matured them, and we don't know it, and we think we have to begin all over again with the litany of words, and that we have to infiltrate them with sabotaging actions worthy of a sixth column – "

"You mean we're to give them the Bible and ask them to make up the doctrine for us! But this is stupid and blasphemous, believe me, my friend!"

"But I repeat unequivocally, we should begin at our final purpose," continued Martinolli without conceding anything. "Perhaps we should tell them that their way of coming to God has been the right one, that God has been and still is to be found in their way of loving one another, in the way they die, and even in their way of believing certain ideas about politics and life... And that their God is a pure God – that perhaps they're right too... Do you understand?"

"No, dear friend," drily replied the Monsignor from Rome, "and I don't even want to."

"Listen," and don Martinolli stopped walking, obstinate as he sometimes was in certain moments. "Why do you think they are so attached to their idols and banners, why do you think they refuse so decisively to listen to our sermons and speeches, and to heed our warnings?"

"Why? Why? What silly questions! On purpose, that's why! Because they want to make a revolution! They want to burn down the churches, stop working, and put everyone else to work."

"Perhaps it's not as simple as all that. Those flags have made them a people, they gave them self-confidence during Fascism. And politics does enter things at a certain point... it has made them understand that their conscience was vital and was worth something... while we, and this is the point, have made them feel that their conscience does not exist, that it was just an atrophied joint, a tree which had never borne fruit."

The Monsignor from Rome started walking again, in the fog

which surrounded the two figures, isolating them in the great square which was semi-deserted at noontime, saying, "Continue! Continue!"

"And even if they're asking for revolution, it's understandable and I'd almost say it was right. The important thing is to teach them what this revolution should be all about, to set its tone… It's like with the children. Didn't you ever wonder why children are brought up differently nowadays? With enough cunning and courage to accept their immaturity and their natural defects, not to suffocate them or humiliate them, but to develop what is good and individualistic in them?"

The Monsignor from Rome turned his gray eyes on Martinolli and asked: "Listen, have you told them any of this romantic, absurd and, if you will excuse the expression, dangerous nonsense?"

"No," admitted Martinolli with a sigh.

"No? And why not, if you set such store by it?"

"I don't believe in it," rebutted Martinolli, suddenly getting angry. "I've told it to you just because I'm afraid not to believe in it. Because I believed I understood it now that I'm about to lay down my burden and close my life as a priest and a man. Because I'm afraid it's an excuse for me, since I haven't succeeded in my task, since I haven't been able to be moved by them… to make them love me… and since it makes me think I have made a mistake not through weakness but because the system is wrong."

The Monsignor from Rome suddenly felt his own burden lightened at this unexpected confession. Martinolli's bitter confusion was transmuted into his own satisfaction, and he almost returned to his previous cordiality.

"My friend," and now it was his turn to take Martinolli by the arm, "your results have been somewhat less than perfect only because your task is difficult, and we are aware of that fact. This is because your task is the same which the Church proposes to perform in the world, only on a smaller scale. Here in this city you are a little Pope, my friend."

"A little Pope," muttered Martinolli.

"For that we know how to wait. And you will support our

goals, never straying from the Church's policies. Don't give in to ideas which are merely products of your physical exhaustion... those ideas which I haven't taken note of at all, do you understand, I haven't heard a word of them!"

His weak attempt at rebellion having petered out, defeated more by the skillful blandishments than by the criticisms of his Roman colleague, Martinolli bent his head and went back to what he had always been.

"You're right," he said. "And then there's the fact that they've resisted me so much, they've fought me all the way..."

They went to eat and the luncheon helped to restore Martinolli to his old self. Even his cheeks got back their former color and when the Monsignor from Rome saw some drops of perspiration on Martinolli's brow, a sure sign that both the luncheon and his admonitions had been digested, he thought it opportune to give the final turn of the screw.

"We'll have Emilia in our hands, my friend," said he as he drank the last glass. "I say Emilia because if we were to burn out certain wastes in these infected consciences, other wastes in other areas contaminated by the same malignant herb could be disposed of as well... Do you understand or not?"

"I understand."

"And now remember, use caresses as firm as a slap in the face, and I do mean firm... and above all, sacrifice on your part, sacrifice!"

"All right," sighed Martinolli. "Sacrifice. I understand."

"Sacrifice and pain... Remember that the Church knows how to wait. But what we're waiting for is a war, dear friend, a war!"

Don Martinolli went with the Monsignor to the station. He waited for the train to pull out. And the train was already under way when the Monsignor from Rome turned around to tell him:

"You have been a good priest. You lack only the final pearl to be a great one. You can give it to us, this pearl, you must..."

"Yes, the pearl," assented Martinolli while the train began to pull out and he ran along for a few yards. "I understand."

He stood there until the tracks were deserted, then he

walked through the underpass. And at that point he understood the limits of that weakness which had been a brake not only on his career (which had begun with too many ambitions) but also on his life as a man, and he understood, too, the emptiness which kept him from the good things he should have desired and accomplished.

He was no longer the able dialectician, a participant in that banal conversation loaded with things left unsaid which had so much influence on the moral destiny of the city, but only a poor lonely priest, dragging himself up step by step amid the smoke from the engines returning from the plains around Padua. And he was thinking mostly of those outbursts of good will, of those attempts to come to an agreement, and even of that hysteria with which he had tried in vain to conquer those consciences which were so important to the Monsignor from Rome, consciences which needed a different kind of love, more open and less afraid, with more faith in life and perhaps even more faith in Christ.

He had never been capable of this love, not toward other people or toward himself, not even as a boy when he decided to remove himself from the common path followed by his contemporaries and become a priest, just because he had a presentiment that there was no other way to save himself from that dark dry weakness which can keep a man at the edge of life.

And these words returned to his mind: "You have been a good priest..." and he smiled bitterly at that. He certainly had been, but for the same reason which was making him suffer. Because the lack of that love which drags and pushes one along, which moves and wounds one, which exalts and leads one into error, the lack of that love which the saints felt was what had forced him into the life of a simple and useless observer of rules and conventions.

But with all this cogitation he could barely tell what it was in himself which had lasted all that time: the fear of suffering, the desire not to apply himself more than he had to, and resentment against everything he thought was against him.

"But why does it all have to be so difficult?" he asked

himself, continuing to walk along the corridors of the railway station until he came out into the square and began to meet people he knew, and in greeting them his attention was distracted from the topic.

II

My mother had told me about how we killed the last Duke in the city. Stabbed by the likes of us, he was left to die like a dog in the street. And his friends had to look at him with his face in the ground where they wouldn't walk even with shoes on. This was one thing I imagined every time I came to think we'd always been equal, and that our pains and pleasures were as old as the walls of our houses.

"Hypocrites!" Mazza used to put it. And he was right, because we'd waited on the Duke hand and foot without ever protesting, and had jumped on him only when he'd wanted to play it shrewd and poke his nose into our business...

What I mean is that we've always been a little like young girls in love; they may attach themselves to someone who uses them, but they can't put up with falsehood, no!...

That was why we never warmed up to Martinolli, just because he never liked to level with anyone or say what was on his mind. (Yes, I agree it was partly our fault if his bishop's – or even cardinal's – hat was still out of reach under glass, but that had nothing to do with conscience.)

Maybe we wouldn't have been so stubborn if he'd come to us not with the smile of a cop but a sincere one that said, "Let's shake hands and see if we can do something together." But first he was afraid, then he cheated, and finally he beat a retreat. He'd extend his arms and say:

"Christ is up there, there where the treasures in Heaven are laid up. Think a little about that. You know where to look if you want to pray." That's about the way it was and that's where it went wrong. Because that was where he played into the hands of some hotheads who could have answered him that the real treasures, for example, were in that ring glittering on the hand which so rarely shook ours. Not to talk of that huge car he disappeared into as soon as he'd said amen, with the sound of all those motorcycles behind. And we were more humiliated than before because he left like that. After all, we weren't going to like him just for the sake of his ideas.

But then, I say, what was the reason for this big fight between us and them, this way of looking at each other that made strangers of us? They were the ones who thought up the reasons and talked so much about them.

Who knows why? Because they were afraid, or just because it suited them?

But the truth is something else and you have to go a little further into it. Let me explain. If Christ was really where Martinolli was pointing his finger, between our roofs and the clouds, let them show us that we could wake up one morning with at least one of our hopes a reality we could enjoy. What did we want? And they, seeing something awful where there wasn't anything at all, God knows what they were thinking. But we didn't ask them to change our houses into palaces or to bring back the innocence of some of our girls who end up God knows where, just like I did, none of that. All we ask is to be cheered up by a handshake, and to have someone pay a little attention to us.

Why did it have to be so hard? Just because there was a river which divided grown people in another way? The evil weed Martinolli was talking about can't be uprooted with high masses or sermons in the square – even if it was really evil, and I don't think it was, just like you can't cure hunger with chatter.

Mazza was right to recite something he'd read I don't know where and which I've learned too: "In the brotherhood of our common tribulations we feel the need of love as is only right, but it seems impossible to us in Italy, where respect is extended only to those who can change it into money, where even love and respect are media of exchange!" Call it a lot of fancy words if you like, but hurrah for Mazza! And he went on: "Is that politics? Does politics perhaps have anything to do with it?"

And then I got up to tell my friends what I'd had the guts to yell at a political speaker in the square, I swear it, with so many people around me looking at me as if I'd gone crazy: "No! Politics has nothing to do with it! I just wanted to say right out that in this country we haven't the courage to love one another!"

And I was all ready to mention names, or rather one man's name, occupation and so forth, if they hadn't grabbed me the way they did that day in front of Farinacci's factory, and instead of one day in jail, I got two. In other words, no one did anything about a rivalry which was stupid and as old as the hills. And you could tell that sooner or later it would come to no good. And I'm telling this not only because I got madder than anyone else, but to show how some wrong ideas can cost a lot of blood. And the ones who have to pay have the least to do with it.

And the ones who accuse us, who accuse us of having done it on purpose to the ones who give orders and who feed us, I'd say it's just some more hot air. We're not mad at anyone, because we're too fond of life. It's just that there've been bosses who've understood us and liked us and we've liked them. And there've been others who couldn't understand us. The truth's all there.

III

The state of affairs was altered by this incapacity to put prejudice aside and unite into one people. And that river which on one side washed a bank with a nice broad treelined avenue was bordered on the other with little rusty iron balconies, medieval gratings and mouse's nests dug into decrepit façades. The atmosphere and attitudes on the two banks were as different as those on two continents separated by an ocean.

But there were relationships, loves, happiness and personal resentment which even that stream could not prevent. There was the same will to live, and to live in a certain way, which had not been violated by recent history, which had pushed those from the other side of the river to fight under risky standards.

And so conventions and judgments changed most of all.

That Mastrangelo, for example, whose family had come to Emilia from the southern part of Italy many years ago and whom Califfa meant when she argued that there are bosses who just can't understand, offered ample excuses to anyone who wanted to misunderstand and exaggerate his distorted reputation.

"That's what Italy's like!" Califfa would say. "All churches and towers on the outside but crap on the inside. That respectable face of his with those pious eyes should be painted and hung on some wall as a symbol!"

Mastrangelo's projects were too ambitious; this derived from his need to take out his frustrations on someone and from some very serious affairs in which Mastrangelo – although partly a victim of the situation – suddenly acquired some responsibility.

"Look, this is Mastrangelo," added Mazza, putting a glass upside down on the table, as he demonstrated the city's hierarchy. "And this is Farinacci, and this is Gazza, and this is Doberdò!" and for each name he put a glass on top of the stack. Then he concluded: "Each on top of the other and they're all trying to screw each other."

It was true. The support Mastrangelo enjoyed, and not just social support, came from the protection which Giacinto Gazza accorded him, for no one knew what reason. Gazza, who cultivated useful people in Ministries, had given Mastrangelo a place in Annibale Doberdò's commercial empire. Doberdò was the real center of power for all the city's businessmen.

People in this position were not likely to be stabbed in the back and could get generous amounts of credit. The passage of their promissory notes was suitably lubricated. In this way Mastrangelo had allied himself with Farinacci and the others (his bricks uniting with cheeses, preserves, salami, spaghetti and perfumes), but there was a difference, at least in Califfa's eyes and those of her friends. The difference was that he was the lowest glass on the pile and while his colleagues had their factories in the new part of town, he had his workshops in the old city. Following a tradition handed down by his father and grandfather, he had always hired local people, and for this reason he represented the certainty, one of the few certainties, of a steady wage.

The presumption that they knew Mastrangelo better than any others had some justification among the people on that side of the river, and it was inevitable that this strange businessman's weaknesses and defects would wind up with romanticized additions and distortions.

On certain evenings, heavily lubricated with Lambrusco wine, Mazza, in his gloomy way, had charged into the usual comparisons and said that Farinacci had only one advantage over Mastrangelo: because of the curse (or blessing) of Farinacci's eternal childishness, women repelled him. But this didn't take into account the family council he always had on his back – old birds who haggled over a fraction of a penny, and if the balance didn't come out exactly right, they grabbed him and put him in quarantine in his office, cleansed by a suitable brainwashing. According to Mazza, Farinacci didn't make any mistakes simply because he couldn't, especially for those purely personal reasons.

"Mastrangelo's surrounded by the most God-awful crew of leeches, thieves and hoods, and it's all because of those women! They flock around him like flies! He's the sort of guy they're after and he's so eager for a night of fun that he'll sign a blank check!"

And that was all Mazza had to say. He fixed his stare on the glass and maybe he really didn't believe any of it himself.

What they were saying was that Mastrangelo had made quite a name for himself as an adviser on religious matters, for having offered to rebuild the bell tower of the Cathedral gratis, and for always being at the head of the subscription list for the Auxiliary Bishop's charity drives. But there were others who kept saying that his sluts went in the service entrance if they didn't go in the front door, and with things keeping up like that he'd taken some beatings that would have ruined him if he hadn't been very good at using the esteem of the banks.

"See the half a billion lire?" concluded Mazza. "That's half a billion he stole in that movie-house business, and that was just so he could be seen in Rome with that whore of a cover girl. With all that money we could have redone our whole neighborhood."

Actually Mastrangelo was just incompetent and didn't know how to handle his business affairs and – apart from his skirt-chasing – he had taken some bad advice. (But what popular fantasy can conceive of a prominent man's ruin divorced from certain excesses?) There were ridiculous purchases of land, apartments that didn't get sold, creditors who were disastrously punctual, and many other things of the sort. And so he came to the inevitable settling of accounts with Doberdò.

Mazza gave a version of that meeting which he assured us was quite accurate. "One day," he related, "he came into Doberdò's office with that baby face of his all pale. Mastrangelo confessed that he was having a few troubles and that once again he needed cash, right away, within twenty-four hours – for the last time, he would swear it.

"Doberdò stared at him and shook his head: 'No! That's enough!'

"This was a blow to Mastrangelo. It was all very well to say that he built houses and that there are times when bricks are as expensive as gold because there are rumors of a devaluation and anyone with a little money to put aside is building houses. But Doberdò gave it to him straight:

" 'Listen, my friend, I'm not here behind this desk to support your whoring around! You've abused my credit too much; I might even say you've tried to grab me by the short hairs!'

" 'You mean you're slamming the door in my face?'

" 'For the moment, yes. Later we'll see!'

" 'That means I'll have to fire some of my help,' stammered Mastrangelo. 'That I'll have to cut down, that I'll have to – '

" 'Do what you think best. This has to do with your conscience as well as your wallet!'

" 'But with Farinacci,' Mastrangelo said, 'with the excuse that the product didn't do well on the market, eh? I wonder if you remember that, Mr. Doberdò!'

" 'That's different. Farinacci didn't act like a fool. And he didn't throw away the money just on himself. He supported a certain line in politics and you know it perfectly well!'

"Mastrangelo started. 'With all due respect for you, I don't give a damn about your politics and I'll keep to my whores. But let's be clear about one thing. If I have to shut down, it'll involve everyone, maybe you too, Mr. Doberdò, because there'll be a strike, and you know what strikes are like around here. It won't be like that farce at Farinacci's and it won't be enough to say "so long and thanks"!'

"And even though Gazza was there, Mastrangelo was grabbed and thrown out. And so after a few days we found out that Mastrangelo had gotten ahold of the personal dossiers of every worker – name, first name, family connections and political tendencies – and he made a cross by the photographs of the hottest ones.

"And as if that weren't enough, many of us have to carry Mastrangelo's cross along with all the other crosses we have to bear, and we're like the birds before a big hurricane."

CHAPTER FIVE

But Mastrangelo's cross was not all they had. Califfa and her friends, on the contrary, had the easy consolation of a calm state of mind, coming from their acceptance of things as they were. And these people, crowded together in old shacks in the shadow of small, deconsecrated churches whose bells were silent and whose interiors were deserted – amid those roofs teeming with cats – could feel this inner peace, often with no prompting at all, like a change in the color of the air.

And there were consolations, although brief, and it was easy to keep one's self warm in them, as if life had changed its appearance – a festival, the birth of another baby, a week of quiet which the women could enjoy in the sun in front of their houses, leaning against the buildings warmed by its rays.

But what made life bitter for them was that they would pass so rapidly from this inner contentment to an inexplicable rebellion of desperate emotions. And this new way of looking at things could burst forth without any explanation.

Califfa was no exception to the rule. And so, when she got fed up with the world, all she did was close the door to her tenement and take to the street which led to the bridge. These walks were able to placate her and calm her down and she carried them out with the naïve astuteness of one acting out something one doesn't understand; it was a walk all behind and belly and it caressed even her desires.

When she got to the boundary of her part of town, she took her belt in a notch, pushed back her hair and carefully and arrogantly straightened her shoulders so that her blouse could hardly contain the soft weight of her still youthful breasts.

She planted her high heels on the sidewalk, proceeding with her eyes straight in front of her without looking anyone in the face, with so much arrogance and pride that the protesting sound of her feet seemed to fill the arcade leading to the square where the town hall was located.

And the street was hers when she passed by, even though there might be a funeral procession there. And her triumph was in looking up at the windows in the apartment buildings and offices, or in the store windows and in seeing, peeping out from the desolate beauty of the things she would not have, the faces of the hypocrites, as she called them, confined in their desire for her like birds in their cages.

She went forward, retraced her steps, and crossed to the other side of the street. And along the route where the air was vibrating with her little act ("You're funnier than a political rally, Califfa!" Cernusco told her), she very carefully omitted none of her obligatory stops.

First the police station to make the cops sweat, nesting as they did in the main entrance, and to see them come out like mice, to make them weep at the arrogant way in which she challenged them. And then the headquarters of some political parties and the buildings along the best streets in town, so that some titled old hens would turn their backs on her from the heights of their balconies. (This was Califfa's image too. She attributed to every flying creature its own capacity to represent human vices and virtues and saw the newer and better part of town as a little hell crowded with birds.)

Cernusco called her from a table at a café in the square to offer her a drink. (He'd lost a leg fighting alongside Guido, but they hadn't tried him, since that lacerated leg had reduced a strikingly handsome youth to a lame man.)

Califfa drank like a trooper, with her hand on her hip, challenging the men at the nearby tables who were looking at her over their glasses.

"You're lucky, Califfa," Cernusco was telling her. "If the Lord above had given me what he'd given you..." and he raised his fist toward the Mayor's balcony, his way of wishing that he might be up there someday. "Because if you want people to respect you in this crazy world, if you want people to know that you're there, you have to have what they have, in your wallet or on your bones, and, Califfa, you've got it on your bones."

Cernusco beat his hand on his good leg and Califfa set out again, but this time toward home. And the last to be teased by her straight legs and her arrogant breasts was the group of customs guards staring at her through the spy hole in their sentry box.

Then came the bridge and finally, when the desire for childish revenge had worn off, Califfa stopped pounding the pavement with her high heels and took off her shoes, since her feet hurt.

Barefoot, without trying to walk in a dignified way any more, she went along her usual street, to the chair by the window, and to her unmade and loveless bed.

II

But those were the days when the people in the large ugly tenements in the old part of town began to wait. The women hung more clothes out on the line to dry and people were working more hurriedly, and Clotilde Braibanti, working more with her imagination than from experience, had put out a sign for some unknown reason with FRENCH HAIRDRESSER on it and had begun the difficult struggle with certain angry hairdos for which only scissors would be any use. They all wanted their hair set, even some old women who were as dried up as mummies and who for the rest of the year limited themselves to scratching their heads and putting a hatpin through the confusion of their hair. Clotilde sweated as she tried to undo those rats' nests and when she knew the worst about them she sent away the girls who worked for her with a wave of her hand and brought out the disinfectant pump.

Mazza, from his building across the streer, was watching groups of skirts coming out of the beauty parlor who should have been ready for a funeral but instead were shining with pomade and with happy curls dangling over their eyes, eyes which should have been reverently closed with a cross made over them. But he did not laugh at the sight, since the ritual had to start that way, and he too tried to give himself a tone and appear perhaps a bit younger, smoothing some hair over the bare skin on his head and trying to right the course of his crooked walk. Mazza straightened up from the wreck of his old age, the women adjusted the curls on their heads, and the smell of their washing spread through the poor dark rooms, and, as the middle of June drew nearer, the sun beat more and more strongly on the tile and iron roofs which concealed those swarming lives from the pity of heaven.

The iron roofs were heating up whole houses, above the unmade beds and the chests of drawers, and even the sparrows were not out there at certain hours of the day. Below, suffocating in the useless abundance of misery, the people were cooking, but they did not pay any attention to that. In fact, they were thinking about other things, about getting flour, eggs, a decent suit, and wondering whether don Campagna would have the nerve to go once more to Martinolli's house.

When don Ersilio Campagna appeared in the sunlight of the street, with his hat pushed down over his head as if he were on his way to a fistfight with Martinolli, people began to feel a little more secure, and to hope that they would win their battle this year, too. In the middle of June, for almost thirty years – that is, from the first year he had been their parish priest – don Campagna hurled himself into the adventure with his eternal air of a refugee (a refugee from the folly which had gotten him stuck in that missionary outpost, a refugee from the bitterness of a priest who was a little too fond of the bottle, from his unfulfilled desire for peace) with his collar undone and his clothes dirty with tobacco and his shoulders drooping, and Mazza dragging along behind.

Mazza stayed down by the entrance, and the poor old priest went up the main staircase already imagining the welcome he would get. He resigned himself to the worst with that spirit of charity which circumstances had taken advantage of far too often, until he arrived at a goodhearted indolence which was prepared for anything. Martinolli was waiting for him. He recognized the three rings of the bell, prolonged but respectful, and he imagined the rest for himself. Don Campagna, struggling with his short breath, would head for the Louis XVI blue satin armchair, from which Martinolli would beg him as always to get up and sit instead in a wooden rocker where there was no satin for him to get dirty. He knew everything after thirty years of such meetings – how he would reproach the poor priest, and how he would begin his speech:

"Don Ersilio, what you are asking me in the name of your parishioners – whom I would call more a mob than a congregation – is neither in the letter, nor in the spirit – "

"Your Excellency, you are right, but the way things are now, if we let 'em have it, maybe we could reason with 'em."

"In other words, I should sponsor a farce, an orgiastic act of superstition, letting it take place in the name of Christ?"

"Excellency, to call it orgiastic is a bit of an exaggeration. Let's say that it's a festival and that they believe that on the night of June 24, by intercession of Saint John – "

"The manna falls on their heads, manna from heaven, which makes them as happy as if they'd won at the lottery. But are you aware –"

"Let them have it, Your Excellency, if they believe in it… and then it's been so many years…"

"Worse, my dear friend, much worse! That's not religion, it's paganism! And the church cannot sponsor paganism with the excuse that it's religion!"

"But, Excellency, these people aren't capable of making fine distinctions. Permit me: you yourself said to me once, when it was a question of smuggling in those machines for Farinacci, that they have the souls of children, that they can be overcome with a trinket, just so long as it shines."

Martinolli blushed with manufactured anger. "So you're implying… out with it! Tell me!"

"I wouldn't say a thing, Your Excellency!"

"I'm not 'Your Excellency'! One of these days I'll be 'Your Eminence'!"

"I wouldn't say a thing, Your Eminence!"

Martinolli got up from his armchair, turned to don Campagna, regarding the old priest he didn't want to look at with a sigh. He was a dull but punctilious attendant and had been for many, too many, years. And when his glance fell on those thin shoulderblades which were pushing their way out of his clothes, and when he saw the wrinkled collar looking as if it were leaning on that neck, dirty with sweat, then he understood that he too was old.

The two of them had grown old together and their youth and maturity had been taken up in the reciprocal observance of commonplaces carried out in the framework of useless protocol.

But with what other people could Martinolli give tangible proof that in that city he was not only a convenient authority to have, but also one who was armed with specific powers, including those of controlling his direct subordinates? Could he perhaps do this with the anonymous priests who brought him their first fruits and fresh vegetables from the country, who would bump into him in church, bringing with them the dust from the hills of the country, and bore him with abuses and bits of stubbornness of no particular importance?

He would not have derived any satisfaction from it. But he got quite some stimulation from subtly tormenting don Ersilio Campagna, who, even though endowed with that intuition which the difficult experiences of his priesthood had refined in him, could not understand why the Auxiliary Bishop took such delight in annoying him. That is, in spite of his guesses and examinations of conscience, he could not get at the obscurest feelings of his superior where they faded into indecipherability, touching as they did on various old mistakes and bitter attitudes which lie at the bottom of a human existence and are not to be cleared up even on the point of death.

How could he have understood that in fussing at him Martinolli was really fussing at himself? In Martinolli's eyes, what was don Campagna but a projection of his conscience, although translated into the most minimal terms? And so, looking at the poor priest, he saw another version of himself, with the rough edges still there and a little used up, compared with his own social good fortune and that ability which comes from a good background and perception sharpened by experience.

Don Campagna was another version of himself which he had picked up and put in the heart of the most rebellious neighborhood to suffer day by day, for the same reasons which led him to suffer on a greater scale, and so that don Campagna would expose himself to those emotions with which Martinolli did not wish to be involved, and finally to experience the poverty of a parish which was as poor as the houses where its people lived.

And since don Ersilio was neither a saint nor a missionary, but was able to distinguish inferior from superior weakness, as Califfa and her friends understood it, and appear tender in the face of the former and inscrutable when faced with the latter, Martinolli ended up by blaming him for the shortcomings of his own conscience.

This was the last of the reasons which led the Monsignor to create an atmosphere of irritating uneasiness when the priest was present. One day don Ersilio clearly heard him say: "You, don Ersilio, are my bad conscience!" and inadvertently from the lips of the Monsignor had come the well-known words:

"When are we going to clear this thicket, eh, when are we going to clear it up?"

The priest did not at first understand, then he opened out his arms, limiting himself to saying, "Eh, what can we do? With God's help..." And what could he add about his work, really, except that he carried it out in the only possible way and that was with the good sense which made him regard all theoretical discussions as useless, since he realized exactly how things were?

"What do you mean, 'What can we do?'" Martinolli reproached him. "Are you aware that your work on a smaller scale is the same which the Church proposes to carry out in the world? Do you know that in the midst of those tenement houses you are a Pope?"

"I?!" exclaimed don Ersilio.

"Yes, a little Pope, but always a Pope! Drive yourself a little more don Ersilio, drive yourself!" and Martinolli put a hand on his shoulder. "And remember: sacrifice, sacrifice!" And remembering how his colleague from Rome had mentioned the same word to him with quite another intonation, a warm satisfaction was added to the other sentiments aroused by don Ersilio's pale yellow face with its dog-like eyes.

He had taken at least one foot out of the grave. And he had avoided a risk. But it would have been so easy, since he had started with nothing, for him to have gone no further than a cassock stained with tobacco, a cold, nearly unfurnished house, the frequent counting of the money in the poorbox, and the nightly examination of his conscience and the losing battle with the feeling that all the years had been a delusion.

And as he touched don Ersilio's shoulders he suddenly pictured his warm residence, the green fields with the red vines which were in his possession, and the comfortable houses of his friends, especially Doberdò's, of his friends who allowed him, playing on a mutual respect, to put his hands not only in their consciences, but also in some of their affairs which were not exactly spiritual.

But don Campagna's voice took him from that accounting. "I'm sorry you're so disturbed, and that it worries you so," said the old priest, believing that Martinolli was standing there like that with his hands behind his back and his eyes in the void to consider whether he should or should not grant his permission for the festival to take place.

Martinolli looked at him for a moment, but immediately went back to his reflections.

"But you know," he said, "you know what the difference is between unreasoned liberality and very bad policy?"

"A hair's breadth, I know," thought don Ersilio, but he said aloud: "No, Your Eminence."

"And do you know what the difference is between a very bad policy and the most Godforsaken disgrace?"

"No, Your Eminence."

Martinolli glowed with luminous satisfaction. "A hair's breadth, my dear friend, a wire as thin as a hair," and the Monsignor pointed to a tuft of his white hair.

Don Ersilio went back to bending his head. "They've already made everything ready, poor people, they're waiting…"

"They pull at our cassocks only when they need us," said Martinolli, pacing up and down the room. He pretended that he was meditating again, to keep the old priest on tenterhooks – and also Mazza, who was standing guard outside.

But the real result, the one he wanted to achieve, was to make the people in the tenements see don Campagna come back late, to have doubts, and to suffer from them. And the fact that they stood there with bated breath on the other side of the river and looked each other in the face, obliged by a superior force to examine their consciences, even though for interested reasons, was one of the few satisfactions the Monsignor had with respect to that stubborn and fanatical sixth column.

But it was vexation and silence which finally caused him to be won over by don Ersilio's timid arguments, because it never even occurred to Martinolli to end his farce with a refusal. That would have been all he needed – to risk the outbreak of a revolt because there was only a hair's breadth between unreasoned liberality and a very bad policy.

And then he was sorry for don Ersilio; he suddenly gave up any idea of revenge when the old priest went away, leaving the smell of tobacco in his room.

Martinolli heard his shoes scraping their way downstairs.

And he thought he also heard his sickly breathing and he could see him in his mind's eye leaning on the rail with his bones dancing in his clothes.

And then he had one of those sudden fits which sometimes assailed him, covering his eyes with tears, and leading him to take his head in his hands and say "Help me!" – less to God than to the personification of his need of consolation.

III

And this was how Califfa's neighborhood could explode in a festival several generations old, a long-awaited break from the cares of the body and the spirit, an exciting way to feel liberated and purified and gloriously happy, although only for one night.

On June 24 a strange sort of dawn was seen rising over the houses of the old city. In the first light of day there were no cries of laborers or noise of trucks on their way to the factories, and not even the shutters in front of the shops were raised, nor even the doors of the apartment houses open. There was a silence until noon, even in the bars. The whole neighborhood looked dead. But behind the impenetrable façades there was not death but the expectation of a moment of life, real, unbridled free life; because people were trying to sleep a little longer to be more wide awake that night when the doors would be thrown open with the first darkness and the streets lit as bright as day. The people would run out into the streets, into the fields, and toward the hills.

On the grass there was to be eating and drinking, and it was love of one's self which imposed the common intoxication, free from distinctions, shame, and the obscure roots of intimacy and egoism. It was an ancient folly, which was interrupted when the church towers struck midnight. Then, under the moon, and on the moist grass, the crowd was silent, the faces were raised to the starry heavens and an emotion was to be seen in their eyes which had but one reason, a common hope handed down for centuries.

No one touched any food at that moment and even the young broke loose from their embraces to look up, waiting for grace to come from those weak and lowered stars in their warm nighttime veil. The noises from the highway, the voices and the music which came from the opposite bank no longer had any part in that time and that space. They had nothing to do with those people who were still as figures in a painting and inspired by the festival to take pride in their race.

Until someone, the first one, rose from his place and, raising his arms and lifting up his trembling hands, covered his face with them, caressing the thin veil of dew there, and shouted: "The manna! The manna!" And it was a cry which spread like a volley of cannon, as if the echo of the countryside brought it with the speed of light from one side to the other of that crowd which had been waiting all that time: "The manna! The manna!"

IV

Yes, the manna. Who knows what they were waiting for? Maybe they thought Jesus Christ was going to fly down onto their new hairdos and cure all their problems, cancel their debts, make them well in the coming year, with bliss in their hearts and a kiss on the forehead like so many children to be put to bed. And how they jumped around on the fields, even the old ones! They waved their hands in the air, laughing and praying at the same time, as if that group of stars were sending down something to eat instead of a good mood.

But then our priest got up, all wrapped in his mantle. The manna which was blessed for the rest of us, was poison for his rheumatism and was likely to keep him in bed for a week. He got up there and all he had to say was "And now let's pray," and everyone got down on their knees around the field chapel with its little Madonna, remembering what he had gone through for them.

So Campagna got up that evening too and I was on my knees like the others and I was waiting for him to finish with the litany and start the party again, especially since I was already warm with the wine, and Califfa, when she's pushed on with a little Lambrusco wine, can barely be kept back. "Amen," said he and then there was a stampede back to the party. We were all eating and carrying on as if no one had had any fun or anything to eat for years. I went back to my glass and I almost didn't care that Guido was at the other end of the bench, suspicious and nasty the way he usually was, and since the wine made me warm, I took off my sweater.

And then Cernusco shouted at me, "Sing, Califfa, come on!" and the others took it up too: "Yes, Califfa, you've got a wonderful voice, no one can sing Verdi as well as you can, Califfa!" I was undecided for a moment, but then I saw Guido, who had more or less come to life and was smiling as if he really wanted to hear me sing. And he said: "Come on, Califfa, let the saints do the praying!"

I was so happy that he had asked me, and in that pleasant way, that I put my hands on my hips and my face to the sky and away I went with *"Parigi, o cara"* with so much energy and passion in my voice that everyone was open-mouthed. And as I was gathering my breath for the high note, I was saying to myself, it looks as if the manna's really bringing me good luck this time!

Because, I repeat, I'd seen Guido looking like he'd never looked before. And just think that he probably already had his plan to humiliate me and ruin me! Will I ever understand men?

In any case, I repeated the cadenza from *"noi lascieremo"* and in the silence, in that field which was black as hell, I heard the voice of Vito Alibrandi coming from the next table, inviting me to do a duet with him.

I felt like a thief who'd been caught; my heart burst and the wind was taken out of my sails. But what could I do? I looked at Guido and he was still smiling, so I closed my eyes and I tried to speed it up, trying to get it over with as soon as possible.

We sang like two crowing roosters and Vito, just to make it harder on me, kept the pace normal, calm and full-voiced, like a singer in church, and he enjoyed making trouble for me.

We went back to *"Parigi, o cara"* and I begged Vito with my eyes, and tried to sing the high notes off key to make him understand what he didn't seem to want to understand, holding the melody back like the bridle of a horse. Finally it was over, thank God, and everyone was clapping their hands. Imagine how yours truly felt. I'd hardly finished the last note when I looked at Guido and I saw that he was clapping his hands too. But he wasn't smiling, and he was his usual suspicious self.

For a while I thought I was going to go mad and, thinking back on it now, so many years later, I can still feel that shiver that came from a presentiment I had even before he opened his mouth. And when he shouted to me, "Wonderful, Califfa, and now show us another duet with him," I felt myself dying even if it wasn't a surprise to me.

"Califfa," he yelled again, meaner this time, after everyone had quieted down, "show us what you do with him when no one's looking! Come on!"

Vito was still standing on a chair and couldn't move, and I held on to Viola, who was next to me, and I must have been crying without knowing it, because my face was wet and that mob of people began swimming in my eyes.

"Come on, Califfa, show us!"

But I was already running through the crowd of people and my shame and anger were behind me, and I felt his last words, his last insult in the distance like a bad dream:

"Come on, Califfa!"

I ran down the hill onto the field, and I didn't stop until I was at the door of Viola's house.

CHAPTER SIX

The was the end of her love for Guido. But right afterward the bottom fell out of everything connected with their life together with a rush of events and a desperate need to begin again.

That night was the last time they saw each other. Califfa stayed in Viola's house, on the bed, with a headache that would not let her think even though she wanted to. She was halfway between sleep and waking, sunk in a kitchen full of children and household articles.

Viola looked at her from the foot of the bed and begged her: "Get up. I'll come with you if you want. Tell him that you'll swear on the head of your poor son that if there's been anything wrong done..."

Califfa didn't listen to her. She stayed there with her face in the pillow and she could taste her shame in her mouth and feel its warm darkness in her guts.

Viola put a glass to Califfa's mouth, to give her a little wine. And she repeated, "Go back to your husband. Why can't you understand? How can you ruin everything that way?"

And finally, one morning, Califfa found the energy to get up and look in the mirror. Her face was like death warmed over and her comb had a hard time making its way through the knots in her hair. But the sun was shining outside and some of the sunshine was coming in the window, and she sat down there on the bricks and it seemed to her that life was putting a little blush in her cheeks once again.

"Go to him, Califfa," Viola was insisting. "There's some good in everything that happens. Maybe after this you two will be able to get along together."

Califfa thought that Viola might be right. Because she knew that Guido would act like a beast, then simmer down. So she thought she knew how he felt. He would be bitterly regretful at having humiliated her in front of everyone, and at having ruined that last hope. But he also had that stupid pride which led him to think more and more that he was alone. "He's always been that way," she would say to herself, "a wild animal that bites first and then yelps."

And she was thinking that it had been just those unusual fits of anger, followed by a disposition to let things go, that had reduced him to the state he was in, kicked in the face by everyone. But the fact was that he was suffering from it, because of her; and his suffering was not like Califfa's. Sooner or later she would get rid of hers; shouting or even singing, but deaf to all pleas, she would get rid of this cancer within her.

Viola tried to convince her; and she started moving about the house, undecided whether to give in, in remorse, with the leftovers of her former feelings – or, rather, with a bit of common sense – to the usual line of reasoning. It would have been a useless humiliation since Guido wouldn't or couldn't have wanted to understand her.

How many times had the desire to break the ice with him, to smile first, led her almost to saying something, to taking him into her confidence? She remembered some evenings when she would move in her bathrobe between the bed and the bureau, when she would get in and out of bed, but could not find peace. The room above had a wooden floor and she would listen to Guido talking to his pigeons, with the loving singsong of a madman, or of a little boy with his toys.

Because her husband was not completely without anything to do; he had a strange trade and it was to go about the countryside buying pigeons still warm from the nest and to raise them for target practice. He called each one by name – Corfu, Athos, Leo: the names of the Partisans in his brigade – and she could tell from his voice that he loved them and that he was thinking of the day when they would be big enough for him to take them in a basket to the shooting range.

And for this reason, Guido never had a joyous Sunday.

Doberdò, Mastrangelo, Mazzullo the Police Chief, and the usual gang that gathered on Sundays, would arrive and sit on their wooden stools at the edge of the field and wait. Guido would prepare the apparatus, caress the birds with his hands, feel their warmth for the last time, and then release them into the air, one by one. And when they flew into the sky, he tried not to look, so as not to see them falling after they were shot.

Doberdò would look; Mastrangelo would look; and Corfu, Athos, and Leo, taken in their first free flight, would fall on the rocks in the stream, or in the little pools of stagnant water, with a thud like rocks. They were Guido's. This was the price of his work. And when it was all over, he would wander disconsolate over the field, gathering up the bodies of the poor dead birds.

He put them into the basket and went back home. So much labor and so much love thrown away like that, for those little bundles of feathers and blood with little or no meat on them, worth only a few lire from the storekeepers.

But that's how Guido was, and so she would hear him talking until late in the night, pronouncing those names as if he were calling someone who could never come back to him. In the night, that solitary voice would torment her. And Califfa would say to herself: "Now I'm going up, I'll talk to him, I'll calm him down…"

But she could go up only a few steps of that stairway because when she found the trapdoor closed, she was reminded of her son and how Guido had acted: he would have acted better if it had been someone else's son! But he had Guido's eyes, Califfa was saying to herself in desperation, his mouth and the same hair; the baby was like a photograph of him, for God's sake! How could he have shrugged his shoulders or turned a deaf ear to her pleas when she had begged him before the baby died: "Find a job, Guido, a job that'll pay you something. We need money to cure him, to make him well. Guido, please!"

He wouldn't listen to her, or if he took a job, he got himself driven away at his first temper tantrum, as if he and his pretensions were the only thing in the world and he had no responsibility. He would pass from one workshop to another and one store to another and his son breathed with more and more difficulty in that sweat-soaked bed where he had only a few more days to live.

Califfa stopped, made impotent by the fundamental impossibility of understanding him, which caused her fear and pain and allowed for no answer on her part. She stayed hours with the thought of Guido who had such tender feelings for a pigeon which was about to die, and yet who was not able to accept life as it is for the sake of his son. And it was at such moments that Califfa understood that the judges perhaps were right after all to condemn him. She understood it with some feeling of being ashamed of herself, but that was how it was; because, as she got to know him better, she also understood that her husband was able to kill a man and then lie down by a woman, gentle and polite as a boy who was just then getting to know the world.

And with the same shame she even doubted that Guido had really deserved the words with which the lawyer had replied to the sentence at the trial: "Now I say to you that Fascism is not dead, Your Honor! No, real Fascism begins now, with this sentence, and it is no longer the Fascism of living men, but of the dead who stink as dead bodies do. And it will be our fault if Fascism returns to take its place in the courtrooms, in the Ministries, and everywhere!"

But Viola insisted and one day Califfa got dressed and said: "All right! I'm going!"

II

I was walking in the middle of the houses and I didn't see a soul. There was only the heat of the sun which prickled, and it dazzled your eyes when it shone on the white houses.

It seemed like I hadn't seen the sun for a long time. The streets were strange, they were so empty. I was saying to myself, it's because I'm still in the country here, and I went on. But when I came to the first tenement houses, I understood that that wasn't it. Something was up. Even here there weren't

74

any children, no men, and the women, the few I met, were standing there with their shoulders to the wall. They looked like they were waiting for a storm on that hot summer day.

They were all lined up there, so scared you'd think they were going to be shot, with their angry eyes straight ahead watching me pass by. I was happy and innocent, as if I'd come from another world, and they looked as if they'd never seen a girl cross the street before.

But what's wrong with them, I was saying to myself, that they're looking at me like that? And meanwhile I was trying to figure out whether I'd have the nerve to go into my house once I got there; whether I'd be able to go up to him and call him by name.

"Guido," I tried to say to myself as I was passing through the Church square – and there wasn't even a dog there either. "Guido... Guido..." But it didn't thrill me at all. Because I didn't believe in it, because it was remorse which led me on, and now I was sure that he knew, that maybe he'd seen it happen with his own eyes.

It was a long time since he'd hit me. And I could still remember when he'd hit me like that, suddenly, without my having any idea of what was coming. And I could see his little-boy face wrinkling up like an old man's and becoming someone else's. And I could still feel his fingers on my lips, thin like the thongs of a whip.

And with those eyes, with that face, he must have killed some innocent people, if he killed anyone at all. But maybe not. Maybe he won't beat me. Maybe he won't dare. He'll turn his back on me, he will, because he won't want to see me or hear me. I'm sure he'll say that's enough of this on-again-and-off-again life.

"Guido," I said to myself again. And as I was passing by, a church bell in the square struck noon. If it hadn't been for the cloud of pigeons which flew around me, I wouldn't have noticed that it was like a cemetery around my house too. The doors were closed and the windows were closed. There wasn't a sound where usually people were yelling from morning till night. But why? Where was I anyway?

And then there was the door to my house. And it was a good thing the sun was making my head boil, because if it hadn't been, there wouldn't have been anything else to remind me that I was still alive and that the silence was real. I felt as if everyone was spying on my shame! I was at the door of my building as if at a confessional – I didn't know where to begin. But it was there that I took heart; because when there's something to do, and not just think about, then I always find the frank face of Califfa.

And I threw open the door, and as soon as I was inside I yelled: "Guido! I'm here! It's me, Califfa!"

But he didn't answer. I went in and dashed up the stairs. No one was there. The kitchen was empty and so was the room above. The bed was unmade. I tried the roof. I pushed open the trapdoor and said to myself, "He must be here, it's only noon." But he wasn't. There were just the pigeons, and when they heard the trapdoor they began batting around in their cages. But the room was empty.

And without really understanding what was up, I began to feel something in the air. I ran down the stairs. And the first person I found I stopped to talk to. It was Bruna, a friend of Viola's, and she was running away from the square when I grabbed her by the arm, and she looked at me like a suspicious dog. I yelled at her: "But, Bruna, what's going on?"

She didn't stop. She shouted over her shoulder: "The cops are down by the bridge. Mastrangelo is locked in his own shop like a thief in jail. And your husband's there, right in the front row!"

God, how I ran after that! And someone yelled at me: "Califfa, Califfa, wait!" But I ran on and on…

III

Mastrangelo thought he had been shrewd. After his meeting with Doberdò, it was true, he had marked the names of the most suspect of his employees. But those were not the ones he fired, as everyone thought he would. His plan was

76

good – namely, to avoid filling the streets with hotheads tied down to a party line and capable of starting riots. He made use instead of a kind of psychological blackmail.

With great care, therefore, trying to know as much as the files could tell him, he had isolated the most harmless and open of his men, trying especially to gather together all those who for one reason or another were not popular with most of the rest of them.

What brotherly spirit, for example, could be inspired by Furlani, a man who'd been involved up to his neck in Mussolini's last gasp, the Republic of Salo, in 1943, and who had not been done away with only because of a feeling of pity for his ten children? Or Afro Ferrari, who had twice worked as a strikebreaker, or Bertinelli, a foreman who was perpetually unhappy and who kept his men under a tight rein as if they were galley slaves?

Mastrangelo, in other words, had changed to another *modus operandi,* described by Farinacci to the Auxiliary Bishop before he had organized the procession of the famous machines: "The main thing is to stop them where they're strongest and put them in a corner where they're weakest – namely, in solidarity. They just can't stick together. Dissension, Excellency, dissension... collectivism is the weakest of defenses. All you have to do is to take out the keystone and everything else falls down. Just get a little rancor started and esteem vanishes and suspicion contaminates everything..."

Dissension had started on that July morning, with Furlani, Bertinelli, and thirty other desperate men kept outside the gate by force, while the siren was sounding and work was starting inside as usual. Furlani was the wildest one of them, and when Mastrangelo's car went by, he jumped on it and hung on so that it took three men to drag him off. He was slobbering, and when he fell to his knees, the first group of police fell on his massive shoulders.

The riot squad took up a position in front of the gates. It was easy to mount a guard against that group, which stopped on a sign from Furlani and began to go back into the square, where the sun had risen to a vertical position over the helmets and the barrels of the machine guns.

But those men who were slinking away from the square where they had been barricaded behind the stones with something to defend, united by a common feeling of sadness, were moved by fear not so much of death as of a future yawning before them like an abyss. The faces, voices and eyes of their children and their women made impossible any surrender to the situation.

Furlani was the first to go home. His children were still asleep, but, driven by his folly, he dragged them from their beds. His wife didn't even have time to cover herself with a bathrobe. He dragged her along with the children into the street in front of everybody, so that they could all see those sleepy creatures, dazzled by the light, and that dried-up woman who was trembling with shame and whose face bore the marks of her miserable life.

Furlani was so angry that he had no further thought of dignity and had no idea of where he was going, dragging that ragged little group through the streets and squares of the slums, with a simple face and a lump in his throat, while the windows opened and a crowd gathered. Furlani proceeded without a word, as if he were running away from a fire.

He needed no words, nor did Ferrari or Bertinelli or the others who copied him and marched along behind him with their children, their wives and their old people, in a desperate and silent procession which grew as it emptied the buildings on its way, street by street and alley after alley.

There was no point in asking aloud for pity and by then it did not make any difference that Furlani had been a Fascist or that Ferrari had been a strikebreaker. They were like so many birds flocking together. People continued to stream out of the buildings: those who were out of work, the boys just getting out of bed, the shopkeepers who pulled the shutters over their shops before they left them, and the women who went along without really knowing why, carried by that emotion which leads crowds when it is accompanied by dignity, stirring up people's blood with its ancient appeal.

Fear was no part of this emotion, not even when the crowd, headed by Furlani and his little flock of tragic witnesses who refused to abandon him, spread out at the edge of the square in front of the plant. There was no fear even when the police found themselves squeezed on both sides when the factory gates had re-opened and were spewing forth more people at their backs; they withdrew toward the wall, holding on to the barrels of their guns.

Furlani proceeded without turning, without a sign, as if that act of rebellion were his alone. From the other side, from the expanding group of workers, Cernusco and Guido came toward him. They were part of a threatening wing of blue work clothes on its way to the left embankment where the police had formed a circle and were waiting. Meanwhile the arrival of more policemen from the direction of the bridge was announced by a siren in that quiet summer day, among those chalk-white crumbling façades where everyone was assembled but where not one voice was raised, and where you could hear people breathe.

IV

And it was into this waiting silence that Califfa burst from the bridge, running barefoot on the stones heated by the sun; and she saw Guido down there, in back of Furlani. And she did not understand what he was doing there or what crazy idea he had taken up, he who had not believed in anything up to yesterday, and who was proud of the fact that he had no political party or any ideas and it did not matter to him what the others thought of him since it's all a swindle, as he used to say, a big swindle...

But now Guido was only a few yards away from those machine guns and he did not seem to see them as he stood there in his old jacket with his hands in his pockets. That moment before the tragedy was suspended between violence and pity. Guido was unaware and without fear, as he knew how to be at certain times.

And that was all that Califfa could see. So she threw herself into the middle of the crowd and shouted: "Guido! Guido!"

And hers was the first cry that broke the rarefied air, like a volley of stones against glass, and while she was desperately making her way through that press of bodies and the common perspiration of rebellion, Guido heard the cry like something beyond creation. It was not the cry of the woman who had betrayed him, not a cry of egotism or fear, but of love, of love freed from shame and guilt. Guido suddenly ceased to be a hollow shell of a man who was risking his life for a just cause simply because he had nothing and no one to save. He was seized with wonder, for Califfa's cry made him a participant with the others in that common intoxication from which he had felt estranged.

"Guido! Guido!" At that moment they could all hear it, with trepidation in their blood. Whatever was to be the end of that drama, he would never again be a man spat upon and betrayed, an unhappy man on whom to take pity. It had taken him so many years to come to this revelation of a moment, to understand, to feel consolation again: so many mistakes to rediscover his sincerity, now, in a brief glance. But it was enough so that he could have an exact sense of everything: of Califfa pushing her way through the crowd, of Furlani, who wanted to hold him back, of the silent crowd looking only at him, the most important of them all, again the partisan who was the first to advance and believed that his was the really just war.

"Guido!" But Guido continued to advance, and in his newly rediscovered happiness, what could it matter to him that the cordon of police was drawing back and then convulsively spreading out on its way to surround him?

The crowd was like a bird beating its wings for the last time before dying. It trembled throughout as if to protect Guido. There were hundreds of faces, hundreds of consciences, all looking at someone who only yesterday was crawling around in corners like a thief. But Guido had come too far forward and suddenly he began to run, shouting in anger and joy at the same time, and when they shot him in the stomach and when he fell on his knees in the square, he turned on his side and looked once again at the sun which had heated his misery for so many years, and the people blotted it from his eyes, maddened and furious as they were, running up to him and over him.

Califfa was in the square by then empty of the crowd, where the police were stationed among their jeeps and where the sun was beating a little less heavily on the asphalt. It was not indifference or madness on her part which prevented her from getting up to follow a poor bloody body stretched out on a jeep, which was being taken away in a crowd of policemen who almost hid it – only its inert arm was exposed, beating against the jeep's side as the dangling hand made a pattern in the dust. She would be able to embrace that body all night at the morgue, or find it in a corner of the cemetery for so many days and so many years.

The puddle of blood spreading out among the wheel ruts, near which Califfa was sitting curled up with her shoulders against the wall, with her clothes torn and her face deformed, her eyes burning with grief, was being dried up by the sun and in a short while the ground would again be dry there.

Califfa did not get up. She stayed there with her arm pointing the way it had been when they knocked her down. And she thought that that blood had sung within her, had been both love and anger to her, as well as fear and exaltation, and had been born in her in the form of her son, with his eyes, his face, and his hands.

And the wind was no longer whistling along the tracks of the siding. The earth had returned to drying itself off in the sun and only a little stain remained. Now Califfa could get up and go away, she could walk across the square with her face bathed in tears and anger, trembling in the shoulders and hesitating and turning for a moment, among the parked jeeps, among the immobile faces of the policemen watching her.

There was only a dusty bush down there, a piece of crumbling wall, two ruts buried in the earth where the grass was growing. And Califfa set off toward the bridge, alone in the silence and the sun.

CHAPTER SEVEN

Annibale Doberdò emerged from the fog, shivering throughout his exhausted and shaking body, with the usual cluster of problems running through his head. His executive Mercedes was being smoothly parked behind him, while the darkened city seemed alive only in the weak light given out by the few shops which were still open. Doberdò crossed the street lazily, in the mist which was shining on his great eyelids which solemnly protected his eagle-like but watery eyes.

It was a bad night in October, with the fog gathering on the silent buildings and buried streets. The fog, the silence… and suddenly the sound of two high heels of a woman or a girl running along the opposite sidewalk. Doberdò stopped at the entrance to his club and his great hatted head turned on his shoulder, diffident and curious, like the head of a horse dragged along by a bridle, in search of that sound. And in the fog was the form of an adolescent white-skinned girl who could be seen walking rapidly along and who vanished at the end of the street, the only ray of life in that desolation, but it was enough: a ray of tender white flesh, straight legs and a youthful bosom under her shopgirl's smock. Annibale Doberdò had time for only rare moments of sweet reverie like that one, conditioned by the impossibility of a fleeting consolation in a body racked with heart disease.

The girl in her squalid overcoat took a final step in Doberdò's sight; the sound of her heels disappeared and the night swallowed her up. Doberdò pushed his homburg back, sank his face into his scarf, and started up the steps of his club. He went up looking threatening and arrogant, tormenting the rail with his huge farmer's hand, just as he did with his adversaries when he sat in his office chair, in every minute of every hour of his tumultuous day; and he did not care that his breath was getting short in his decrepit lungs and that the wheeze grew as he came up the steps under that cathedral-like vault, across the drawing rooms hung with chandeliers and caressed by a funereal semi-shadow.

Doberdò went up, rocking on the red rail, and tried not to look at the ruin of his body in those mirrors which faced him and assailed him from everywhere. He went up the steps pulling himself along by sheer will power, and in the meantime he was smiling at the white face of the girl veiled in the fog. Then his diseased breathing began to infiltrate into the reading room.

Farinacci put his jacket back on; Police Chief Mazzullo came with dignified haste out of the men's room and established himself in an armchair; Mastrangelo and Gazza put up their pool cues, annoyed; and Mastrangelo adjusted the knot on his necktie, while Cantoni the lawyer, who was the most diligent of them all, opened the window so the smoke would blow out, and put the newspaper on the little table at exactly the right spot, delicately folding it. The only one who could sit there with his leg on the arm of a chair without disturbing his lazy pose was Count Pedrelli, even if Doberdò's wheezing coming along the hall was no longer a warning but a threatening presence, among the potted plants wilting in the autumn, and with the waiters rushing to take his things with the unctuous lightness of a cloud of harlots.

Doberdò spread out his arms and kept right on walking while his hat, his scarf, and his coat were taken off him as if from a dummy in a store window. The form of his hunched-up back was exposed, with his short jacket. He proceeded with his hands clasped behind his back toward the glass door behind which Pedrelli, sheathed by centuries of nobility, was enjoying his privileges. These included nesting in the armchair and barely rising when Doberdò, who among many other things was president of the club, opened the door. Doberdò's watery, shrewd little eyes wandered about the room, passing over the usual faces wrinkled in their deferential smiles.

A life full of errors, of ingrained folly, of the elegant plotting of a nobleman in great difficulties, could all be pardoned in someone privileged enough to be able to greet Annibale Doberdò by raising his backside barely four inches from his chair while the club's president, with a "Good evening, gentlemen!" as cordial as a death sentence, passed on trembling legs among the notables who flitted about him. The old lion walked to the end of the room and only when he allowed himself to fall into the red leather armchair which was his by right, and only when his hand had seized the newspaper put there next to him (the knew, he must have known, that it was Cantoni who had put it there) did the atmosphere revive with a slight bustle of voices. Doberdò's breath down there, between the curtains at the window, eased off slowly and almost died out; the faces in the room were all pointed at him, ready to smile or start a conversation, but only if he wanted to, only if he were to deign to turn that large white-haired head.

But Doberdò did not turn: he continued to stare at the newspaper, even if he did not read it. He knew perfectly well what was going on in those minds, where the right phrase, the boot-licking compliment, was being dreamed up, ready to jump at him like so many crickets. Farinacci's promissory notes, Mastrangelo's labor troubles, the "Excuse me, Mr. Doberdò, but Rome is asking..." from Mazzollo, the Chief of Police, even Gazza's dirty politics and Cantoni's poetic sighs, so filled with sentimental delusion... Doberdò shrugged his shoulders. He was too tired. His profile sank farther into his newspaper, and he read it between fits of dozing.

And then Farinacci leaned submissively over to Gazza and said: "Certainly his position now is as interesting as it is difficult... But it's worthy of his talent, worthy of his talent..." and Gazza nodded, contemplating the chief recipient of his petty political favors with the tenderness usually accorded a sleeping baby.

But Doberdò was not thinking about situations. He was

looking at the fog piling up behind the windows, and he was wondering where that girl had gone; he was thinking of the heat of her breath, of her eating amid the laughter of a poor table, of the red of her mouth, and he was thinking of the girl undressing, freeing her fresh breasts before going to bed. He imagined the little shafts of light in the darkness of the fog and the night. An anonymous shopgirl stretched lazily out in his brain in this rare moment of peace, and he smiled to himself again, resting on his chest the head which controlled the destinies of the city.

II

The fog was enfolding the banks of the river, the fields and the farms, and the lights were lit outside the house doors. At times they looked like bomb explosions in the depth of the night, when the wind changed and brightened the mists around Viola's house.

Poor Viola, Califfa was thinking during those nights when Viola went out to ply her trade, when she would watch her going down the street, keeping close to the wall, her hands recognizing its cracks as if she were blind, in order not to get lost out there in the middle of the country. And it was Califfa's job to station herself at the door until Viola reached the first building, shouting and singing from there so that Viola would know which direction to take so as not to get lost.

"Volare, oh, oh... !" and finally from that black inferno would come Viola's voice to quiet Califfa down: "All right! All right!"

Then Califfa would go back in and close the door after her, saying to herself: Give her a hand, God, if You're out there! She would sit by the stove and it would seem she could see Viola there, with that pale sickly face of hers and those eyes which had seen better days. Once they had been shiny with youth, but now they shone with fever as she held her shawl around her shoulders, trembling within it, that poor woman of forty who looked as if she were sixty.

She shuttled across the street so that the police would not see her, and then she ducked into a cheap restaurant where there was a room on the second floor with a little table, a toilet, and a camp bed with a mattress. It was as cold as hell, and when the windows blew open the cold air and the fog would come in. Viola lay down on the mattress and held her breasts tightly as if she were going to give birth. She prayed that the night would go quickly.

Usually they would eat and raise hell. And people from the other side of the river would often show up, a little because of the wine, which was robust, but especially because many people were talking about that whore who had been through quite some battles, according to a lot of men, but had survived them all and really put out like she enjoyed it.

And every time she did, her fever got worse, so that at the end of her night's work when Viola came home and Califfa heard her sick voice and ran out to meet her, she found a poor, worn-out thing, panting and burning up with fever, who trembled in Califfa's arms. She would bring Viola back to the house and rub her back to give her a little warmth; she would put her to bed and get in with her and hold her the whole night.

Her poor head sought peace on Califfa's shoulder and the two streams of their breath came together, Califfa's cold and clear so that she could not close her eyes, Viola's heavy but deep as well.

It was then that Califfa learned how long the hours of a night can bee, and how cruel that light which never comes to whiten the windows or at least to console you with the certainty that you could call someone if you felt you were dying...

And so Viola would set out on her *via crucis* and Califfa would stay home by the stove, counting the hours with the trains as they went by (she knew those trains well, because for a month or so she had slept in a railway warehouse). There was the eleven-o'clock local and the Milan express at midnight, and in the calm of that house, with the wash on the line and dripping in the kitchen, all that could be heard was the breathing of Viola's children.

If she were to move the clothes line, she could see those creatures in one great bed at the end of the room, piled up one on another in a confusion compounded of love and tender egotism, with their little arms on the covers and a happy smile on their faces. She went to put the small hands under the sheet, but first she held them in hers, and that flowing of innocent blood and shaking of delicate bones made her understand what was good about life, more than any sermon in church could.

And she was also thinking how foolish Viola was, because those children were not born by accident: Viola had wanted them all. She had so much desire for life and so much faith in mankind that Califfa was ashamed of having gotten so fed up with life when Viola would tell how she decided to let herself get pregnant.

"I know it's not good, Califfa," she confessed. "But when I run into certain important people in my work, people who have made a success of life, and they're handsome and intelligent, I wonder how they've gotten where they have and I want to have a child so bad... The man gets on top of me and does what he wants and then he goes away. And I stay there and think about it. If I have a child this time it'll have his blood and maybe even a little of his brains, and if he's made a fortune, why can't his child make a fortune too?"

And so the little Honorable was born, with a nose just like Giacinto Gazza's, who by then was Doberdò's hench man, but whom Viola had serviced when he was an honorable member of Parliament.

The little Honorable (Viola had given them the names herself and that was what she liked to call them) was sleeping with his head leaning on the shoulder of the Poet, who was ugly, with those warts on his big head, and just think what he would be like when he grew up with his overcoat around his shoulders and a bundle of newspapers under his arm. He looked like a caricature of Cantoni when he went along the arcade before supper. ("He is a little ugly, but look at his eyes, Califfa," said Viola, caressing her son. "Look and tell me if you don't think this one was born to think.")

And so they were all asleep shivering in the cold under that dirty sheet, even little Mazzullo, and if Viola had told the truth, even little Doberdò. The last-named was a large three-year-old, as pushy as his father, who was snoring like a grown man and who struck his brothers as he turned over, making them draw back toward the edge of the bed. A little Duke, who had hardly opened his eyes, was asking for some food and heaven help anyone who couldn't give him some.

Califfa stroked their foreheads and she smiled and almost stopped thinking about all her troubles of the past few months, about the death of her husband and what had happened afterward. She was thinking of Viola combing her children's hair and saying in a happy tone: "Here's the city in miniature, Califfa!" and she laughed and laughed with a contagious sort of smile.

III

After Guido's death (and Vito Alibrandi had also gone away, with his good looks and his high-handed ways, and they said he took the train to Milan to clown around in his shorts with the soccer team), I had lived like a bird. I felt dried up, as if something had burned me.

Tomorrow I'll move, tomorrow I'll put an end to it, I'll decide on something. But I was still there. Four months had gone by and I was still being supported by Viola.

"But no!" she flared up. "What do you mean supported? If you're taking care of my children, that's already something, Califfa, I swear to you, that's beyond price." Yes, but it couldn't last forever. You've found a life again where you can do whatever you want, whatever it costs, as easily as you can choose your clothes in the morning. So... that's the way I was, even if I knew that my only freedom was to head straight to ruin, because I could already say that it was all over.

I knew it, but I couldn't find the strength to decide. And if I stayed that way, using up the days living off other people, it was because I was waiting for something or someone to decide for me. Then, once I had started with something, nothing would be important to me any more, and I wouldn't turn back. I was tired of rebelling.

But meanwhile I still had that hurt inside me. What a summer I'd passed! It was awfully hot there and everything was so dry it looked as if it was made of dust. And down there in the city everybody was still crazy. One innocent death wasn't enough and there were still strikes and a lot of people were taken down a peg or two, but everything went back to what it had been before.

I thought I was going crazy in that place, which seemed not a part of this world to me, and I couldn't even open a window because there was so much dust that would come into the house. And I couldn't even take a walk outside, the sun was so hot. I was a prisoner of myself, of others, of everything, and whatever little bit of affection I could gather together when I could find a way to console myself would disappear right away because I didn't think I was worthy of it.

I felt that way when I saw them tearing down the house where my son had been born and had died, or when I was walking in the grass where I'd made love, and I could tell you exactly where and when it was. And in spite of what had happened, when I passed under Vito's windows, which were always closed now that he'd gone away, I thought they were like a funeral there on those broken balconies where the grass was growing.

But I would come back to the old Califfa who could keep on going and feel tender as a baby when I saw the stone they had put where my Guido had been shot down like a dog. And now it was planted there under Mastrangelo's windows like a slap in his face, and all he had to do was to raise his eyes from his papers to see it on the wall, with the carnations I put there every Sunday.

GUIDO CORSINI, WORKER, DIED FOR FREEDOM, FOR JUSTICE...

Poor Guido – putting him in his grave, they had finally given him a job and work clothes... In short, I had wept for him and I had felt some remorse, especially because some people said it was my fault, and that Guido was so desperate because I'd treated him so bad, just imagine... But let's let that go. I'd gotten very worried and then I thought I'd gotten over it.

And so on certain beautiful clear mornings I took Viola's children by the hand to bring them up the hill to the nuns' kindergarten and I had an awful desire to give up everything and escape. When there wasn't a fog up there by the convent you could see the whole city's newer part, all big and white. Farther on was the plain and Doberdò's chimneys. And it seemed to me as if that bit of valley in the midst of the trees was the nave of a church, since I could also hear the voices of the young nuns moving about in the meadows. They looked like awkward little birds without the strength to fly, just like me.

The children took me by the hand. But I couldn't keep my eyes off the bottom of the valley, which attracted me like a precipice. And I was saying to myself: "Get away, Califfa, get away!"

But where? Viola was keeping her eye on me as if I was one of her children. And when she saw me like that, looking up at the sky like a crazy woman, she shook her head and tried to cheer me up by acting the clown, amid the water drums and the wash. "Califfa, what can I do to wipe that dead expression off your face? If I had those shameless eyes..."

In other words, she pummeled me with good cheer and I was docile but I had let go, and she wanted my bitterness to be like hers, where there was always the thread of a song and of hope. And my laugh was supposed to be like hers, like an animal which accepted everything in life.

And finally one night there came this package for me. And there was a dress in it with sequins and things. Now that I think back on it, I smile in pain, but that evening it seemed too good to be true.

"Viola, but have you gone crazy? Whatever made you...?!"

"Oh, don't think I stole it, that thing there. I took on one more man for a week and I rented it for you!" and she laughed.

Poor Viola, what could I do except hug her, together with

90

the silk of that dress which was the cause of everything else that happened? That dress made me look like something out of a magazine, and she laughed with pleasure to see it, and it gave everything back to her, her youth, her body which she had enhanced by means of sweaters borrowed from me and my thrown-away skirts... And when I turned around in front of a mirror, I could hardly recognize myself, and I pulled in my tummy, stupid and childish – and I wanted to cry.

IV

When the opera season came and the faces of the tenors and prima donnas were to be seen on posters of the Regio Teatro throughout the city, with their hair all done up, covered with powder and affected smiles, Viola rose to a happiness which had remained buried in the bitter residue of the other days of the year. As a matter of fact, this was the only thing she lived for, and her obscure and bizarre mind was eased most of all by this emotion which had been passed down to her from her father, mother and ancestors.

In fact, it was much more than an instinctive joy that seized her when, in the great foggy streets among the plane trees in that deserted part of the city, the lights of the theater were turned up, and the bejeweled and befurred better people came out of their cars and suddenly, up there, the sound of the orchestra's first note was distributed from the windows of the cupola opened to the night.

This was one of Viola's rites; it was a religion for her. After all, what was a year spent in dusty places off the city streets, hidden like the rustling of mice in the darkness of neglected or guarded rooms, a year of desperate dialogue with God, made up of love which was thoughtless perdition, when the opera season finally arrived and, inebriated and liberated, she could push her way into the happy crowd and with her eyes closed take in the perfume of that easy life? Her savings had permitted her to pass with head high like any respectable person, to climb the stairs to the last gallery.

And to make herself feel more alive in that state of intoxication, or better, through that generosity which was so sincere in her, Viola brought along her girl friends, paying for a season at the opera for them too.

In short, it was a month of mad spending, of weeping covertly in the humble angle of a bench as a Violetta faded away on the stage, a Violetta in whom Viola saw herself guiltily reflected, and of joyous content at the exultant music of Verdi's *Otello...*

This peaceful life began that afternoon when a happy and obscene Viola was wandering about nude in the living room of her house, and her girl friends – also naked – were pouring water into a tube, getting ready for their bath. The poor rags they all wore were lying on the chairs, and while Viola hopped into the tube with a song on her lips, Bruna unhinged her mouth in an outburst of joy as if it were the first bath of her life; Anita, who had been a hairdresser before taking up with that crew, was heating her curling irons on the fire so she could set their hair.

What life there was in those splashings in the tub, in the laughter like that of little girls in love, and in the singing coming from that poor house and spreading from there to the fields around it – even the workmen on the scaffolding of the new buildings could hear it.

The evening enclosed the house in darkness and made Viola impatient as she smiled at her reflection in the mirror, at her restored purity. Until the music began in the smoky semi-shadow of the full theater, caressing a lazy audience which was as intent as a cat on a mouse... But that evening, while the orchestra was filling up with the city's prominent citizens, Viola and her friends, dangling their curious heads from above, were not laughing, nor did they even wink. They were not moved by what the orchestra could offer for their innocent amusement, since the theater for them was not between those curtains of flaming red velvet above the illuminated heads of the musicians in the orchestra pit, but this time at the other end of the hall, where two policemen in dress uniforms were flanking the people as they came in.

"There she is! There she is!" said Rosa suddenly, glowing in the satisfaction of having discovered her first, and as the others piled up behind her with a shiver of emotion which soon changed itself into tears in Viola's eyes, Califfa, hesitating at first and then the ironic mistress of her beauty, came up the stairs, escorted by an usher like a lady among ladies and gentlemen, poured into the dress Viola had rented for her, and holding in her hand the ticket which had cost Viola a week of bread and cheese.

Califfa advanced, dazzled by the light and trembling with emotion. But perhaps because of the fear that seized her as soon as she had taken her first step in that world where she did not belong, or because of an impulse to escape and the pride that led her to resist it, her body had an arrogance that made her better-looking, and taller. And her hair, held in a brooch of false gold (and how much work that hairdo had cost Anita), made even whiter her shoulders and her protruding, undefended breasts.

Feeling a little more sure of herself, Califfa surveyed the galleries, looking for Viola and her friends in the crowded half-light full of laughing faces, and it was with an imperceptible but visceral jolt that Mazzullo the Police Chief, sitting with his family next to what had been the Royal Box, came upon her as he examined the crowd with his opera glasses and studied the hesitant challenge of those legs caressed by the fringe of the dress. And there was a little jolt for the amazed and happy Pedrelli, enough to make him stop his nervous fingers on his nose. And Doberdò arrested the gesturing arm of Gazza with a grip of iron.

"And how is it possible, Mr. Doberdò, that there be a plan of reconstruction supported by the Communists, which was dreamed up just for the sake of ruining, I said ruining, this ancient cit – "

"Who's that?" grunted Doberdò, pointing to Califfa, who at that moment was sinking into her seat.

"Who's who?" asked Gazza.

Doberdò pushed the neck of the political secretary in the appropriate direction and Califfa's face appeared to the myopic and inquiring eyes of Gazza – those eyes, that mouth, but especially the eyes with the light shining in them, while she turned once again and, having finally found Viola's waving hand, smiled properly at her, just as if she were smiling at Doberdò, at his angry elephant's head above his black tie. Gazza was furious that he was unable to give a name immediately to that bewildered but laughing face, because with Doberdò he took pride in his cunning in bedroom affairs as well as dirty politics. His anger was somewhat quieted when Pedrelli, whom he asked about the girl with a sign from his finger, had to extend his arms. He didn't know either.

But now the lights were dimming and while the trumpets were announcing the beginning of *Aida,* a large tear was flowing down Viola's cheek, and she let it get as far as her lips and fall from there onto her coat, because she had never before in her life felt such satisfaction. In Califfa's happiness, in the hesitant pride of that face which exceeded in beauty everyone around her, Viola finally felt some relief of the urge she had carried in her all those years: to enter a crowded theater with head high, just as her friend had been able to do so well, and to sit among the rich and noble, animating the air around her, attracting the glances of the men, as Califfa was doing. And even Viola could take some of the credit because she had been the one to insist the night before:

"No, Califfa, you shouldn't come to the gallery… it would be an insult to you: you're made to sit in the orchestra."

And now because she finally felt that urge relieved, Viola didn't mind that the Eternal Father had given her that face which she had recognized for what it was even when she was a girl. It was a face ready for the street, a face in which too much of everything could be read too easily, and which had always kept her back from any progress.

She leaned her forehead on the marble of the column and, smiling to herself, turned her eyes to the ceiling shining with gold and fans, and the sea of faces below which was helping her miracle along. The miracle was concluded the next day when a florist's messenger came up on his motorcycle to the most run-down part of the city's periphery, carrying a great bunch of flaming roses which he could hardly keep on his bicycle's handlebars, along the dirty little street almost buried in rubbish among the wash hanging out to dry on the line.

The bouquet of roses, put in front of the unused fireplace, brightened up Viola's poor kitchen, perfuming the air with its wealthy generosity. Viola could hardly believe it, nor could her friends who came in to enjoy the marvel, holding back as if the sound of their shoes could dissolve that burst of flame on the mantelpiece.

And it was with a trembling hand that Irene Corsini removed from the cellophane the card addressed to her, on which a name was written: *Annibale Doberdò*.

PART II

CHAPTER EIGHT

And in this way Irene Corsini accepted that cross of affectionate pity and sorrowing sympathy for those in error with which the people from her part of the city – resigned for centuries to sin deriving from misery – follow the girl whom life takes and transports far from their common destiny and the bitter collective struggle. They pass over a bridge, those poor bitches, attracted by an enormous amount of trash characteristic of a life of ease, and suddenly their struggle becomes a private hell, a great regret which will imprison them in the years to come, a slow recall to life which with the passage of time will perhaps lead them back to the youth they lost in crossing the frontier of those waters, in looking back for the last time at their happy but desperate houses. They leave on an obscure journey even if they go no farther than a few yards. But those girls do not cease to love the ones who stay behind. They have learned to sin. But in their world, sin is only a way of expressing emotion in the heat of an intoxication forbidden by life's insidious mysteries. That's enough – and it is of no importance that the world can pronounce in their faces that cruel and insolent word: whore.

The great affection continues – as a matter of fact, it grows more acute, as always happens in the face of death, illness, and everything which nature creates and destroys beyond men and their will. Could these men and women closed up in the narrow circle of their existence perhaps bargain away the only abundant good in their existence, and that is pity – for someone confined to a bed, or someone like Guido Corsini who seeks death with the final burst of vitality of one who doesn't want to participate any more? They couldn't. And the same goes for those poor girls whom hunger and loneliness drive to seek their death beyond a bridge in the respectable streets of the new city, today as centuries ago, without anything having changed in the least.

The whores are the flower of that discouraged youth, and one can see a bitter pride in them as they disappear into the light of an unknown life, born again in the death of their real feelings and of their pride, because that world of forbidden contentment where they are going will have to admire, before corrupting and destroying it, the proud and savage beauty which carries with it the beauty of an entire humiliated people, a banner of genuine and healthy life.

And so Califfa passed that bridge too, driven in part by Viola, but much more by the need to survive by relying on herself alone, to avoid being a burden to anyone, following a rule that her pride would not let her violate, although her pride itself had been violated. For this reason, perhaps she herself could not have related how she had passed to that bed and that little apartment rented for her in a nice building on the river, from the last dubious caresses of that bunch of dried-up petals which Viola had thrown into the trash with a sigh.

It seemed to Califfa that she had been led by a series of facts and emotions which were too logical to belong to free choice and thus allow for regret, or for the possibility of opening in a woman the wound of shame so difficult to heal. And she had not felt any sense of shame or guilt. She accepted the fact that she was a whore, and in the very name of all those who had preceded her in a mad escape from difficulties which were quite like hers, and in the name of a fatality which had become a right and obligation and made that flight inevitable for anyone like her who had been reduced to the point where she had no one and no more reason to keep herself respectable.

"Doberdò!" Viola had said. "Annibale Doberdò, the biggest man in the city!" And Califfa had agreed.

Certainly no one would have been able to understand the truth she understood unless they were among the ones she had left behind in the tenements, who knew what hunger was and were familiar with the hearse which takes away the young and the old from that slice of tormented city; where a puff of wind could burn up years of sacrifice, anger and struggle, leaving you with empty hands. And then you have to start all over again, until the next puff of wind comes, with the punctuality of farcical destiny, and ruins everything once more.

And it was for that destiny, so as not to give it the satisfaction of fighting it, but to humiliate it by forcing its hand, that she had gone up that stairway in a nervous, giddy state. And this changed into anger the first time she took her clothes off in front of him.

"The first time, you shouldn't think of anything," Viola had advised her. "of nothing at all... You have to act as if he weren't there."

But that wasn't how it was. Taking off her dress, throwing away her last stitch with her eyes closed as Viola had thrown in the trash the only roses she had ever had in her life, Califfa had thought of Guido and how he had died by the wall. She thought she knew how he had felt, just before he died.

They had chosen two different ways to die, he throwing himself against a police machine gun, and she rising nude in a semi-darkened room, sitting on the edge of a bed, and allowing Annibale Doberdò's heavy finger to tickle the small creases in her skin and descend along her back, toward her unquiet hips in the fold of the sheet.

And in this way Irene Corsini died to her past, and allowed herself to be violated for the second time in her life, as she gazed at the curtains in the windows, full of wind and white moonlight, those curtains she had once so strongly desired when she was a girl standing on the bridge over the river, and which one day were to be hers.

In the happiest period of her life, when her virginity vanished in a fit of madness, it had been like the rustling of the trees, or of voices in the night like some music which only she had been able to hear. And there was that sound of happy workers' voices raised in song in the wind around the outskirts of the city.

"When you're in bed with him, close your eyes and let him operate. Don't think," Viola had said. "Don't think and don't remember anything. That's the point."

But as she died, she had thought of her brothers and sisters, while Doberdò's wrinkled lip curled over the curve of her side and that difficult breathing, of desire which never succeeded in becoming real desire, rose up in the darkness of the room.

And after that death, it was not long before she got used to everything in a resigned sort of way, after her first stupor was over. And Califfa accepted it humbly with no bashfulness, diffidence, or fear, abandoning herself to the inevitable progress of fact and emotion. And so, living her new free life supported only by her nostalgic memories, Califfa got used to feeling Doberdò's lip separate itself from her flesh like a flabby beast, and to seeing her lover get up from the bed and disappear toward the bathroom, with his breathing sounding bitter in the darkness, until the roar of the water drowned it out (but could one call loving what that man did, moved by regret for his ebbing life, as he enjoyed in her the last trace of disappointed and wasted youth?).

"Being a whore," Viola had said, "is like getting into a bed that's not yours. The first night it's hard to sleep, but then…"

Yes, that was true. And so she got used to smiling at Doberdò, greeting him before hours of pretending during which his body never did give way to real pleasure; but she did begin to feel at home there.

The curtains with the Greek design were hers and they glided over her body when she slipped out of the bed and came to the window, which she touched with a hesitating hand; and the geraniums rustling on the balcony were hers, too.

And she was reminded of what Guido had said as they looked at the buildings of the new city: "We'll live up there, you'll see. One day we'll be able to manage… and we'll take our children up in elevators, and each one will have a room of his own…"

And now it was all hers. And that shiny bathtub was hers too, that bathtub where she lazed around in soapy water and gathered her wits about her, as if she were in a womb of a mother who could have defended her from life and from herself. Before, at Viola's, she had never had enough water, and baths in her old washtub had been annoying and humiliating to take. But now she would have liked never to get up again from those tepid winds which blew over her skin. To sink like that ever farther down, to disappear in that heat of found felicity, without ever asking for anything else.

And she learned to walk on those tiles without being nervous about it, on the same tiles which the servants had forbidden her to walk on in her shoes as a little girl. And she learned how a woman can go out, deluding a slightly mistrustful porter with her nonchalance, the sort of porter who greets you in the morning and whose tone of voice at night can ruin your evening, as if you'd stolen something from him. (Viola's first bit of advice had been just that: "The others, the ones who wanted to, the ones who insinuate, are all the same in this country, where choosing between good and evil means being able to or not. Act as if they weren't even there! Act like you can smell 'em!")

She even learned not to be afraid of that sound of an immense world lying in wait which assailed her when she stretched out her hand to the telephone and took the receiver to her ear before she went to bed, not to call anyone, but just to hear that sound which gave her a sense of her own solitude, making it encounter a barrier of alert silence which protected thousands of lives unknown to her.

She tried dialing a number at random and her heart beat wildly. A number: a silence, a voice which could mean everything, and then a basic aggressive fear. And when she put the receiver on the edge of the bed and that sound – questioning and oppressive as the life which awaited her the next day – spread out in the strange room, she once again became the child sleeping alone for the first time who seeks out her mother in fear caused by overwhelming solitude and the first revelations of life's cruelty.

Her eyes filled with tears while the telephone's signal continued to beat in the darkness and she saw her mother again; she remembered certain nights in which her young mother had come up to her bed to touch her when she was sick, to hold her hand, and she had discovered for the first time, in the light of the lamp, the real color of the hair of that woman who was always too distracted by her anguished life, and who in that moment was bending her head to kiss her.

And she bade that image goodbye as if she had not done so many years ago, and she talked to her: "Goodbye! Forgive me!" She had not always been a good girl and she had ended up in that bed. She kept on listening to the call from the outside.

Sleep finally took her, and the voluntary damnation of that signal lasted all the night, in the room which was lit occasionally by the headlights of cars.

II

Califfa soon learned everything necessary to remain in the game she had accepted without debasing herself. She learned not to be astonished at trifles and not to be dazzled by riches or overly impressed by someone who had more money than she did. And she learned to see in being well off an inevitable consequence of her ruin and not personal calculation or a means of revenging herself on her past, and she learned especially to understand and put up with the malignity and wickedness which a whore, when she's a good one, inevitably attracts around her.

And according to the nth bit of advice from Viola, which she gave out with much seriousness, "To be a whore, Califfa, is easy and hard. You have to have humility and you have to be forgiving. It means understanding men and waiting for their bestiality, but also being able to forgive it."

Califfa looked at her, barely raising her eyes, with an intimidated little smile: "Like the monks…"

"More or less, Califfa, more or less. You feel them digging around in you, as you make love as much as you can… and if you can't love and understand, you can die from it."

And Califfa took this advice too. Everything her new life offered her, in fact, continued to involve her pity, her anger, her nostalgia, but not the dignity which was buried but not dead within her, dormant in her sinful lethargy.

Until one day Annibale Doberdò took her out of town. He took a country road without telling her anything, as if he'd planned no fixed itinerary. Califfa, who was still like a little girl when she got into the car, had such fun looking out the window that at first she did not realize where they were going.

And suddenly, when it was too late for her to ask him to stop, with an emotion which made the blood rush to her head, she recognized the poppies in a row on the side of the street, the little valley, the wall with the holes in it, and the large gate.

She asked herself why they were going there, but she did not have time to ask herself anything else, because he made her get out, ushering her along the path through the graves. She looked around her and for a moment she thought that she could not find her son's grave, that little slab of marble which the rainwater had made yellow, hidden by the weeds in the paupers' part of the cemetery.

There was an expanse of poor names and poor faces in which she saw a little gravestone staring out, and she ran forward in happiness. It stuck out, with the name stamped in the marble in golden letters, and above the group of sculpted angels was the head of her son, carved in the marble as if he were still alive, with the waving hair and that smile just like the one in the only smiling photograph she had been able to keep.

Her son was smiling there where the green stopped being a rotting mess of plants and where the light and the air could come in. He was just as she remembered him on that afternoon she had taken him to the photographer in his Sunday best, and he had not wanted to smile, and she had fixed her affectionately angry gaze on him.

She squeezed the head and she felt the living flesh within, as she had when she awoke from the deluded anger of childbirth.

Annibale Doberdò came up to her, put a hand on her shoulder, and at that moment Califfa understood that she had been urged beyond that bridge not only by a fatal law, not only by desperation, but most of all by an unconscious, vital need for happiness, just a moment of happiness before she died. And she also understood that, however long her adventure might last, she had one more reason not to be ashamed: Annibale Doberdò was a man one could respect and whom one could love in a nice way too.

It was all the way Viola had predicted, saying goodbye to Califfa on her departure: "Happiness, my girl, is a great beast. You will wait for it and you will wait for it some more, but nothing happens. Then you act like a saint and it escapes. Then when you think you don't even want it any more, when you think it's stupid to believe in it any more, it hits you from behind and grabs you here, in the stomach, and it squeezes you until it hurts…"

III

And just think that on the afternoon when I'd thrown some rags in my suitcase and went off I hadn't the courage to come into my own house. Really. He'd written me on a card: Such a street, and number so and so. And then he had said what I thought was just a line and nothing else: "Now you've slept with the mice long enough. With a face like yours, what do you plan to do, be a tramp?" In other words, I had the right to wear furs, the way he told it, with a hat and gloves, and to walk in the streets like a prize dog.

I repeat that it all seemed just a line to me, first, because Califfa needs some convincing, and, second, because I was listening to him as I sat in that huge car of his on a seat that was like a mattress, which humiliated me. And then maybe it was just a line, because it was only later that I saw Doberdò act differently toward me. Who knows, maybe he felt comfortable with me, and, to tell the truth, I made him feel young, because I understood that that was what he was after.

And it was easier for me, since I was afraid of him only that first night in his car and I felt uncomfortable only the first time he undressed me. And I understood that at first he didn't want to let himself go with me – I couldn't understand him right away either! And it was only right. How could he tell that I'd mean so much more to him than his usual girl friends – because of what I was like and what I'd been through? In short, I was a little reserved too, at first.

But when a woman begins to understand that a man who could just as easily shut the door in her face and walk off after he's been satisfied is still looking for her and needs to talk to her and to hear her talk – then if she's not stupid, her heart goes out to him. It was the opposite of what had happened with Vito. Because the presents came later – but presents never meant anything to me, and it certainly wasn't with presents that he was able to have me the way I am when I believe in someone, and that is good-looking, happy, and able to cure a headache better than I don't know what – I say the presents came laser, but first there was just his desire to have me near him that could console me.

"Califfa," he would say, and he wanted me to sit down so he could put his arm around me as if I was his daughter, "I like you just because you're you." And how should I be? Maybe because he had a house bigger than City Hall, or because he moved like the Lord God Almighty? None of these things meant anything to me and I told him so straight out. Because in so many years I'd learned to scratch under the misery to see what a man's made of and pay attention only to that – even if he was eating nothing but bread and water like a man in prison – and I could do the same thing with all that abundance.

I don't mean to give the wrong impression and say that when I got to know him better and realized that he was more or less like the others I would have dropped him like a hot potato and taken away my things and closed the door. No. I swear that no matter what happened I wouldn't have turned back at all. Because I'd given my word. Because I didn't care any more where I'd gotten to. And Califfa when she's decided to turn over a leaf, for good or bad, stays just the way she is.

I just mean that when I could see that Doberdò was a human being, in spite of everything they said about him behind his back, I began to put some spirit and enthusiasm into earning what he was giving me, not like so many whores who don't give out with one more smile or one more word than they have to. They think all they have to do is open their legs and that's it.

It was awful for him, poor man! Good God, he had a family, wife and son, and a mob eating off him worse than the police, all telling him *Yessir, Yessir,* and ready to put his shoes on for him if he'd ask, even some big shots. And was it possible that none of them understood what I understood so well? That you can't keep living off a man just to see how many people he can support?

Because a man's a man even if he's gotten into so damned many affairs that he isn't his own boss any more, and he can't be squeezed like a lemon. Otherwise, what'll he do? Keep on squeezing and he'll lose his taste for life, and the one who can have the good things of life just by stretching out his hand has to forget about the things that can really make him happy, and he ends up alone like a dog.

And that was what I thought. And it was the way I acted too, and when he came to see me, even if I felt rotten inside, I did all I could not to burden him with it. I tried to put him at his ease, to put his head down, to stretch out... God knows, I didn't feel like acting the clown for him. But I pulled myself together and told him some stories about my mad world, where people really laugh when they laugh, with their blood and not just their lips – not the way they did in his world, where people are stingy even with their laughter. You couldn't call bread bread or wine wine and you couldn't call a spade a spade in his world, so I couldn't care less if they sounded like silly stories of an ignorant girl – all I cared about was that they were good.

And now he would change when he came to see me. He was a new man. He'd come into the apartment all exhausted, and when he went away – never before the small hours of the morning, and that because he was happy with me – he had such color in his cheeks that it was a pleasure just to look at him. Maybe the next day, if I'd seen him behind his desk, with all those people who looked up to him, I might have been impressed too. But in the apartment, sitting in a chair or stretched out on the bed, no. He was like my son, he who could have been my father – and I had to encourage him. Certainly it was a little comical. For me to pull him out of his doldrums would take a crane. And he would say to me:

"Califfa, Califfa, who'd ever have thought we'd get on so well together… and that you were like that?"

"And what'd you think I'd be like?" I'd ask him.

"Eh," he'd answer, "you don't know what bitches some women are… They're like melons and you can't see what they're like from the outside."

And when we started talking about hard things (but it wasn't that I prevented him from talking about whatever he liked, for God's sake; he would be able to do whatever he liked, and if I didn't understand, I was still happy just to listen to him), I'd just uncork a bottle and that'd be all there was to that. But every time I raised my glass that way, now that I was in control of the situation, I always laughed, who knows why, when I was happy with him, and I'd remember how stupid I'd been the first day.

"Califfa, why do you laugh so much?" he'd ask me. "Come on. Tell me." But I was still laughing without answering him. How could I tell him that when I had come to the address on the paper and found myself before the elegant-looking building with that gate with the lights by the names, I was stupefied. I was standing there with my suitcase in my hand and I didn't know what to do. I was there, but the porter in his hat and uniform was coming.

Just imagine – he didn't even ask me what I wanted. A girl dressed the way I was and with that suitcase with the string around it so it couldn't open by mistake – what could he have thought? I might have been a thief. He stared at me and stayed right there behind the gate, like a policeman, without doing anything else. And he had an expression like he was going to murder me.

So what could I do? Stupid as I was, should I have taken my suitcase and run away? And meantime I was saying to myself: "I don't dare, I don't dare! I could never dare! Mother of God, I can't even pray to you now! How did I ever get involved, Mother of God?"

And so I went off walking as if I could find courage on the street, with that suitcase which was weighing me down and which was full of useless things. Up and down in the city, and at noon I was eating my roll down by the railroad tracks and I was thinking: To hell with it, and to hell with you too, Viola!

I was hungry and I had such spots in front of my eyes that if I didn't sit on my suitcase I'd have a dizzy spell And just think what there was at my house. He'd said so himself then and his words were all I could remember: "You don't even have to do the marketing. The superintendent's wife will do that... Just open the icebox and eat when you're hungry!" God, I said to myself, how can I have been so stupid! I've never been afraid of anything before!

But it was only when it was beginning to get dark that I felt strong enough to get up, take my suitcase, and jump down the railway embankment, and who knows when I would have if the janitor'd been there then? It was dark and it was cold and foggy where I'd passed the whole afternoon like a statue. And I was back at that damned building after I'd marched all over the city like a soldier. I stuck out my hand and pushed the first button I came to.

The door opened and I barged in. And when that fellow came up and took me by the arm, I hit him with my suitcase, mad at him as if he'd done I don't know what.

"And where do you think you're going?"

"I'll go wherever I want! I'm going to my house! To my house to do whatever I damn please!" And up the stairs I went (it was the third floor, first door on the right, he'd told me). "Here are the keys, if you don't believe me!" and I waved them at him from the stairway.

"You could have told me that before."

"You can just take that hat of yours and go to hell!" And I opened all the doors and windows and turned on all the lights with a lump in my throat, like I was going to die. I threw myself into the nearest chair and covered my face with my hands. I knew I had done it!

CHAPTER NINE

"There's the bitch," said Gazza, when he saw Clementina Doberdò appear at the head of a staircase in the building facing his office. This happened punctually at six o'clock every Saturday afternoon, so punctually that no one knew if it were Clementina who came forth from the door as soon as Martinolli's church bells sounded vespers, or whether it were the Auxiliary Bishop who gave the signal for the bells when the woman called him on the telephone to announce dryly: "I'm coming!"

"The bitch!" repeated Cantoni the lawyer, who was lounging in Gazza's offices (the offices were strictly political, and administrative in the larger sense) in the hope of being put on the list of candidates for the next election. Always, as if the apparition had not been habitual for many years, a certain emotion took possession of him whenever he saw her. He had been smiling at Clementina that day many years ago in the middle of a living room bubbling with chatter. Studying him with her myopic yellowy eyes and with a hint of contempt in her voice as if she were spitting the words in his face, she had said to him with a loud voice worthy of a Pope so that everyone could hear: "You are a man I simply cannot stand!" And this sentence pronounced so far in the past, this unreasonable antipathy, had transformed him from a lawyer and humanist with brilliant promise into a defender of rural thieves and prostitutes.

Clementina, pallid and tense, appeared on the staircase in her black dress, with a veil around her neck. And the idea that she was on her way to a funeral instead of vespers was

111

given not only by the color of her face and clothes, but also by the obstinate way she gave herself on one side to the arm of Annibale, her husband, and on the other to that of her son, Giampiero, the way she gritted her teeth as she came down the steps, the way she let the two of them propel her along the city's principal street.

It was not a spiritual pain which contorted Clementina Doberdò's face and caved in her body, but an acute physical one, a subtle torture against which she had fought aggressively so as not to let people see what was going on, from the day her legs had been weakened by a slow but progressive paralysis. Refusing a cripple's wheelchair, disregarding the advice of her doctors, and driven on only by the pride which had animated everything she had ever done in life, she persisted with her last ounce of strength in traversing the expanse of street which separated her house from Martinolli's church, every Saturday at six, just as she had done in the days of her youth and in her vigorous maturity.

Religion had nothing to do with this pitiful walk; there was the angry desire to enjoy once again the fruits of a life given over to struggle and intrigue; the deferential greetings from the people, the bows, the tipping of the hats which saluted in a cloud of smiling homage the person of Clementina Doberdò, the real force behind Annibale, the real creator of Doberdò's power.

Batting her eyelids, which were not used to the light, Clementina went down the staircase to the gate, as deference was granted her haughty way by the kindly and ironic resignation of her husband, who had been torn from the cares of his office for the occasion, and the adolescent embarrassment of a son who was probably too low-pressured to be a real Doberdò.

She looked around, investigating, and shook her head contemptuously in exchange for Gazza's bow from his nest behind the glass. (She did not even have to lift her eyes toward the balcony. She could imagine the political secretary's precipitous bow. He was one of her many creatures, and he had been molded and remolded by her now skeletal and trembling hands, which always knew where to light.)

The procession had begun, and the feet of Annibale and Giampiero, trying to adjust to her pace, went separately past each and every slab of the pavement, humble and tolerant, marching along that *via crucis* which exposed them to the malignity, rancor and envy which served to delude Clementina, and to remind people of the story of the man who was certainly the most pathetic in character of "the father, the son, and the holy ghost," as Cantoni had ironically called that group.

And Doberdò was thinking over his story too, as he held that dry hand which clutched his and his eyes wandered in the fading light of the day over towers, roofs and silent little squares of a city made enchanting by the evening.

II

And he was seeing the same city many years before, made up then of gardens and carriages, military bands, and dances in ballrooms. All those places were vibrating with curiosity about the first political stirrings, the first signs of indignation which had risen at that time from the tumult of the streets – from the depressing defeat of the poor, held back but in obstinate revolt – to the consciousness of the upper classes. And traces of this indignation were to be found amid the smiles of the landowners' daughters and the stupid gallantries of a flock of noblemen who had roosted on others' wealth so as not to have to dirty themselves with reality and pain.

And he saw himself pulled in one direction by the city, which continued to smile in ignorance and considered the changing times only as fuel for the idle chatter of its living rooms, and in another by the rebellions where the farmers ended up with their faces to the wall. The prospect of slow starvation pushed numbers of them to seek a speedier death under the volleys of the Royal Cavalry.

A small landowner and proprietor of that little jam factory

which was spreading its smoke over one of the few tranquil suburbs (since Doberdò, a young man with color in his cheeks who was ready to roll up his sleeves himself, employed as many as he could), he should have stayed with his own people, with that mad gathering of proprietors who were already financing the first squads of bully boys, thinking that Fascism was the only way out. But he didn't; he was with the opposition.

They said that the memory of his father was too strong in him. The elder Doberdò had been of peasant origin and a Socialist in every fiber of his being, who had pulled himself up by his own bootstraps but without trickery. This made it impossible for Annibale Doberdò to close his factory's door in the face of those women who came to sit in front of his plant, mute, hungry, and silent, spending the night there like tragic figures waiting for a miracle, with their children wrapped up in blankets or clinging to their breasts which were as dried up as their souls.

Doberdò always opened his doors to them at last, and his factory was finally changed into a kind of charity ward. Under those iron roofs, looked upon with contempt by the gentlemen in straw hats who drove by in their carriages just to laugh at Doberdò, hunger turned into hope, but at the cost of so meager a profit for the proprietor that the factory was seriously threatened with bankruptcy. But Doberdò pushed himself hard, cursing and making wide use of his thick red-haired fists.

And one night when the Fascists had broken into his factory to smash and destroy things, they had seen Doberdò appear at a meeting of the proprietors in his shirt sleeves with a revolver in his belt. He threw open the door and looked at them one by one, alone against twenty of them, with so much anger in his face that the others were frightened. And he came forward, knowing full well toward which of those frightened faces to advance.

And a slap resounded through the silence of the hall. No one who turned around at that moment could have told who had been slapped, since the victim had taken it without batting an eyelash and his face was vacant like the others. He was a saint, but stupid, they said of him. He supported the Socialist cause and the people's cooperatives. According to his more conservative friends, he was ignoring, or pretending to ignore, the great trial which was ensnaring Italy. Along with hordes of people like him, they thought, he was helping to prepare for the final downfall.

But on close inspection, Annibale Doberdò proved to be something less than a total saint, and the crowd of farmers who loved and respected him could certainly never imagine some of his real feelings, which he concealed even from himself.

He raised his voice in pique – or better, in ambition – and took pleasure in passing through the crowds which feared and respected him, and among those who hated him but were forced to take account of his explosive personality. And to this was added rancor for whoever possessed more than he did. But most important of all was Doberdò's plain weakness. Contrary to appearances, he was a weak man inside. Even though he did not dare to betray his humble origin – and he took advantage of it whenever it suited his purpose – his subtly ambiguous personality aspired to something better.

Doberdò was motivated not by the profits which the industrialists and the agrarian proprietors were preparing for themselves by supporting the looting and murders of the Fascists, but by the social refinements of a world which escaped him, the worldly prestige of a reputation he did not possess, and by a style of life crowded with cultured and elegant people. But more than anything else it was by young women, whom he pictured in his mind as one solid mound of tender white feminine flesh. For Annibale Doberdò would do anything for women, whether it was the betrayal of an ideal or the complete collapse of appearances.

For all that his peasant origin had allowed him to be a stupid saint with a great deal of vitality, it also threatened to involve him in the grossest gaffes of the *nouveaux riches*. And Annibale Doberdò officially ended his struggles with himself – giving reason for ironic triumph to those who had opposed him until just before – on a day which must have remained engraved on his memory for the rest of his life like a condemnation, a day which he greeted then as a miracle and as his own salvation. That was the day when the stately carriage of Clementina Marchi burst into the courtyard of his country house, bringing with it a noble name and the troubles of a family with an *entrée* into the best society and a pile of protested promissory notes.

It was a minor affair – the sale of some land, just enough to plant four poppies on, nothing more. Annibale Doberdò looked at her black hair wound around that proud little head; those clear eyes which were so much on their guard, in which could be seen her youthful desire that the precipitous fall of her family stop short of the very bottom; those legs and that body whose elegance heightened a certain sensual arrogance – and he felt lost. He groped around in the darkness of his impatient desires and irrational ambition.

But Clementina Marchi, studying him out of the corner of her eye, between the signatures of the notary and the recital of the legal formulas, observing the face of a social climber in those new times and the chimneys framed in the window beyond that head seething with desire, made an exciting calculation that was as immediate as it was exact.

And in this way the refined and astute name of the Marchis became the propelling force within the horny shell of that earthy vulgar-sounding name Doberdò. The factory stopped being a charity ward where "pity's products are prepared" as its owner's enemies murmured; and that empty chair in the agrarian meeting was where the "stupid saint" was defeated for the first time, and in a vulgar manner. It was a moral defeat which only Clementina, sinking her hands into the virgin gold of her husband's property, enthroning herself in his mind, maneuvering, negotiating and threatening with every resource of a gangster and a calculator, prevented from appearing a humiliation, by wrapping it in the light of financial success and business strength.

Annibale Doberdò stopped looking his farmers in the face, not because of any contempt for them, but for shame brought

116

on by his vanity which sometimes made him want to weep. He forgot how to take off his jacket and roll up his sleeves. And he tried not to pass by the place where people like him left the imprint of their blood on their last trip to justice; and he closed the window when the prisoners passed by in gray files, perhaps never to return – an example which should have opened people's eyes – under the balconies of his new town house, on their way to Ustica, Ponza, and other hellish places of imprisonment. He even allowed someone to take his father's picture from the desk in his office, that frank and sincere countenance, a source of nostalgia for his peasant background, and consign it to the darkness of an anonymous room.

Obeying Clementina, supporting her frantic class-consciousness, pretending not to know about her adulteries, which were wild but with men of appropriate social standing, and giving in with resigned happiness to her all too rare moments of wifely tenderness, Annibale Doberdò became the living symbol of a class of people whom Fascism was to enrich without dragging them along at its downfall, whom the priests had to bless even in their sins, and to whom the war was to offer the bitter flowers of speculation from the desolation it caused.

Doberdò multiplied his factories; he coupled tomatoes with cheese and put industry side by side with commerce; he came to know the mechanism of the Swiss banks, the web of government financing, the progress of funds which do not exist, and that jungle which allowed one to make a friend fail in order to raise one's self, with one's feet on his head, higher still in the sea of money flowing in and out; he financed at exorbitant rates and was generous to Fascist hierarchs and members of Parliament who were later to be generous with his name in a country swelling with undigested poison.

He tolerated it all, in his half-lit parlors filled first with the black of military uniforms and later with the black of priests' cassocks. And the idea he had of himself was that of a fat heavy Christ nailed to the cross of success, but one who underwent his suffering in the heat of a success which gave him no pain whatsoever.

All he had to do was to throw open the windows of his

office and count the chimneys in the city's sky and see how they multiplied on the blue of the hills where he was born, and painful memories, in which his parents, brothers and sisters and childhood friends burst into his mind and tightened his stomach, went away again, calming down in the slumber of his conscience. It was easy, too easy for all this to last through the years, but meanwhile that which was to become his prison later gave him a feeling then that he had achieved freedom.

And the telephones multiplied and with them the calls from cities he had not heard of before – London, Paris, New York – and his companions of another time disappeared forever from business life. In that he saw freedom. Freedom for everything. Even the freedom to dial a telephone number and to hear the voice of a young woman, and suddenly that unknown voice, that face, that flesh, those bones, which could be beautiful or ugly, could all be gathered into his mania for universal possession.

His name was enough – Annibale Doberdò! – for the unknown voice, be it of faithful wife or innocent virgin, to collapse into servile stupor before him, the number-one man. And Doberdò was happier at this stupor which had neither name nor face, but only the exciting tone of a possible offer, than he would have been at the actual granting of their favors. Because it allowed him to conjure up a bed as large as the world, with so many fresh young naked women all ready for him as he passed by, touching them and noting the difference between a breast here, a behind there, and skin somewhere else, intrigued by their different ways of offering themselves and of being women.

That was his freedom. Transient fantasies which the telephones would bring back, taking him from Paris, London, and New York, from cheese to sauce and from shoes to ham. And in the little spare time he had, he tried to read, to inform himself, giving scope to the stamina that allowed him to be at his desk at dawn and not to come away except for a brief troubled sleep.

And so he had no time, or perhaps he tried not to have any time, for such considerations, or to find out what was thought of him in the city which ate Doberdò foods, wore Doberdò clothes, and read Doberdò papers. Did they love or hate him? Without being too aware of it, he didn't care too much whether it was love or hate; the important thing was that people not be indifferent. And how could they be indifferent to that name spread over the city, to that man buried behind the highest window in the town's only skyscraper, which was lit into the small hours of the night, so that all people needed to do was raise their eyes to see the traces of that light?

Saint Doberdò, a patron saint and no longer a "stupid saint."

But if he had had more time, Annibale Doberdò would have become aware that the city, without either loving him or hating him, harbored feelings for him that were worse than indifference: namely, the benevolent pity extended, beyond their apparent power, by those who are weak and empty-headed.

It took many years for him to feel their glances on him, and for a long time he understood nothing and was not aware that people were devouring the most intimate facts about his family life as they met him. And they were looking over his shoulder to the reality, to where the proud and punctilious Clementina Doberdò passed by.

Clementina Doberdò was now dragging herself along on her evening walk between the young Giampiero and the shaking Annibale. The first lights were being turned on as hats were raised and people bowed, and Annibale Doberdò was thinking and remembering; and he was thinking of the dull exhaustion with which the decline of his maturity was assailing him.

Was it just physical fatigue? Or was it a weak heart, as his doctor had been telling him? But a weak heart does not make a man bring out his father's picture from an anonymous room to the light of his desk – that poor, dear face looking sincerely out from among the telephones. Nor does it bring an ambitious man to stop at a poor house in the country with the desire to stay there, maybe to eat a polenta and to sleep on a great hair mattress.

But, above all, it does not lead a man who can play at

politics, love, and the funds and fate of other people to get up from his desk where millions are swirling around like balls on a roulette table, to walk to the window which dominates the horizon and look toward an obscure corner of the city among the poppies, where the lights of the dead tremble at the end of a solitary night.

An Annibale Doberdò who steers a whole troupe of vassals and yes-men, tolerated by him or created with his hands, from Farinacci to Mastrangelo to Mazzullo the Police Chief to Martinolli and to so many others seated behind desks which really belong to him, and who gives time, thought, and affection to a poor girl whom hunger and loneliness have brought to him like a little fawn driven in by the cold, this Doberdò is no longer the Doberdò he once was.

III

And that afternoon the walk came to an end, as it always did, in the nave of Martinolli's church. Clementina, Annibale, and Giampiero sat down in the first pew, where Doberdò's family coat of arms shone in the half-light. Martinolli put on his stole and disappeared into the confessional.

The two sacristans raised Clementina by the armpits and placed her respectfully by the grating, and she went at her confession with the same energy and the same hysterical madness with which she had once attacked her love affairs, trying to rub out one kind of life, in that moment, with the same ardor she once put into her pursuit of sin and success, with which she then felt herself satiated.

Doberdò looked at her for a moment and felt pity and contempt, almost surprising himself. But, as he often had in recent times, he also felt a subtle, irresistible hate for that imploring face, for those trembling hands, and for that body which neither the years nor disease had robbed of its nervous elegance.

He looked around and fixed his gaze on the altar bathed in the last light of day which was coming from the great windows. Yes, he was no longer alone. He thought of Califfa

120

and a brief moment of contentment took possession of him and isolated him. He understood that a day was coming which he had long awaited, a day when his contempt for that wife and her dreary exhaustion, his sweet pity for that son kneeling beside him, and his paternal indifference could invade him without there being any particular consequence; a day in which his sleepy nostalgia could fade away forever.

Because now he was not alone. He could go to the building by the river and go up to the apartment, kiss her, caress her, and teach her how life was lived among happy people and allow her the girlish surprise of one who knows everything and yet nothing about life.

He was coming to understand that the most genuine freedom of his life consisted in this participating charity in which were summed up his cowardice, his renewal, and everything which he could have done and which he had not done. But was it charity or vanity? This state of happiness, of a happiness which was finally his own, and this understanding that nothing else is of any importance – was not this perhaps the last act of his ambiguity?

He could sink down with a renewed awakening of his senses by the side of that woman who so powerfully brought him back to the humors and simple habits of his forgotten origin. He could slide over her warm smooth skin; and he was grateful to her for having come to him at just the right moment.

With her, he would try not to get lost again, in the same way he would try to prevent her from getting lost now; a poor girl who, like him, was likely to forget what she came from, which she should not do. He was going to make her happy. He was going to defend her.

It seemed to him the only way to approach death with a peaceful soul.

"O God, I thank you for her beauty... I ask your pardon for the shame which I will prevent her from feeling, for the peace which I will try to give her..." This was the prayer which he pronounced at the altar, fading away in the darkness, on that Saturday afternoon invaded by the bells.

And when his son Giampiero touched him on the shoulder,

to alert him that it was his turn, Annibale Doberdò smiled to himself as he realized that it was the thought of a whore which had freed his spirit, and that it had been his sins which restored his purity.

He got up, walked across the nave, and knelt in front of the same grating, behind which he could see the pale outline of Martinolli's face. The farce had begun, because Annibale Doberdò's sins were also partly those of Martinolli. And the Monsignor knew this well. For this reason, he descended into an abyss of bitterness when Doberdò drew near to the confessional. He was the real sinner, nailed as he was to the recital of some of his own sins, with the ironic twist that he would be able to forgive in another the same faults which were gathering within him and crying out for forgiveness.

"Father, I allowed them to ruin a man."

Martinolli knew perfectly well who this man was and how they had ruined him, but he was obliged to ask, with a sad tone of voice:

"Who is this man? How did it happen?"

And Doberdò, enjoying the game, said with that subtle perfidy which was so typical of him, "He was a businessman, the father of three children, he was about to go bankrupt, or rather, we made him go bankrupt."

"Could he have been saved?"

"He might have been, perhaps."

"And so?"

"There were certain interests involved..."

Among those interests were those of Auxiliary Bishop Egisto Martinolli, who was trembling in the dark of the confessional while that voice continued implacably in its common accusation.

And when he came to the amen, after Doberdò's face had gone away from the grating, he stayed there, with his head against the wood, without the force to move aside the velvet curtains and come out.

"Amen!" and Annibale Doberdò's steps, which were going away cleansed and at peace with God, resounded in his brain until he became dizzy.

CHAPTER TEN

That's how it was. I was living on easy street, but I don't know who there was to envy me. I had plenty to eat and drink, and all I had to do for anything I wanted was open my mouth. But I wasn't making anything off it. For me, robbing a man like that, who respected me and treated me like a daughter, would be like stealing in church. In other words, I was well off in my cage, and at the beginning I didn't even feel tied down to those three rooms with balcony. And this was because it's not true that a girl who's been officially branded a whore and catalogued apart for the benefit of the hypocrites is locked up there in sin, waiting for her boss's pleasure.

I had that idea myself when I took my rags into that house. I don't know why I thought I'd be chained up like an animal. Maybe it was because of him. He was so different from other men, a gentleman from head to toe. Because he understood without anyone having to say anything in so many words and he tried not to bear down on me too much. Anyway, the day went by fast, and I'd need three of them in one to do what I had to do, and I'd find myself closing up the doors and windows at night, being sad that another day had gone by.

I'd spend the morning at the house. I'd always slept late, but there I got up almost at dawn. Just look, I would say to myself, now that no one's pushing you, now that you could easily sleep until noon, you act like you had to run out and open a store. And I could see all that green from my bedroom window! And it was so quiet early in the morning! Imagine me used to all those children and neighbors and

123

their noise from as far back as I can remember... I could hardly sleep, and the nicest thing about it was that in the day I would even talk to myself, just so I wouldn't go crazy.

I'd take a chair and sit out on the balcony, because there was the nicest breeze coming up from the trees, and I'd talk to myself just like someone in a booby hatch. Califfa this and Califfa that, and meantime I was taking in the whole apartment, which was neat and clean.

And then, about eleven, Gilda Fumagalli, my teacher, would come. She was an old maid who'd probably been to bed with a man only once in her life, but that'd been enough, and how, because she had a son thirty years old. She wasn't a very impressive little woman to look at, but she gave herself airs I didn't like – she the brain and I the dope, she the saint and I something up from the gutter.

Everything I said was wrong and I couldn't guess anything right, not anything at all. And after all, I hadn't asked that old bag to come to my house and act as if she were my boss.

"Ah, come on! Don't take it so hard!" Doberdò'd say to me. "The important thing is to learn, and Fumagalli – as far as patience goes, there's no one like her." And just to keep him happy, I didn't say anything. I would sit in front of her and I would open my notebook and it would begin. Read here, multiply there, write me a little theme, listen to me, obey me, this way and not that way, and not the other way either. But who was she anyway, the Queen?

All morning she'd be there making life miserable for me, just because he wanted it that way: "Clean her up for me. She's an intelligent girl, you'll see; she understands everything!" I'd hardly finished third grade, just imagine, and the way the schools are where I went, the teachers were taking a risk if they looked the other way. So I had a hard time with the pen, even though I'd always had something to say, because I'd always liked to listen to other people – that is, I learned more from my ears than from my eyes.

In the morning, school; and homework in the afternoons, for me, at my age and with all the other things I had on my mind. And the things she told me to write about! "The Happy

Days of My Childhood" or "The First Trip I Ever Took," and once even "How I Remember My Father." Either she was stupid or she was doing it on purpose. I think she was trying to get my goat and shame me into telling the truth. But I didn't fall for that and I tried to talk about the fathers and trips and happy days of someone else I knew. But one day Gilda Fumagalli got out of the wrong side of the bed, or something. Anyway, she just went too far. No, dear, that was too much! And I refused. I slammed the notebook shut and told her there was a limit to everything.

"What father, what vacations? Stop pretending! You and that hypocritical face of yours! You know perfectly well that I don't know who my father was and that as for my childhood I was screaming with hunger, and if I took a trip, it was to the cemetery, there and back."

You should have seen her. She was red in the face and her eyes were burning, she was so excited. She said that from someone like me, from a woman in my category...

"So that's what you're getting at, you bitch! What do you mean, someone like me?" I began screaming.

"You certainly have some nerve!" and she said she was going to tell someone we both knew all about it, because she had been able to make a lot of other hot heads roll. And then, and these were her exact words, with that gutter face of hers, she called me "an untrained and vicious animal!"

Animal? Who was an animal? Oh, Gilda, let's be clear about one thing, and I went around the table and if there hadn't been the cord of the iron in my way so I couldn't get to her, I would have taken her by the hair and shown her what kind of animal I was.

"Stop! Please stop! I've got asthma! There are some things I simply can't do! Oh my goodness, don't make me run. I didn't mean it in that sense, I swear to you! I meant an animal in the sense of the force of nature!"

I stopped in front of her and she was like a parrot with its feathers taken off, hunched up in the corner, trying to look sweet.

"Oh, so that's what you meant! But I'm telling you now

right out that you've made me mad and that I want you to get out of here! If you know something about me, watch out because I know something about you too. And if I tell him that's all I can stand, it'll be so much less for that tomcat of a son of yours, who shouldn't go around getting into debt all over the place."

And you should have seen her afterward! *Yes, Mrs. Corsini* here, *No, Mrs. Corsini* there. I made her respect me, and how! And I went to ask Viola's advice, to see if I was doing the right thing. I called her up on the telephone, but not because there was any need of it, and not that we couldn't get together either. It was just that I knew what a thrill she got going into Braibanti's beauty parlor like a cop and yelling *hello* into the phone as if it were a loud chorus from Verdi's *Otello!* And all the girls could see who she was talking to!

Viola, Viola, what a voice she had, what emotion. It was as if we were at opposite ends of the earth. But from my window I could see that hilltop with her sheets on it hanging out to dry.

And then she was silly. The only time I could bring her into the house, I practically had to drag her by the hair of her head, because she didn't want to hear about going up. "But *I* live there, me, Califfa, not the Emperor!"

"Yes, yes. But I'm not dressed right. I can't go up in this, and with my hair a mess..."

"But what do you care about your hair? There'll just be you, me, and the four walls." So when we came to the entrance of the building and that guy comes up looking like a priest in his black jacket, she didn't see me as Califfa but as someone else, and I really thought it was bothering her. But that afternoon I dragged her up the stairs, and as soon as we were in the living room she saw a bunch of roses even bigger than the ones Doberdò had sent, the ones she had almost cried over when she had to throw them out. So what did she do? Viola realized suddenly that they were for her, to thank her for what she'd done for me, and she began to sniffle and I had to keep up with that flood of tears because, who knows why, when she's happy, she's like a shower in summer.

And there was more than just the roses. On the bed there was a new dress from the best shop and near it a bag with matching shoes. To see her in new clothes from head to foot, to see her walking around like a decent woman, just once... She couldn't stop the tears. It was a ball and she couldn't keep her eyes or her hands from anything, even the faucets in the bathroom, the cords on the curtains, and the light-switches, so that after she left my little apartment, it looked like a battlefield.

But the fun I had seeing her made young again was worth that and more. There was that surprise on her face and all those embraces and thanks for me – and him – and I thanked her for when she helped me when I was discouraged. And I think she'd not had many days like that, because I can still remember how she left with that load of flowers and packages. And I was there imagining how happy she'd be going over the bridge on her way home, with the money she'd let me slip into her bra – she who was barely keeping alive and whom everyone liked so much – and I wanted to look at the sky where it was getting dark; and it made me shiver.

And so that was my day, that was how I lived like a whore. And at the end of it, when he called me up, for some reason or another, to say that he couldn't come – and that was often – I would go back onto the balcony to lie down. The dark hills were pretty, all lit up, like the city was. And from there it looked like mine.

Or, walking around, out there in the dark, so no one could see me (what would we have said to each other, me and the people who'd known me as a kid, if I'd seen them? What could I get from them but a look that meant they were sorry for me?), I would go back to my old neighborhood. I would go back there, being careful to take the sidestreets, like a police spy. Only a few months had passed, but the streets and houses seemed very different and I resisted the temptation to touch with my hand the misery I had lived in until so recently, and how! But I couldn't sleep and I was unhappy all the next day. It was a vice and there are some vices you just can't give orders to.

It was bothering me, and I almost felt like it was my fault that those people were having such a hard time, and the long and the short of it was that they ended up buzzing around Doberdò in a way that made me ashamed. Sometimes it's better to get killed than ask for money, I swear it. I was ashamed, I repeat, ashamed. It was lucky that he had me sit next to him and laughed even before I started talking: "I get it, how much do you want, Saint Bernard?"

He called me Saint Bernard, and he was right, because I never touched any of that money, I swear that too, and he knew that perfectly well; if not, he'd be the first to say no, I won't give you any. So it was nothing but a pack of lies when they said later that I'd had him give me all those checks (who knows what impression that gave?) and they accused me of stealing. Califfa hasn't ever stolen and that's always been her rule, not even a pin! That money was to make a kid better, or to let some family have some peace, because I knew that when there's no money at all, everything's ruined, even with the best of intentions. Was that stealing?

They should have been in my shoes when I'd wake up at night on the other side of the river and see the lights of their windows. I knew everything about them: who was trying to quiet a child, who was sick. There was a name that went with every light. And it might sound a little corny, but it was as if they were there in my bed and I could hear them breathing in my room. And I couldn't sleep any more, not even if I closed the windows so I wouldn't see the lights any more and so I could hide in the dark.

"Tell us you were playing the saint," they challenged me when things were being settled up – something people would say who won't ever understand anything even if they live to be a hundred! It was no good to talk with people like that; all you can do is tell them to go to hell, with their titles and their damned respectable faces... A saint! No, not a saint! Sainthood had nothing to do with it; maybe it was the heat. That's what everybody blames their mistakes on. But what can you tell them to do? What's the good of shouting yourself hoarse? The main thing is that your conscience isn't bothering you and that you don't have any unsettled accounts with yourself, because if you did, you'd really be a thief.

And I could show my conscience with no fear, even when I actually did exaggerate a little with Doberdò – the twenty-fourth of June was getting close. I remember it like it was yesterday, one night after dinner, with me here and him at the other end of the table. I asked him for a favor and I didn't have the nerve to look him in the eye. And I said to myself: This time it's too much! My God, it's too much!

But it wasn't too much at all. A gentleman like he always was, he just asked me why, and when I told him, he just answered that he'd arrange it himself. And he was as good as his word.

II

And it was Doberdò's word which allowed don Ersilio Campagna, for the first time in all those years, to avoid humbling himself in front of the Auxiliary Bishop, to obtain that act of "unreasoned liberality" which differed by a hair's breadth from a God-awful disgrace. That was because Doberdò found himself next to Martinolli one morning of that same week in a field near the city at a cornerstone-laying ceremony, one of the many, one of the too many, as Doberdò was lamenting:

"Pretty soon there won't be room for a cauliflower to grow around here! I'm against cornerstone layings, decidedly against them! I'd rather have cauliflower!"

"But this is for a school," Martinolli had objected, "not for speculation in real estate! For their souls and their minds, not for their bodies! It's for our children. Where do we want to leave our children, eh? In whose hands?" And so Doberdò let the Bishop extract from him that sigh of resignation which meant his name would appear in the financing. And after that rapid, intimate ceremony, as they were going back along the path crowded with officials, Doberdò said nonchalantly: "My dear don Martinolli, do you know what people have told me?

That sometimes you're a little prissy, prissy not to say a martinet, and a martinet if not a stubborn old man!"

"I?!" asked Martinolli with an awkward smile, without understanding.

Doberdò had glanced at him, then suddenly lengthened his stride and, leaving him behind, he had stepped among the dangling bars of the first scaffolding, saying just, "Let's not make such a fuss over their manna, dear Monsignor, let's let 'em enjoy it the way they want – maybe even with your blessing!"

Martinolli stayed there and stared at him, suddenly understanding the situation and knowing all too well the curve those shoulders could take on and the meaning those half-statements could have when Doberdò was seized by those unexpected fits of brusqueness. And this was the reason why don Ersilio was informed that that year, as an exception, not only would the festival not encounter any objections, but that the candles could also be lit in the chapel, "used for the purpose," Martinolli wrote in his note, "of innocent festivals, and not only to brighten them, but also for the purpose – may God support it! – of attenuating certain ambiguous and pagan aspects of the situation, whose recurrence, regrettably enough, is effected…"

After reading the note, don Ersilio was uncertain. And the following Sunday too he was suspended between satisfaction and a regret which he tried to drive away, when he announced the Bishop's generous decision during his sermon, adding that (just this once) he would not be obliged to ask for the mediation of some spiritual reserves to which he could always have turned in case of trouble. They were not needed now, but they must not be forgotten. The congregation therefore should thank Monsignor Martinolli and say an Ave Maria for him, since he had so spontaneously done something for them.

And don Ersilio had a touch of regret in finding his problem solved even before he faced it. If he were to lose this one merit in the eyes of the parish, what other tangible proof was there of his usefulness? Because the little fuss he made in showing that he could open a door which actually was already open constituted quite a store of credit. And for this reason he was in a very bad mood, also because no one had asked Martinolli for anything.

But that was an exceptional year which was to see real manna descend on the poor part of the city. Three trucks loaded with spaghetti, cheese, and canned food, all products of companies Doberdò represented, came one evening to the main square in the old quarter and began unloading. Addressee: no one and everyone. There was no bill. Gratis and for the love of God, said the drivers, and they looked, as if anyone needed to be told, at the canvas covers on the trucks where the donor's name was written in letters a foot high: "Doberdò Doberdò Doberdò" above and below.

And now the windows were opening and faces were peering out and someone was saying that it really might all be a joke; but the bags were full and it sure did look like cheeses. Finally Viola burst into the group that had gathered around the trucks like flies, and, rummaging among the bags and boxes, said they should all be strung up if they still didn't know who should be thanked for everything. But if she hadn't gotten that telephone call, Califfa thought later, who knows if Viola would have had such faith in her that she'd understand, and that she would be so sure in front of those presents, which were beginning to disappear into the houses, among the waving of arms and chattering of the women?

Then the square began to empty, and when Califfa passed by in the first hours of that night there were only the empty bags stacked up on a sidewalk and a slight odor of cheese where they had been split open and divided up.

And the following night when there was the festival, Califfa stayed with Doberdò to listen to the singing, the music, and the shouting, which the wind was bringing up from the fields around the city to the balcony.

"He asked me, 'Are you happy?' and he took my hand. Happy? I wanted to tell him yes, because I could hear how happy my people were – then I thought of Guido, and Vito that night, and I started to cry... The party went on all night.

And when I got up the next morning, what did I find? That they had tied a bunch of violets on to the grating of my balcony, as we always do when we feel gratitude, because the violet is the flower of our city. I still have those flowers, and I'm still wondering how they managed to climb up there as far as the balcony, that night when they had the festival..."

CHAPTER ELEVEN

Waking from a difficult dream, Doberdò was shaken by a shudder which drove him back under the covers, and he had to suck in his stomach to drive it away. And afterward a veil of sweat formed on his forehead. He had assaults of chills and fever which were repeated during the day, and Doberdò bent his head, pretending he was concentrating when he had people in the office, to drive off this obscure threat. And when he lifted it from his hands, only then did his face seem to open out to the light, and a shadow of astonished alarm passed over his little eyes. He felt faint, and his heart stopped in the sudden abyss for an instantaneous but seemingly interminable pause.

Then again there was the other dizziness of telephones, words, and faces which took his mind off the first vertigo. And it was as if chance were playing with his weak heart, surrounding him with pretexts capable of isolating him in the horror of that illness.

"It's a stupid mocking kind of chill, Doctor, which I just can't understand."

The doctor explored his breathless chest and, listening to that far-off clogged-up heart, tried to reassure him: "These things are inevitable, I would say almost salutary, when the blood pressure is being normalized. When the body reacts, it's a good sign."

"It's not my body, Doctor. I'm the one who reacts, and I don't react well – sometimes like a child and sometimes like a madman!"

Like a madman... Annibale Doberdò repeated it to himself the day when Farinacci's mother died and he betook himself to her house to leave his signature in the mourning book at the entrance to her building, and to pay the body the minimum of respects which convention allowed. It was early morning and the streets were almost empty, silent under the moon which day had not yet cancelled out.

And in his mind's eye he saw the wrought-iron bed on which old lady Farinacci was probably stretched out at that moment and it seemed just yesterday that he had had that idiotic affair with her – there had been only one time – on that same bed which he recalled at that moment, so distinctly that he could even count the curly leaves carved on it and hear it thumping against the wall.

But twenty years had gone by, twenty years figured up in the twinkling of an eye, as if they had just passed in the preceding moment; and it seemed only a few hours ago that he had kissed that fresh and stubborn woman, only the night before that he had left her with her panting little belly, alive in the darkened room, alive, to find her cold and dead the next morning.

Doberdò was again seized with a cold shudder. He stopped and leaned against a wall; and when it had passed, a strange feeling of well-being took possession of him, as if there had been a catastrophe which had involved him with Signora Farinacci in the same mortal danger and only he had come out of it.

He was inspired by the survivor's feeling of exultation, and on his way up the stairway, among the smoky funeral torches, he said to himself: "I'm alive! I'm alive and she's dead!" and he was light and free.

He signed the register, shook Ubaldo Farinacci's hand, and sought for some appropriate sentiments to mutter, but all the while the commotion and sadness on all those faces and the low hum of their voices were transmuted into so much more exultation for him. Farinacci took him to the room. It was marked with the smell of burning wax and he repeated to himself: "I'm alive! I'm alive, by God!" and when he recognized the roses stamped on the walls, and then that bed, a great happiness took possession of him.

He glared at the rigid feet of the corpse, swollen in their shoes, tied together with a ribbon.

"Annibale, kiss me, kiss me..." and he saw himself again, nude and surrounded by the roses which were climbing to the ceiling, bent over, kissing her from her breasts on down as far as her knees and those little white feet, then so alive, to the reddened nails of those trembling fingers now rigid and swollen in death.

He was free to be happy in the face of death, to despise, insult, and deride it; free to get out of that room and that building, to look at the women, and to caress the curls of a child passing by, and to feel the heat of the sun on his face... He was free to realize that the Farinacci woman was dead and that he had survived to remember a day he had suddenly reappraised after having forgotten it for twenty years.

He felt so full of vitality that he quickened his step along the streets which were filling up with people by then...

II

He preferred to walk to the office, because the smell of the lemon trees along the avenue made his breathing easier, so much so that he was walking along with his eyes half closed, breathing deeply. He was reviving under a sky already warm with summer, and the railing of the bridge was warm too as he ran his hand along it, enjoying the roughness of the stone; and the voices rang in his newly liberated head, coming from the windows filled with sheets and mattresses, or from the slope crowded with old houses. Voices and smells of nights he had experienced, of live awakenings, of the will to live.

And it was of no importance to him, in his happy walk in the dust, that his shoes and his trousers got dirty, or that perspiration obliged him to take off his jacket and undo the collar of his shirt.

And for this reason the secretaries saw him appear that way: dusty, with his jacket on his arm and his necktie undone, but with color in his face and with his eyes still looking out the illuminated window from which the city lazily spread out.

Monday was a bore for Doberdò. There was a succession of unavoidable appointments, announced by the lighting of a red bulb on the table where the secretaries sat; every light had a name and it was Doberdò who would push the button on his desk and, according to the amount of time his finger stayed on the button and therefore the behavior of that light, the secretaries would know if the caller were to be admitted and, if so, for how long. At ten, Gazza, in a slight state of agitation, was brought into his office. On Monday Gazza had to summarize all the editorials in the Sunday papers, because Doberdò's eyes were tired and on Sunday he refused to pay any attention to anything written.

"We are in the hands of braying asses!" began Gazza with the passion he knew how to pretend when he had to show that if he did not earn his money with his political predictions he at least did so with suffering. "Asses, I would say, stupid asses! And please realize that I say this with great disappointment, with the bitterness of one who believes in the Christian Democratic Party, who was a Christian Democrat when the others were just Communists, all Communists."

Doberdò smiled, and he noticed that Gazza was trying to raise one short, unquiet leg onto the other knee, a gesture to symbolize the heat he was trying to put into his words.

"Stirring up dissension among factions, leaking certain deals that are inevitable in any government... But why? I ask you why!" And Gazza pounded on Doberdò's desk.

"Here's a man who doesn't believe in anything... I'm paying a man who's never believed in anything," Doberdò thought.

"'At just the right time, we'll confront people with a dramatic choice.' The *Corriere della Sera* says it so well, I'd say it always says it well!"

"I'm alive!" thought Doberdò, staring at the bent and agitated form of Gazza.

"'...because that mob of eggheads under Fanfani's banner...'"

"I'm still alive!" and in front of him the air was luminous and tranquil.

"And as Missiroli so aptly puts it, so very aptly…"

And above the trees were the hills cleansed by the good weather, where one could count the houses in the little villages…

At ten-thirty the stockbroker arrived. The red eye of judgment blinked but a moment on the secretaries' table. Before he went in, the broker took a good look at the red light, whose secret he knew, and he hoped each time that it would shine for a second more, for one second more would have meant a nice raise for him. "What's a second?" he sadly asked himself. "Just time enough to breathe… A breath to pay the rent with…"

And when from the partially opened door Doberdò saw the hat deferentially leaving that bald head to reveal the broker bathed in frightened perspiration, he inevitably thought: "He bothers me. I don't understand why, but he bothers me. He's a good man, but I'll have to replace him."

"The market has had what can be characterized as an active course, sir, but with a tendency for prices to become stabilized…"

"I'm still alive!" thought Doberdò again.

"…upward signs are to observed in Finsider, which has just finished selling a new stock issue…"

And now the clouds were moving toward the horizon, making the light more uncertain.

"… and, if I may, I would suggest that you concentrate on Finsider, concentrate on Finsider. I think you will find that I am right."

"I wonder if it's going to rain," thought Doberdò.

"Finsider!"

With the fear of rain, the sense of his own fragility came back.

"Finsider, Mr. Doberdò!"

Doberdò continued to stare out the window at the sky, dumbfounded.

"Mr. Doberdò!" repeated the disconcerted broker.

137

Doberdò came to. "Do you think it's going to rain?"

The bewildered broker looked at the sky, then at Doberdò. "Yes, perhaps, probably. A little rain at last, eh, Mr. Doberdò, with all those dried-up fields…"

To Doberdò's disgust, he backed up: "Or perhaps not… No… it'll blow over…" and he smiled, to look more optimistic.

After he sent the broker away, it was time for Giampiero Doberdò's tutor. "I'll tell you frankly, the boy has me a little worried," said the teacher. "He's intelligent and he learns perfectly well. He absorbs, digests, assimilates, but…"

"But what?" asked Doberdò.

"He doesn't give back anything, or he doesn't want to."

"I don't understand."

"I mean he keeps everything bottled up within himself… that he doesn't work together with his teacher… that even though he's physically weak, he's presumptuous and headstrong with his companions and teachers."

"A shithead!" thought Doberdò.

"He doesn't fit in well, because he's surrounded by persons unworthy of him. I'd advise some other kind of school more suited to the boy, which would be able to give him a more tangible sense, I would say, of a certain position, which, after all, it is his duty to acquire…"

"My son's a shithead!" And Doberdò brought to mind the beach at Viareggio that summer of 1946. Through the umbrellas and the swimmers he saw that fellow coming along the beach wiping the sweat off his face with his handkerchief – he never took off his pants, his shirt, or even this shoes, and he barely turned up the cuffs of his trousers on his hairy legs. Under his arm were some books and at his side was Clementina, still magnificent in that green bathing suit. She and her friends were butterflies around the light of that famous brain which was dispensing wisdom. He was a moderately famous literary man who changed the subject as soon as Doberdò came up, substituting De Gasperi for Proust and the works of the Constituent Assembly for James.

Doberdò was seated on the sand, looking at his naked feet

and pretending not to notice how embarrassed his wife was because he had thrown cold water on those conversations which were inaccessible to him. "A shithead!" he was thinking then on the beach, just as he did later in his office. But his mocking suspicion in the office was not with him long, because the sun reappeared between the clouds and the window. The room became invaded with it, as was he.

"... The boy's not doing his best; he's not reaching his potential; his trans – "

"Open the window!" said Doberdò without listening to him any more.

Voices, sounds, and odors entered the room. Doberdò half closed his eyes and sighed. "There! Can you smell it? That's the perfume of the lemon trees... the chestnut... the wheat... Do you know when the wheat begins to sprout?"

The tutor, embarrassed, had nothing to say. "Really, I wouldn't know... You know what I teach is Italian and Latin."

"That's bad. You shouldn't ignore certain things."

"Well, as I was saying, the boy –"

"Forget about the boy! Open the other window!"

And the doctor, who was ushered in at exactly eleven-thirty with a flashing of the light which lasted longer than any other, found Doberdò excited and trembling, a relaxed Doberdò who wanted to joke, and gave in only when the stethoscope was wandering up and down his chest. Far away, in the anonymous buzzing of the city, he heard the sound of a funeral bell and immediately he saw those feet in their black stockings. His heart sank and he had his usual shiver.

"Relax! Have some fun! And get some peace and quiet," said the doctor. "But why won't you pay any attention to what I say?"

Doberdò vacillated, struggling with himself, and finally achieved control. And when the examination was over, he stayed there stripped to the waist; and then suddenly he grabbed his undershirt, shirt, and jacket, dressed in a hurry, and rushed out of his office. He didn't look at anyone. The German engineer (twelve noon), the Lombard industrialist (twelve-fifteen) and Martinolli (twelve-thirty) all got up from their armchairs in astonishment, as Doberdò, buttoning up his shirt, shouted to the secretaries:

"Call up the Countess and tell her I won't be home for lunch!" He went out with his good mood back again and he would have liked to add: "Alive! Like a child or a like a madman, but alive!"

And, turning down the elevator which the doorman had opened for him, he preferred to walk down, humming along the way.

III

This was his first vacation in many months, that flight in the car with Califfa at his side. She had been hauled out of bed, having been up late the night before, and was trying to wake up and to understand where she was going. She was still jarred by Doberdò's bursting into her room, by the light which had inundated the bed and freed the room from the shadowy smell of sleepy young flesh, while he, with those drops of happy perspiration and his rosy cheeks, looked like a bell-ringer sounding the resurrection.

She had time to put on a dress and wash her face and off they went in the car, running between two dusty banks of daisies as soon as it got out in the country. And now Califfa was staring at Doberdò with some fear, since she had never seen his eyes so small and lucid before, and she did not understand what was happening to him. And probably Doberdò himself didn't understand that urge to run away, to escape. His soul was confused, as was his mind; the only thing that was clear was the agitation which was driving him on and making his hands tremble on the wheel.

If at first it had been the idea of an absurd survival, of a danger averted, now it was only the necessity of burning up this vitality which filled him and led him to push down on the accelerator with the wind whistling through the open windows, out into the green. He looked at Califfa curled up

140

on the seat and caressed her bare knees. She continued to stare at him with her face supported in her hands. Images, pictures, and sounds were still buzzing around in his mind; the doctor's words, the gray countenance of the gray Gazza, the telephones in league against him, the agitated secretaries he had made fun of, just as he had of the German engineer, the Lombard industrialist, Martinolli, his wife, and life itself. How he wanted to drop it all and escape into the country! And he had. Now they could all fend for themselves, especially since they were so sure of what he should do...

"But where are we going, Mr. Doberdò?" asked Califfa, who could not bring herself to call him by his first name in spite of their intimacy. Doberdò turned an astonished face to her, as if he had just realized that the road had become a stony track where the car was bouncing up and down between two huge fields red with poppies. An extraordinary shimmering rose above the grass, and the singing birds kept losing themselves in the sun. And at the edge of the fields were clusters of houses with sheets waving on the clothes lines among lazy voices. And life itself was with him in the face of Califfa leaning back in the seat, in his open mouth and thick lips.

And now Doberdò was beginning to understand. It wasn't only the lights and telephones waiting in ambush for him that he was fleeing, but he seemed to be rising up in the great light. He felt as if he had successfully passed the Last Judgment, already light, already free. In that instant he understood the life of light in its absolute purity, when it is not just mixed in with things but above them. Light was his vacation, his youth found again, the religion of his fear of death. He stopped the car. He leaned his head on the wheel. "God, I thank you for this light, and the fact that I'm still alive..."

"But what's the matter with you?" said Califfa, shaking him. "Don't act like that, you're scaring me. Are you sick or something?" And the idea of being sick brought back the image of those swollen feet tied together with the ribbon and once again he shuddered. He opened his eyes wide to bring in the light and, motivated by a presentiment, held Califfa to him and drank in the young smell of her neck and hair, as if he were going to bid her a last farewell there in the light of the countryside.

"The important thing is to be alive, Califfa, alive! That's the only important thing, don't forget that!" He helped her out of the car and they walked across the meadow, taking with them the wine and a picnic lunch he had bought before picking her up. They laughed as they tramped through the grass and he was not sixty years old any more, but thirty, twenty, eighteen. He was still the boy who lived in the smoke of his little factory, the one who stopped to pick the poppies in the ditches, to cover his land with them. They roughhoused around on the grass, and the baskets flew into the air. She ran off and Doberdò even caught up with her, running on the grass which pushed down under his feet.

They found some shade by the city walls, in the middle of some vines. The distant countryside flashed back and forth in the noon haze and it seemed that they were looking at it through a veil of water. Doberdò felt a strange thirst and a desire to get drunk on that wine, which the doctor had warned him to have only two fingers of in a glass ("Two fingers and no more! If you have any more, your heart will palpitate!"). He turned the glass around in the light before emptying it and said: "You know, Califfa, for twenty years, I've been missing the cicadas…" He turned his head to hear better the sound which was coming down from the trees, confused with the buzz of the flies: "…and the flies. Twenty years as if there hadn't been any flies or cicadas…"

"And what's so special about a fly," observed Califfa, shooing one away from her buttered bread. "Just an ugly little bug!"

"No, no! The fly flies upward, into the light! Look at him a little." And Califfa sat there with her bread still in her mouth and she watched the insect flying up among the trees in a series of spirals toward the sky.

"It's the only beast that really understands the function of light, and its poetry, that knows how to amuse itself with it in a civilized way. Do you understand?"

142

And Califfa answered: "And why should I understand it? You say some things so well, I enjoy not understanding them. Everybody tries so hard to understand, but sometimes it's nice not to understand. Just to say that's the way it is and that's all."

Doberdò smiled. He poured himself another glass of wine. "You'll come to understand everything when you realize that you can't ever understand anything."

"Oh!" said Califfa, filling her mouth.

"How can you understand light? It's there and that's the way it is. There's nothing else to be said." And Doberdò felt comfort in that commonplace philosophy which he had kept to himself for years, from the day when Clementina had peremptorily forbidden him to come out with banalities like that among the prominent citizens who frequented Palazzo Doberdò. But now he could let himself go; there was only the countryside listening to him, with Califfa hanging on his every word.

"Because, you understand, the life of a man like me is like that of a worm, which starts out in the light and digs and turns farther and farther in, to get to the marrow of God knows what... You get it?"

Califfa stuck out her chin, to indicate neither yes or no.

"And when he arrives, he realizes that there's only darkness and cold in that marrow and that the light was outside, and that it would have been better if he'd stayed outside. It would have meant less trouble for him, and fewer humiliations..." But by now the wine was encumbering his words and making his eyelids heavy. His fingers moved more slowly, his glass overturned on the ground, and heated sleep overcame him.

Califfa took the food from his hand, covered him up with his jacket, stretched out next to him, and fell asleep herself.

Doberdò was dreaming so clearly that his thoughts appeared logical to him in his sleeping state. He dreamed he got up and went across the field, taking Califfa with him. He got to the edge of it and already he could see that house with the collapsing wall and the windows flapping on their hinges like clothes on a line.

("But, Annibale, what do you care if that pigsty falls down one of these days? With all those other things you have on your mind, you want to think about that pigsty." That's how Clementina would talk about it, and so he had to drive even that gentle memory back into the dark recesses of his mind; the memory of himself as a boy, in the house filled with mothers, fathers, uncles, and cousins happily playing around on the roof under the weathervane, like the other boys, with the cheerful odor of the wine coming up from the depths of the kitchen. What was it to raise up a wall, put some props under the ceiling, and fix some windows? That stubborn old Clementina made up these things just to anger him, but he said not a word and took no initiative, just so he could at least eat his soup in peace. And so the weeds had grown by leaps and bounds, all the way up to the roof, so that the house looked like a great fountain in which the streams of water were the beards of vegetation that sprouted out of every hole and waved about in the air.)

And it seemed to him in his dream that he and Califfa went in, and there was a table and a fireplace and even a bed with a mattress. (To hell with Clementina!) And he saw the dust coming in the window, and there was a fire in the fireplace. It was beautiful and wonderful to his newly opened eyes, as if it were the first fire mankind had ever seen. And then the polenta slipped down on the plate, and the two of them grabbed it, ate it, and washed it down with some wine. And at the end there was a strong cigar to tickle his nose. And when the noise of dinner was over, there resounded in the evening silence his personal announcement that his good health had been confirmed – which was also his unalloyed vengeance against the Gazzas, the Clementinas and the Giampieros – a belch.

(He had awaited it for many years, years of searching among the remains of his physical well-being, of imploring a belch from his stomach, at least a little one. One day when in an unexpected awakening this vital push had arisen within him, Martinolli the Auxiliary Bishop had been on his right side and Clementina on his left. And so he had had to reject that gratuitous present from his tummy, and humiliate it, pushing it down with a wrench of his insides.)

And he dreamed that a happy Califfa saw him take off his office clothes, like a recruit on leave, disgusted with his uniform and happy to get out of it. And naked he slid down beside her in that bed where he had had his first desire as a boy, and where in long nights when sleep was a weak ash over the burning embers of his lust, he had thought what his first woman would be like – and his last.

The polenta, the wine, and the fresh air, the roughness of the sheets, the creaking of the mattress allowed him finally to do justice to Califfa's young body. And after love-making there were the stars, a sky crowded with them, seen through the open window. (And it was here, in that bed, with that poor Madonna hanging above its head, struck by a blow from his father's shoe when the old gentleman was furious and in a very bad mood...)

And he dreamed that Califfa was sleeping like a little girl, with a hand under her face. Her breath was caressing his cheek. He was far from the waiting, the doubts, and the anxiety to discover and to hurry life up. And looking at the window trembling in the starlight, how could he think that there was an office with too many telephones, a city commanded by a name, a wife called Clementina and a man like Gazza who didn't believe in anything? No it wasn't just a flight. His vacation was beginning then, in Califfa's breathing, sweet with unalloyed purity.

But the night passed and dawn came. The lights disappeared and the grass gradually became visible; the birds began to sing, and with the sheet flung to the foot of the bed, he could turn where he liked, because Califfa was not Clementina and would not bark at him: "Annibale, can't you be still? Have some respect for someone else's sleep!" (And away he would go, trying to make himself smaller, way over to the other edge of the bed, moving his legs slowly, as if he were staying clear of a mine, legs he would like to raise up under the covers...)

Dawn spread over the fields and there was the milkman

with his horn. Its sound rose from the winding road, an insistent and aggressive sound, and his mother was muttering from the next room: "Oh, Carlino! Him and that horn of his!" Now Carlino was blowing it right outside the house and his mother jumped out of bed and shouted: "I'm coming! I'm coming! Just stop blowing that horn!" (Milk! A bucket of milk, milk with bread, with polenta, with that horn... It had been years since he'd had any milk. "No milk for a colitis case," said the doctor. "It's poison for you!")

Gazza stopped sounding his horn when his car bounced out of a depression and he caught sight of Doberdò and Califfa down there stretched out on the red blanket on the grass. He braked his car with a little laugh and threw himself onto the grass, shouting: "Mr. Doberdò! Thank God I've found you, Mr. Doberdò!"

Doberdò heard that voice rise from the bottom of his consciousness, like a foreign body pushed up from the bottom of still waters, and with his last confusing cluster of images still in his head, he pushed open his eyes in time to see Gazza jumping over the ditch, running toward him and taking off his hat as he came.

"Mr. Doberdò, but what are you doing here? It's already five and at five-thirty we've got that member of Parliament from Rome... It's a good thing I've sniffed you out. As I was saying to myself, who'd ever guess where you went?" With a snarl, Doberdò scratched his head and looked over the fields, where the sun was beginning to go down, and he looked at Califfa who was waking up and rubbing her eyes. A little bird sang above his head and he looked up with a smile.

But it was only when he turned his head to Gazza that the vital burst of energy arose from his invigorated stomach. And this time, with his eyes wandering around in bitter awakening, he did not hold it back.

CHAPTER TWELVE

Viola, in her own way – that is, with that cast of mind which made her suspicious of everything and everyone, and all too ready to speak, but which invariably ended up by betraying her – was therefore advising Califfa on an adventure about which at bottom she knew just as little as her friend. But could Califfa have taken those bits of advice seriously, limited as they were by so instinctive a warmth and often deformed by bad faith and ignorance as well? Not that Califfa did not ask for them, it was just that she preferred not to clear up any ambiguities. The sordid ramifications of Viola's life still had too vivid an effect on her, and, more than anything else, Califfa had too great a need of a pretext to cover her mistakes, and too great an antipathy to gambling with the remains of her reputation, to take her friend's advice.

Thinking over her character, Califfa realized that in Viola there flourished a priestly spirit, a religion of life which was all her own. And even though she had been destructively critical of some church customs, she had taken in others, absorbing their good sense, which, according to her, made it possible to avoid some traps.

And even from the rather weird examples with which she used to adorn her ideas, there came forth this regurgitated, overturned religion of her own advantage. As for instance when she tried to teach Califfa the commandments she had received and adapted to the present times and circumstances: "What's the point of honoring your father and mother, the dirty bastards?" "Watch out for your neighbor; he's your worst enemy!" "Have no other gods but yourself." "Bear false witness whenever it's convenient!" And especially: "Steal whenever it seems a good idea, especially from the ones that have. If you're good at stealing, who's going to look in your pocket?" And she had other principles like those.

But she would invariably conclude: "But, Califfa, you always have to be careful! Stay on your guard, Califfa, and remember, put your paw out, more for taking than for giving, and then take it right back in, as if the earth were shaking!" And this was what the two friends always disagreed about, with Califfa smiling. And she would react:

"But why? Why should I live like a hermit when I haven't anything to hide, and when I can hold my head up better than anyone else?"

"The damned poor!" answered Viola. "It's true, and your case just goes to show it, Califfa. If they have an inch, they want a mile. And nothing that happens teaches them anything. They still look for trouble!"

"Leave the poor alone," insisted Califfa. "Just answer me. I've spent months on that balcony and in that bed, with a little breath of fresh air only once in a while, as if I was doing a life sentence. I have a man who'd cover me with gold and who insists on taking me out to have fun when the sun's shining and everyone can see me... to make me feel free. And he doesn't understand why I insist on staying in that house, since I'm young, healthy and happy... But no! Should I sit here like a bump on the wall? If only it was worth it, being locked up like this!"

Then Viola took her by an arm and stared at her. "Listen!" she said. "Let's look each other in the face and talk frankly to each other! If you have a yen to do these things, that's one thing, but it's another when you tell me you don't understand that when someone reduces herself like that, whether it's good or bad, she has to forget about certain rights. Because no one will have anything to do with her, because you have to keep your eyes open, since it's easy for people to say awful things about you. And what do you think it would take to cut your throat? Yes, you, just because you've been so lucky!"

Califfa was silent a moment, when they would meet for

their pathetic discussions in the shade of that garden behind the house, in secret like two thwarted lovers. Then she said: "There's always gossip, even if I don't go out at all. They couldn't care less whether or not I'm closed up; the gossip can go through walls just like that. You understand how much need there is of a face to see for there to be gossip in a town like this with a man like that."

"Yes, but – " Viola tried to interject.

"Don't 'but' me! As a matter of fact, if I was going to listen to those people who take it on themselves to bring me the gossip at my house like it was bread, I would have gone long ago. As if there was nothing to talk about in this damned town but Califfa! Wives, lovers, priests, whores, and thieves, they're all taking on Califfa! As if I was the only one they could throw the first stone at!" (And what fun it was to give her to understand things which were not even true: that an "amen" would soon be coming for her as it had for all Doberdò's other women; and what pleasure it was to let her knew that Doberdò had not lived like a saint. But Califfa, along with everybody else, knew all these things already, and was well aware that he was fickle in matters of the bed and that the others had lasted just long enough for a taste and that was it.)

And Viola shrugged her shoulders, almost offended. "But listen, if it means that much to you, do what you think best. I'm just telling you what comes into my head. But if you don't like it, it must mean that you don't really like the whole idea."

"You're right," admitted Califfa, sitting on the little wall with her head in her hands. "You're right."

And Viola kept at her. "But look: you have a wonderful place to live; and you have another piece of good luck having a man who respects you, not to speak of the money; and you want to risk everything? To be seen with him, to show off the clothes he buys you and to tell people the hell with you, you can just die with envy? I don't blame you for feeling that way, Califfa, not at all. But for someone like you, who's walking a tightrope, it's just stupid!"

Califfa looked at her with a bitter smile and shook her

head. "No, Viola, you're not right there. And you don't understand... I'm too hot-blooded to calculate anything and I've never done it and I never will."

"And so?"

"And so I've already paid too much for life, just because other people were different. And what has it gotten me? I'm going to play it differently, Viola! I can't sit back thinking of what I'm making for another day! And what difference does the money make anyway? What good does it do me if I go back to zero? I'll go back to zero anyway if that's where I'm bound to go. But as long as I'm here, I mean to enjoy every minute of it!" She took Viola by the arm. "Try to understand, Viola! Try to understand!"

And a lump came to Viola's throat. "What do you mean understand? They're bitches and they're just waiting for you to hold up your head, because you've been lucky, because you're beautiful, because you're young... just waiting for you to stick your neck out!"

"Then I'll stick my neck out!" yelled Califfa in anger. "It's better to stick your neck out than to be afraid of them! It's better to stick your neck out than to measure life with an eyedropper, even though I've swallowed a lot of bitter pills! I want to get out, and laugh, and dance, even if I am a slut, without worrying about it, and the hell with the rest.

You say I haven't the right, but I have, Viola... I have the right to my conscience, the right to what I've suffered for!"

Viola had no more to say. She sat there in silence looking at the point of her shoe.

II

And so one night when he came to my house he told me there'd be this party, out in the country, I don't remember where, but there was no use talking about it... oh, no!

Another night looking at that face of his, with all the best reasons in the world, and even just to make Viola happy – and maybe she was right – another night like that, No!

So he said, "What?" and he almost didn't believe me. He did only when I put on that dress I'd always left in the closet (what would I have put it on for anyway, to show off in front of the pictures on the wall?) and he was always complaining that the money'd been wasted. And I pushed back my hair the way I know looks better, then on with my gloves. I grabbed my purse and off we went.

But when we're in the car and Doberdò's about to take the road to the right, I say to him: "No, this way, please…"

"But that's not our way. The party's this way."

"Just a little out of your way, please…"

He made a wry face and with a little burst of speed there we were beyond the bridge and the car began its way through the narrow streets that were dark as hell and full of all kinds of noises. He looked around him without understanding any of it. The walls were scary and the little lights here and there were so dim you almost saw less with them than without them, and then there were those pigs lying around in the doorways with their mouths wide open, looking at that great big car in the middle – and there were times when it could hardly pass, the street was so narrow.

He was sweating to keep the car on the road and maybe he thought I was going crazy, because I kept telling him to go on, go on, and the more I did, the worse it got. If only he knew how hard on me it was smelling all those smells again, and seeing those cats running off, with the dust on the doors and windows, as dead as if no one lived in 'em. If he knew what I felt as I recognized each wall and every suspicious face and the wash on the line; I could tell him who slept on this sheet and who on that. So much so that I hadn't the strength to say anything to him when he jerked the wheel, trying not to run into a column and said, "But where the hell are we going? What sort of dump are you taking me to?!"

I just held in my gut and sat there without saying a word, like a fool.

"But what's the matter with you? Why are you playing this act?"

Then I showed him. "Up there, please…" It was a rundown

little street, with lots of cat peepee and a baby howling up there as if it hadn't eaten for months. He turned and suddenly stopped, because where could he go? In that battleship of a car in between two walls which were almost touching each other…

He turned off the motor and looked at me. "And now what? What do we do now? Look at each other?" Then I let it all out and told him I'd brought him there on purpose. And I knew it wasn't any fun, but just for that I'd wanted to bring him; I wanted him to smell it and hear it with his own eyes. He looked around, looked at the cracks in the walls, the weeds, the cans, and listened to that damned crying.

"And now that I've seen it? Tell me what it's all about, Califfa, because mysteries give me a headache. Come on! You can talk!"

And I tell him that in that house where there's that child crying and where it would take just a tap to knock over those water-logged walls, I was born and my mother died, and if it hadn't been for him to drag me away by the hair of my head, maybe, who knows I'd die there too.

"I'm sorry," he said, and you can tell he has a lump in his throat just exactly like mine; I can feel my eyes fill and I burst into tears. And I hold his hands, those big hands, like a good priest's, which I liked so much and I told him, "Don't get mad! I just want to say one thing" and he stroked my hair.

"Go ahead!"

"You swear you won't get mad?"

"Yes, I swear it."

"All right, listen. You tell me come on, be seen, come out, let's go, let's do something, and if I don't, you get mad. But I don't say no just to make you mad, I do it because I'm scared, because here where you can see it, I don't ever want to come back, just to wait to die young! Never, do you understand?"

I must have been crying and not knowing it, because he was drying my cheeks and asking me: "And who says you've got to come back here?"

"I know. If it were just for you to say, I'd be happy. But you, with all that reputation you have to defend, with everyone else trying to protect it – let me finish, because maybe I know better about this than you do – for you to be seen with a slut like me!" My heart was bursting as I said the word and I was even afraid that he'd not understand me and that he'd get mad.

But instead, what a nice man he was! He took my face in his hands and told me calmly, but with a look in his eyes which was worth his swearing a thousand times, he told me that when people were sincere there wasn't any shame involved with anyone, and as for the others, he didn't care, he didn't have to account to anyone. If anyone had any accounting to do, it was they who had to account to him, his wife and son included. Wouldn't that be wonderful, after he had tried to keep them under his thumb all his life, a life given over to the greater glory of his own comfort, to arrive at the age of sixty and not even be his own boss! And let 'em talk if they wanted to, let 'em talk! What did it matter to me since it didn't matter at all to him? Let 'em see me with or without Doberdò, it would be the same thing, or worse; so that it was better to cast the die, if there was one to cast.

And I remember so well the last thing he said: "You told me yourself that there are things you don't understand, but which you like all the same, because that's just the way they are... And so? Just remember that one of those things is on my mind right now and it concerns you. A nice thing, but if I were to tell you now, you wouldn't understand, because perhaps I don't really understand it either. But it's beautiful, and that's what's important!" And then: "Just be yourself, Califfa, beautiful, sane, and proud as you are. And as long as I'm around, with my feet on the ground, no matter what they say, I'll worry about you, and God help anyone who gets in my way. If you like, I'll swear to that too!"

No. He didn't have to swear. It was enough for me and I was happy. And so we went to the party where all his friends were. Imagine how Viola would have taken it if I'd gone and told her that the die was cast and that I was breathing easier.

But how could I make her understand what I had felt when I entered society – let's call it that – holding on to the arm he offered me, without being scared a bit, or even impressed, and that when my anger had died down, it did me good to look 'em in the eye, all his friends one by one. And to see how those eyes were looking me over, but without being able to do anything about it, and to make them understand that now I was there too. Oh, yes, I was there, all right, and seated at their level!

Oh, no, Viola couldn't understand. She didn't even know what it meant to shake those hands while he introduced me, as if I didn't know them perfectly well already: "Mr. Farinacci, Mrs. Corsini. Mr. Gazza, the Chief of Police" and even him, Mastrangelo!

Those moments were worth a lifetime, if you'd lived like I had, moments which still give me my only consolation today as I look back on them, my only reason for going on! If you could have heard me in front of them, me, one of the many girls from the slums, a slut, but on his arm, and with my looks... to discover them as they were... and to listen to them as they talked... Oh, Viola, Viola, if you could only have seen how nothing else was important to me, that I didn't care that I acted crazy or that I'd lit a fuse, as you say, with that Gazza, who started buzzing around me right off, trying to be nice. He was showing off with all his stupid airs, and just think that he'd been in politics for so many years in our city, and they talked a lot about it, and even said that he might become a Minister in the Government since he was such friends with so many big shots!

And I forgot to say that when I found myself next to Mastrangelo, so close I could smell his sweaty skin, there was a gnawing inside me. How I cursed to myself, seeing him smiling at me, and I smiled back with some looks full of poison, and I wanted to spit in his face, if it hadn't been for Doberdò. But I felt great all the same that he had to bow his head before me, Irene Corsini, called Califfa!

After her first appearance, Califfa was not judged definitively, because Doberdò's usual group of friends had been trained to accept certain kinds of eccentricities and had seen others like her exposed in this way to the concession of momentary sympathy – which was obligatory, after all, given the delicacy of the situation – but also quite likely to disappear from that solemn and lazy arm. In short, Califfa was one like so many others, even if they had been impressed by her beauty, bearing, and conversation – and by that impudence which showed signs of a natural pride though it instinctively avoided insults. All these good points made them believe that she would last longer than usual, but that there was no real change. And even Martinolli, summing up the opinions of others, limited himself to a smile, so that when Doberdò sported his whore about town, he said that it was almost better that way, and that if a man like that allowed himself certain caprices, it was a good sign, a sign of a head free from a lot of nonsense which was much worse. The Bishop was soon obliged to eat his words.

But the certainty in most people's minds that it was nothing more than a passing whim soon collapsed, and with such an outrage to established values as to raise the inevitable scandal, all the more so because Doberdò went everywhere with Califfa, almost without exception, after this episode:

When September began, and the sides of the hills took on the dark color of ripening grapes, and the hunters' rifle shots resounded under a foggy gray sky, Count Pedrelli would open the gates of his Renaissance villa. The ritual, which had remained unchanged for generations, was still carried out under the pretext that it opened the hunting season on the estate, but actually it was to allow Pedrelli to summon great numbers of nobles and persons in authority from every region and to play the card of his high rank with such consummate skill that it would be good for another year. Princes would come from Venice, Rome, and Palermo, and, well knowing what fertile sparks can fly forth from the friction of a certain nobility with a certain kind of politics, Pedrelli, with his sense for secret alliances, as incredibly well informed as he was shrewd, would fish in other people's troubled waters. Although preferring representatives of the majority, he did not omit political extremes in the laborious drawing up of his guest lists, in conformity with the elective principle of his elastic conscience, which, after he had wasted a fortune, had kept him from the bottom and had enabled him to escape from the wreck of that crown with nine balls, stamped on his engraved writing paper, which tied his ancient ducal nobility in tortuous and unexpected ways to some of the oldest families in Europe.

And so when the party began, Pedrelli acquired a vivacity at other times unfamiliar to all who knew him, and continued his tightrope walking, jumping from princes to members of Parliament with full acknowledgment of his political incongruity, just to raise up clouds of approbation about his effete and obsequious figure; until the presentation of the final bill, when the show was over and the moment had come for everyone to say goodbye, and he wandered around with his figurative begging bowl.

And it was enough for him that they told him to his face that he was a marvelous host and the genial master of the house, even if, behind his back – and he was well aware of it – they all looked on him more or less as did Gazza, who would exclaim, "That clown!" when he recognized the coat of arms on his invitation. But at the same time, with just a bit of pride, he turned the gold decorated paper around in his hand, and as Pedrelli's Latin motto shone in the light ("Nomen ad sidera supremum") he saw himself advancing slowly along the entrance road on the day of the party, well aware of what it meant, and feeling that gravel under his feet, having those people looking at him, and exchanging bows with those heads.

It was a privilege and, like all privileges extracted, however arbitrarily, from social reputations, it enhanced one's standing. It was one of the many blank checks Pedrelli distributed in exchange for other more substantial checks, not blank ones, but equally stimulating.

And thus there was no invitation which was not accepted; on the contrary, the social importance of appearing among the decrepit waiters who knew what a farce it was, among the unchained masses of greyhounds, the crowded benches, the gunshots and the hustle and bustle, created secret ambitions which for the most part were disappointed, because Pedrelli, measuring up fortunes and social standing with an eyedropper, made use of his invitations to accentuate the disappointment of the ones who weren't invited and to stimulate their urge to compete, to make them come cautiously forward with some specific favor.

And so Vittoriano Pedrelli sold his dream, transforming it into tangibles with the ingenuity of an alchemist, deliberately rhetorical and naturally cynical, but a careful student of other people's pretensions – pretensions which at least for a day became joy of the spirit, because on that first Sunday in September in that crowded green valley there was no one who did not feel among the elect in that precarious paradise, whether because of the penetrating force of Parmesan cheese in the markets of Europe or because of some concession accorded to a Pedrelli in spirited combat with his own weaknesses.

It was therefore with a surprise that passed from disbelief into horror and a premonition of his own downfall, on that Sunday morning, when the party was under way in the most auspicious manner and with an air of perfect success, that Pedrelli saw Doberdò coming up that path with Califfa. While the two figures were still in the distance, he had one moment of happy doubt because he thought he recognized the form of Clementina Doberdò in the movement of that cape – she had not shown herself since the onset of her illness – but he began to sweat as soon as he recognized that arrogant gait and that vulgar mannerism of holding her purse almost to her chest, and the unconcerned way her hair was done up in a ribbon.

He stood there undecided and was tempted to rush down and stop them, or at least do something about it, and he set out, while Gazza watched the scene in silent horror. With an awkward jump, Pedrelli left behind the flabbergasted member of Parliament whose turn it was to be attended, but he was put off by the sure, decisive advance of the couple. What was to have been a dash petered out in a shaking walk, and the two men came up to each other, Pedrelli like a soldier who has come out of the trenches and is already resigned to giving himself up to the enemy, and Doberdò, fresher and younger as he turned his head around, drinking in the amazement caused by his appearance at the side of Califfa.

Clothed in its little skull adorned with graying hair, Pedrelli's brain was like a turtle turned over on its back waving its feet around in frustration ("A woman like that, a woman like that in here! My party ruined! Oh, my God, after centuries of tradition!"), and Doberdò, reading the Count's bewildered eyes and that crease of a mouth which was supposed to be taken for a welcoming smile, could see that brain thrashing about, and it accentuated the subtle cruelty with which, during the previous evening, he had dreamed up this mortal blow to the ritual which for too many years had been the official consecration of his boredom, his emptiness, and the useless myths in which he had once believed. This was one more step in his farcical game with himself and others, after his revelation of life (not as he had lived it but as he would have liked to enjoy it and as he had let it pass by) had been transformed into a desire to make up for lost time, into an urge to reaffirm certain truths and to set up his ill-managed life on another footing.

"Welcome…" stammered Pedrelli, and he was forced to bow and kiss Califfa's hand.

Doberdò did not even look him in the face. "Thank you," he said and dragged Califfa off, leaving Pedrelli with his head leaning a little forward, in a gesture of homage which actually was an acceptance of his weakness and defeat.

"I hope you will have a good time," he added, making a sign to bring them bad luck.

"We certainly will," and Doberdò and Califfa continued on their way, exchanging greetings with old acquaintances who were still unaware of the situation, with Califfa's hand in that glove which, as it passed from mouth to mouth, looked like a leaf trembling in the wind, ever downward on its way to the ground.

"A whore," repeated Pedrelli to himself. "In here! Everybody will know about it! Anywhere but here! The party's ruined!" It was fortunate for him that some black clouds appeared on the horizon and ruined the party before Califfa could. With a great noise which announced a storm, rain began to pour on the estate. There was a flow of water in the air, a running about and a screaming of women under the roofs of the pavilions, and Pedrelli, who didn't give himself a moment's peace, tried to distribute umbrellas to at least the most important of his guests, blindly obedient, even as he rushed from one tree to another, to his calculations of maxima and minima, because even an umbrella given at the right moment can have its value.

"Your Excellency! Prince! Duke!" he cried as he got muddier and muddier, while above his head the sky gave vent to its fury and all the while he was murmuring, "Thank God! Thank God!" because the rain, breaking up the crowd, had confined Califfa and Doberdò under God knows what shelter, preventing surprise from transforming itself into a curiosity which might be dangerous.

CHAPTER THIRTEEN

Bruna's son – she was a friend of Viola's – had died the day before. He was drawn out by months of fever and you could hardly see him in that large hospital bed, racked by labored breathing, his hands stretched out on the cover as if he had wanted to raise himself up in his exhausted agony to come down from that cross of a bed where he was steadily more bogged down in death.

One more to cancel out. And not even the medicines which Califfa had been able to get for him had done any good. They were too late because they had told her too late. She had been with him before he died and she remembered how she would look at him in that huge dark hospital room, without being able to take her eyes from that face which would shudder, a little less each time, like a dying butterfly before it extends its wings. And Bruna, on the other side of the bed, worn out by sleepless nights, had let herself down, with her head on her arm, for some silent weeping, so that no one else could see it.

Califfa's son had died more or less in that way, and that explained the numbness which penetrated her senses, that solitude like a chill on the stomach, even though death was no surprise to her by then and it did not sadden her since she was used to it. It merely left her with a feeling as if she had just gotten an undeserved insult, and she felt her usual embittered anger.

She went out of the hospital when there was already a little light on the roofs of the houses, and she was sharply reminded of many other nights like that when the city can

160

only be a witness for you – and you don't want to go home. She passed the rest of the night tossing and turning in bed, and in the morning she still had him before her eyes, and she knew everything even if she had not seen him die.

She brought some more money to Bruna, but she didn't want to see the dead creature, nicely set up in a bed which could be seen from the kitchen. And there was that air of sterile order which death brings in those houses most neglected and most corrupted by misery, and Bruna's was one of them. Califfa had had enough of it, seeing her dead son, and suddenly she thought she saw him in a bed just like that one, in a house with the same air. So she went out of the kitchen and began walking with her head down, without being aware of where she was and without even knowing where she was going.

She did not realize how long she had been wandering about, sitting on the benches in the street or staring at a shopwindow without taking anything in. But when she came back home the streetlights were already lit and a light fog had given the night a bitter humidity – and he was there waiting for her. He had heard about it and he said: "Let's go out... that way you can forget about it for a while."

Califfa let him take her out without saying anything, but she was still very depressed when they got into the car. However, in that season there was the smell of land waking up which she liked so much, and in the dark the fog had suddenly disappeared – even though there was a light smell of putrefaction rising from the river – and the trees, shining with dew, were passing by in a splendor she hadn't noticed before.

Then they came to the Po and Califfa realized that they were going to a kind of party. "Gazza's giving it," said Doberdò. "He's celebrating a business success." They had set up a table on the bank of the river so that they could see the other side. Everything was so nice, with the new moon and the lights from the little villages on the bank reflected in the water. But Califfa did not appreciate the sight and with her stomach feeling as if a rope were knotted around it, she

161

didn't even want to eat, although Gazza, who'd already had a little to drink by then, shouted that whoever didn't eat offended him.

Califfa couldn't keep her mind off that face and how it had stopped shaking with life under that skin. And she couldn't stop thinking about that big iron bed with that tuft of hair she had caught a glimpse of, just a black streak between the blanket and the pillow. Bruna's hand did not want to separate from hers when she wanted to get away, and Bruna, once Califfa had gone from the kitchen, would have nothing and no one to attach herself to. There was just that tuft of hair between the posts on the bedstead and the silence of that house which death had made neat and orderly.

And that was why she hardly knew they were talking to her. And when Gazza passed his hand in front of her eyes and asked her, "But what's the matter with you? What are you looking at?" it was as if she had suddenly been dumped there, and all of a sudden she was ashamed of herself and it seemed terrible that no one respected her grief and that she had to look joyful when she didn't feel that way at all.

It was a bad moment that gave her some pain. She took a glass in her trembling hand and pretended to drink, to pull herself together, because the temptation was strong to give it all up and escape into the night, into the countryside...

And that's how it was. After a while, I didn't see anything any more. Maybe it was more my fault than theirs. Anyway, I felt like I was full of gas from head to foot and that I'd blow up if someone touched a match to me. My God, I let go that night! And now that I think back on it, I still don't know how it happened.

It was just a temper tantrum. No matter what they did to me, it was still just a temper tantrum. I should have been able to understand them, and realize that they'd had a little to drink and wanted to laugh and kid around, and so it wasn't the time or the place for a scene like that. But when I get into such a mood, there's no stopping me...

Anyway, they were talking about millions, houses, and cars

162

as if they were loaves of bread, as if no one amounted to anything unless he had 'em. They said their two cents' worth about finance, and went on. But then Gazza began talking about religion, and equality. I thought he wanted to get at me, clever as he was, but I thought I understood him, all the same. With the wine they'd already had, including him, you can imagine what it sounded like.

And so between one glass and the next, they began talking about Jesus Christ. Gazza talked about Christ as if He were one of the gang, and I remember clear as day what he said just before I started to spoil his party, as if he was saying it now, because afterward I thought about it a long time to see if I'd been right to do what I did.

So he started. "I wonder," he said, and he looked at Doberdò, who was letting Gazza have his head since he could see that he was half crocked and making sheep's eyes at me, and maybe he could tell what I was thinking. "I wonder, ladies and gentlemen, what Christ would do if he were alive today, thirty-three years old – whether He'd get mixed up with this gang of hypocrites!"

Cantoni, who looked as if he'd been bending an elbow too, tried to tell him that when everyone was in a joking mood, it was better to talk about sports and women, with all due respect to the ladies present (and I wasn't the only woman there, there was the wife of Mazzallo the Police Chief and some other women I can't remember any more). But Gazza wouldn't stop and he kept on talking around and around, never coming to the point: "I think that He'd make some pretty good compromises, shrewd as he was... At least He, the Son of God, would understand, I should hope, that you can't fight a battle of ideas the way we do with fools who use the enemy's words like a bunch of monkeys," and he was talking so loud that they began looking at him from some of the other tables.

"Come on, Giacinto, that's enough," said Pedrelli. "And besides, you'll have such a hangover you won't be able to sleep."

But Gazza was really on his way and couldn't be stopped.

He said: "To have certain riffraff in your house, at the same table – and even in the same bed!"

And just think that I'd told Doberdò over and over again: "Please don't put me in certain situations. You know what I'm like. Be careful, because one time or another I could lose my temper."

"So lose it!" he answered with a laugh. "Who's forbidding you to lose your temper?" Maybe he didn't think I was serious; maybe he thought I was talking as Califfa and not as his girl friend, but if he ever had any doubts, poor man, they all left him that night. In other words, hearing them talking that way – because Pedrelli and Cantoni joined Gazza just a little, because it was fun to see how everything was getting more exciting – hearing them talk about religion just because they had tongues in their heads, without love or respect for anything, as mad as they were drunk, I began to tell them a thing or two, and I put so much into it and I needed so badly to get it off my chest that Gazza there was a sight, with his mouth open, with tears in his eyes like a kid.

To tell the truth, I let fly only when he said something I thought was against me, just a little phrase with a tone of voice like a priest, the way he usually talked to hint that certain people in the city stank and that they could be smelled in the best of neighborhoods and that for this reason, with the new town planning, they'd have to clean up in a big way.

Viola should have been there to hear me when I threw back his town planning in his face and told him that I'd give everyone there a shovel, and no planning at all. A shovel for everyone, and put 'em all to work so that Gazza would get a big hump on his back like Cantoni the lawyer had, because it's easy to talk about town planning when you have a full stomach, but just try it when you've been as hungry as I have, and when you've had to trample honesty underfoot and when you can't do anything about death, and you become a whore because there's nothing else you can do!

And all hell broke loose in the restaurant because the waiters were coming up to tell me not to shout so loud and the managers were too. It was awful. "That's enough!" said Doberdò to me. "Stop it!" But I couldn't and I shouted like a

164

crazy woman even when they were dragging me away, it seemed such a good time to tell everyone openly what no one had had the nerve to tell them. And there were some things I'm ashamed to tell about – I was crazy, and I don't know where I had the nerve, with Doberdò dragging me away by the arm and me still looking at them, sweating. I could have killed 'em all.

I didn't listen to Viola's sermons at all and I wasn't prudent. I let go as long as I had the strength and then when I'd boiled over I started crying, because that's the way I am – I shout, then I cry like a stupid little girl – and I started sobbing on Doberdò's shoulder. I was as ashamed as a baby, and I understood what a mess I'd made.

It was nice of Doberdò to say that it was just nerves and to add that bit about Bruna and her son. They'd had expressions on their faces, especially Gazza, that he'd never forget. And that's how the party ended up, and when he got me into his car face to face I was waiting for something awful. But there wasn't anything like that. He looked at me for a minute and before he put the car into gear, he said to me – and these were his exact words: "You were right. If I'd had your frankness sometimes in my life… But you shouldn't take it so hard!"

I swear that's what he said, and for the rest of the trip he talked about something else.

II

Gazza did not seem to give any official attention to that outburst. "She's a weird one," was all he said, pretending to mitigate that fact with a vaguely felt admiration. "She's got quite a temperament, and I'd say even a flair for the dramatic. Yes, a flair for the dramatic is the right way to put it." And later when he was talking with Doberdò it even seemed that it was Doberdò's fault, because Annibale, with more feeling than was usual with his brusque manner, said to him, among other things: "I'm sorry about that, but you know how women can be at times..." And Gazza, humbly putting forward his hands to interrupt the excuses which, for all that, had already come to an end, found that frankness adorable:

"Her spontaneity is so feminine and so aggressively vital. Mr. Doberdò, if only we had such open sincerity and such courage of our convictions in this conformist world, rotting with moral opportunism... You know full well, Mr. Doberdò, you know full well..." But within himself he already had quite enough reasons for not being at peace, and he cursed Califfa, more than anything else because she had caused him to pass a very bad night. The bronchial catarrh which afflicted Gazza when he was nervous shook his stomach and intestines and it took camomile tea and perequil to make it go away. It was a night passed between the bed and the window, waiting for the day, with his wife, stupefied with sleep, coming and going with cups of tea; and he would say to her "I don't need you, no one's looking for you, that'd be all I need!" between bouts of coughing into his handkerchief.

Gazza's moods reflected these crises and it was hard for him to recover from a setback, especially when the desire for revenge was accompanied by the possibility of its being consistent with his tactics. Since Doberdò was paying him, he thought, he had the duty to act in his interests, even at the risk of running into opposition with some of Doberdò's momentary pleasures. As is known, a man, especially a rich and prominent man, is always in a state of precarious equilibrium between success and ruin, and all it takes is one false step to bring about his downfall. And thinking in this way with so much duplicity even toward himself – because the truth was that he saw a competitor in every person who came at all close to Doberdò, whether man or woman – he had always kept his guard up. He was convinced that knowing more than others about certain people was the equivalent of having a blank check, even if the information he finally got was often banal, and even if the efforts to get it were often useless.

For this reason there had not been any amorous adventure of Doberdò's, except for the most casual, in which Gazza had not meddled, preferably with the discreet assistance of the authorities. "You never know," he would say to himself, "it can always be useful..." So much the more so because the third pawn to play whenever it was worth it was always Clementina, who might be shaken from her massive disinterest in her husband's erotic adventures to ask for an explanation.

And this time his own personal rancor was involved. The following afternoon found Gazza at the railway station with Mazzullo the Police Chief in his wake as the Rome Express was pulling in. He threw out one of his half-requests which Mazzullo was so good at understanding without the necessity of anyone drawing diagrams. One day, in fact, when Gazza was laughing about it with Doberdò, he had said of Mazzullo, "That one's like a hungry dog ready to pounce. There's no need to throw him the bone. All you have to do is to make one move in that direction."

In other words, the relationship among the three of them was more or less this: as Sgorbati stood to Doberdò, so Mazzullo stood to Gazza. Could the Police Chief possibly forget how that report saying "a brilliant, excellent, promising officer," which had remained buried for years in a pile of memoranda on one of the least-qualified desks of the Inspectorate General of the Police, had been seen suddenly to move to quite different piles of paper? Until one day Mazzullo, with his wife, son, and maid, had found himself at the station surrounded by luggage, and, opening his arms as Gazza ran up to him, had exclaimed: "Giacinto, dear Giacinto! Many thanks!" An embrace followed in which the little Gazza disappeared into the huge bulk of the other man.

What seemed not at all clear to people was, after all, quite logical: that a Police Chief, and one with such an authoritative appearance as Mazzullo's, was waiting for a hint and even served as a chauffeur when Gazza left for Rome with those files in his briefcase, each file marked with the name of a case or a firm.

There were notes on every folder, and Mazzullo, while Gazza went off to get his ticket, was allowed to look through them, so that often, even too often, and to the great regret of the Chief of Police, he would find his own name, and Gazza would say as he went off through the station: "Take a good look. Make sure everything's all right!"

Mazzullo looked through the papers, observing those red and blue pencil marks hurriedly scribbled on the folders: number one, *Death of Mrs. Farinacci: the whole estate: insist!* Number two: *Pedrelli: the highway: arbitrary use of the right of eminent domain!* Number three: *sample lot of typical Doberdò products for the Yugoslav group: get it going: urgent!* And, finally, number four, where all that was written was *Mazzullo!*

The Chief of Police barely disturbed the papers in the files which concerned him, hesitating as if he were afraid to see those documents before his eyes again, because there were still some tricky problems there, thanks to the frequent crises in a city as difficult as that, which Gazza was able to deal with, to tell the truth. That was why he was leaving for Rome, and after his most recent electoral failure his principal activity had been that: to get off the train at Rome, get his suitcases into a hotel, take a shower and begin what he called "pointing the compass" toward the right corners of the Ministries – but one needed a magnetic needle for that! Without that, what could you arrange?

Along those corridors, up and down those stairs, he was a fish returning to its native waters, and he knew how to knock on the door, how to get his foot in it, how to throw it open – whether with authoritative decisiveness or with deference – and how to shake hands, smile, or allude to joking threats, whom to invite to lunch, and whom to promise some folding money. He went up and down with the fervor of a conspirator, well informed about the most obscure clause in the law, a small and brilliant shuffler of papers, and in that moving about among hordes of clerks, secretaries, and legal paper familiar to everyone, he traveled miles as if on a pilgrimage for the interests of his clients. And it was only on rare occasions that it fell to his lot to take the train back with an inscription on the folder – *Not settled! Has to be better organized!* – which meant that more money was needed.

And so that afternoon Gazza was on his way as usual to his twice-monthly appointment, and while his train was coming into the station and after he had said his usual "So long, stay loose!" to Mazzullo, he waited until the last minute, to give the impression that he did not attach too much importance to the matter, to throw out, before he took up his luggage: "Oh, wait a minute, that woman, write her name down, Irene Giovanardi, Corsini's widow, find out a little for me what she's like... you know, I think she's a little off, I don't think her health is too good... Can you?" And he got on the train, well aware that Mazzullo would give the right interpretation to the word "health."

The express train moved out of the station and Gazza, turning to the window, repeated a "So long" full of promises and Mazzullo the Police Chief waved one hand, putting the card with the note on it in his pocket with the other.

Some evenings later they met again at Doberdò's house. They went out onto the terrace, and with the same distracted air Gazza brought the conversation around to the subject, but he certainly did not expect the answer he got from Mazzullo.

"What?!" he said, stopping his walk. "Not even a note? Never even been picked up!"

Mazzullo opened out his arms. "That's how it is!"

"Never worked as a prostitute?"

"Unfortunately, no."

"But isn't there anything at all in her file?"

"No!"

"But my dear man, it's not possible, allow me. In this country where everyone, and I mean everyone, has some little affair that's hurting his conscience, a woman like that must have something! Maybe in one of those raids on the call-girl houses..."

Mazzullo clicked his tongue to make his negative reply all the more incisive: "As far as the files are concerned, she's clean as a whistle, except for some very minor disturbances of the peace."

"Oh, the files!" Gazza said, while he paced about the terrace with tiny little steps. "The files can be useful only up

169

to a certain point, the way those government offices are, including the Ministry of Justice, dear friend, including the Ministry of Justice. Remember that other girl of Doberdò's, the one – what was her name? – the one who looked like a saint too, but when we looked into the matter a little. Because if we don't open the eyes of our – "

"Found guilty of prostitution," Mazzullo promptly helped him. He had a perfect filing cabinet in his head. "But look, she wasn't from here, she was a Sardinian, from Nuoro, and Corsini was born and brought up in this town, so…"

"Yes," Gazza admitted. "But I'd look a little more into those disturbances of the peace…" At that time, he didn't pay too much attention to the last name of Irene's husband, to that Guido Corsini to whom he gave a real name and face only later. And when he did, he called up Mazzullo and told him that it might be useful to his investigations to know that there was a bandit, condemned and killed by the forces of law and order… And Mazzullo should certainly remember because in the margin it was written that Gazza had had to make not one but three trips to Rome.

"But who would have realized it was that Guido Corsini?" he said, shaking his head. "It's a small world, isn't it?"

III

One night I was in my bathrobe getting ready for bed when I heard such a ring on the bell that I thought something terrible must have happened. And when I opened the door and saw Viola on the doorstep looking like something the cat dragged in, and so out of breath from climbing up the stairs she couldn't say a word, I was sure of it.

"The cops!" she said, dumping herself into a chair. "The cops!" I had to wait for her to catch her breath before I could understand anything. Finally she calmed down, took the drink I offered her, and said: "The cops came! Two of them!"

"And so?" I said.

"About you!"

"Me! But you're crazy!"

"But what do you mean crazy? Was I crazy when I told you to pull in your horns and to be a little quieter?" And she told me two cops had been all over the neighborhood that day asking about the life, death, and miracles of yours truly, as if I were being canonized. The excuse was that there was a certain investigation pending. "I know what these investigations of theirs are!" she said. "In this stupid place, the more innocent you are, the less they leave you in peace!"

I was waiting for God knows what, and for this I burst out laughing and said to her: "But Viola, why do you always see the Devil under every bed? The reason there's an investigation is that I've asked for a passport, that's what. Because he wants to take me to France. To France, understand?"

"A passport," she laughed. "But what sort of dream world are you living in?"

"Now, that's enough. But sufficient unto the day is the evil thereof!"

Viola looked at me with a sigh. "It's no use, you'll never understand me, not even if I were to light a fire under you. But my conscience is clear now, now that I've told you, and in time!" And she made like she was going to go away, but I wouldn't let her, and I made her stay. To keep her there, I showed her the new record player he'd just given me and I even persuaded her to take a nice bath in the tube and she began to paddle around in there like a kid and she stopped worrying about the cops.

I was looking at her, and I was thinking to myself: Why? Were all those things she was saying exaggerated? Just think of it... Not that I had to worry about anything, because it seemed impossible that with so much freedom proclaimed to the right and the left, and after so many revolutions and wars to be free, a girl couldn't do what she wanted to even between the sheets, but without stepping on any one's toes... I could believe that people might say awful things about each other and that other people were just beasts, but the police – that was something else. No, not the police. But I was still naïve then, in spite of what I'd been through already.

171

But meantime I went along my way, without giving it another thought. And I was enjoying my new life of a whore, which also gave me light and sun and the possibility of doing what I wanted whenever I wanted to. And then I would enter the best shops and I was Mrs. Irene Corsini, and that's who I was when I walked up and down streets in the center, where so many respectable people who would have avoided me were saying hello because they wanted to or because they had to. The men would tip their hats and the women would smile at me, and I didn't care any more who hated me behind my back. And even the fear of saying something wrong which used to paralyze me when I had to say something in front of educated people, or my fear of having a pen in hand in front of a blank piece of paper, was almost gone.

Good for Gilda Fumagalli, she taught me well. Because of how I'd made her get into line and her being afraid she'd lose what little he paid her, she'd become a sort of missionary for me. And you should see how well she treated me. By then I could even tell you what the capital of Japan was and that you don't say "haven't *no*" but "haven't *any*." "How intelligent you are, Mrs. Corsini, how intelligent! I've told Mr. Doberdò, you know, that in less than a year you've made enormous progress. What wonderful progress! And if it weren't for arithmetic, I'd say you know more than someone who's gotten all the way through school!"

All in all, I was keeping my head above water. Aside from that scene at Gazza's party, I had always known how to behave, and I thought I had been shrewd, and I'd never acted that way before, so that now I could sleep calmly and I understood that he liked me much more. And this was very important with Doberdò, because if he didn't like someone, that someone might even become Pope but Doberdò would still beat him like something to be kicked out of the way. And just think that everything had been so easy for me. "Just be yourself!" he had told me. "Just yourself!" And I had not changed a bit, not even when he would ask me what strange things I was up to, and this didn't happen just once, but many times, because when we weren't making love or traveling around, he was full of ideas about how he was going to make me over.

For example, one day he said to me: "Starting tomorrow, I want you to learn how to ride! There's a stable I have where the air is so healthy, early in the morning, that it could raise the dead. You'll have fun and it'll be good for you."

Another girl would have asked if he was crazy, and, to be frank, I didn't understand the reason why he should have me riding when the sun was just coming up. (How could I know that he was doing it for a reason I'll tell you about later?) But I didn't try to stop him. I remember I just said, "Me, on a horse? No! I've always been afraid of them!"

"Yes," he insisted. "Tomorrow I'll tell Pedrelli to go to my stable every morning to teach you to ride, for free. He knows a lot about that sort of thing." And so I say to myself, okay. We'll go riding if he wants me to – I've tried so many things, I might as well try this. It'll certainly be different! And there I was trying out this new feeling with Pedrelli, poor man. You could tell he'd eat me alive if it weren't a question of doing Doberdò a favor.

He was mad as a wet hen at having to help someone like me, in a place like that where he thought he was the cock of the roost, and where if the people thought something was a bit smelly, it wasn't the droppings of the horses on the bridle path. But later, when I understood what it was all about and realized that Doberdò had done it on purpose and cooked up that mess for Pedrelli – that is, as well as showing me off, it was one of those schemes only he was capable of to humiliate people – I got a kick out of showing what I had up front when I got on the horse, and what legs I had as I rode, to some of those little girls who were just blossoming out, and who thought they were pretty hot stuff, but who were flat as boards.

IV

But what made her the happiest of all and what she remembered most pleasantly of those vacation months was

173

when Doberdò, who among the many positions he had was also president of a football team, had Califfa ride in an airplane one Sunday. There were just the pilot and her, and the plane seemed like a little red box which trembled over the grass on the airfield. They put her on board, put a great bunch of flowers in her hand, and told her that that day she would be queen of the game and that she was to throw the flowers onto the field.

The name of the team and the day were written on the ribbon which held the bouquet. Califfa remembered the date: the fifteenth of November, but the weather was still warm, and green was in the air, and the fog was still not heavy. They left the earth, Califfa with the flowers in her arms, and she wasn't afraid, and the earth jumped up and down in front of her eyes. It was green, yellow, and dark. And there was lots of wind in her face. But afterward when the plane was in the air, how peaceful and serene it was for Califfa.

She went up and up and it seemed that she wasn't alive any more but had been called by God. And she had a desire not to go back to the earth, but to continue to rise up with her light body, which had no more thoughts and no more guilt.

All she could see of the city below was roofs, and she was trying to find Viola's house, and her house on the river, but it was no use. And she went back to looking up, in the middle of those clouds that came by her, and she would say, "Thank God!" for the happiness she felt when she went up to one of them. And then right afterward she was afraid because the world was big and she was small; and then it felt good to stay there, holding her flowers, and she felt less guilty because she was thinking: If the world is so big, what difference does it make if there's someone named Irene Corsini whom people call Califfa and who works as a whore God knows where?

There were burnt fields under them and still more red roofs, but when the plane banked, she saw the roofs over her head and heard that yell from the stands. And there was a black something which began flying around in the sky, almost breathing, and there were so many heads and so many

174

people down there where the players were in the middle of the field, and they were so very small. Finally the pilot had to grab the flowers from her hand, and the bouquet sank down with a flaming burst of the roses as they disappeared into the air.

The pilot wanted to return to the airfield, but Califfa begged him to show her a little more sky. And so as they went away from the field and the shouting faded away (it was the shouting of her friends who were there because they knew she would be on the airplane), Califfa turned a moment and remembered Vito and how he used to play down there. And he was the best of them, and she used to wait for him behind the goal.

But then there were the clouds in front of them and the woods on the hills, and there was the light of the sun, and Califfa was able to breathe completely freely and already she was thinking of nothing.

CHAPTER FOURTEEN

For some weeks Clementina had been declining her maid's help in getting out of bed. On the contrary, once she had decided to come out from under the blankets, she not only no longer gave frantic pulls on the bell cord, but if anyone knocked on her door to offer help there were words. These were mornings of cold, foggy light. She who was used to being on her feet with the first clattering of the pots and pans in the kitchen below, and who could not stand lying around in bed because she considered that to be robbing time from life, stopped a minute to stare at that painted angel which was flying about on the ceiling among great bouquets of roses. She studied the strokes of paint on their cheeks which were laughing with good health, the small penis almost completely hidden in the drapery, and in front of this explosion of manly well-being she sighed: "How stupid men are! What windbags!"

And as the light grew brighter in her room, with the clock on the Empire bureau striking the half-hours and the quarter-hours, her sleepiness slowly changed to unease, with the boredom of certain thoughts. Yes, it really was unease she felt when, having thrown off the covers, she regained her usual energy and, sliding onto the floor, holding on to the head of the bed, stubbornly insisting on doing everything by herself, she succeeded in getting into her clothes. She could not deny it, at least to herself: she felt an unquiet curiosity which drove her to move the armchair to the French window leading out onto the balcony and to plop herself into it there, disturbed in every fiber of her being.

An admission which was bothering her had led her to say from between her teeth: "But really, that stubborn old man! Is he really indulging in that nonsense at his age?"

The balcony of Doberdò's house on one side faced the bridle path in the park, and Clementina's eyes were wandering over the trees and over the deserted track until she saw Califfa and Pedrelli coming around the bend, appearing and disappearing among the trees and bushes in their silent ride together. The thump of the horses' hoofs could be heard even up there, and Clementina was squeezing the arms of her chair, seeing how Califfa's horse gracefully combined its cadence with her bearing as she passed by that point where Clementina could best see her, lowering that head of hair kept in place with a ribbon to avoid a blow from the branches.

"That stubborn old man!" repeated Clementina, and in the kitchen down below they could hear her foot beating anxiously and impotently against the floor as it accompanied her thought: "This is just too much! Enough!" It had been almost a month, in fact, that Califfa had been enjoying this infantile aggressive role, displaying her full breasts and her legs on the horse's side which brought other skinnier legs to mind – with Clementina as the audience, her firm judicial face behind the French window among the red splashes of the curtains.

At first Clementina had felt an ambiguous pity, which had made her smile, rather than resentment or anger (feelings which Clementina allowed herself only on more important occasions) at this indication of her husband's triumph, so reduced that it was pitiful. "Have fun while you can, poor kid!" and she felt sorry for the girl now to be seen in the park at the most critical moment of her absurd adventure, because she would soon disappear as she had come, like all the other girls, after some months of bedtime fun, disastrous months that would lead to a ruined life.

Clementina already knew all about it: the usual rented apartment and poor Gilda Fumagalli, who had to climb up those stairs like a servant; a more or less generous monthly allowance according to how generous the girl was; and finally this finishing touch by that ingenious Pygmalion: the rides in the park to expose the product, with the forced complicity of Pedrelli, to hit Clementina, to humiliate her, to offend her.

Poor Annibale, Clementina was thinking, shaking her head with a smile, and a certain amount of pride which was not at all absurd. This was because it was the fragility of these caprices or revenges of his and the ingenuity behind them which made Clementina understand that she was still the stronger, as she had always been, and that Annibale was still solidly in her hand, like an eel seized by the throat which moves nothing but its tail. And she was not even surprised. Annibale had grown up on a farm, and he'd die like a farmer. "You can't make a silk purse out of a sow's ear!" Clementina would say. And it was just the sort of thing you could expect from temperaments which couldn't fit in very well anywhere, those treacherous tricks which in the case of Annibale were directed to subtle vengeance and even more to making up for a setback which had kept him bitter for much too long.

"Yes, go ahead and ride," murmured Clementina, studying Califfa – and the irony of that amusement reminded her of a day many years before. It was just a moment of that day, only a moment, but it was both disastrous and decisive.

"An historic moment," Clementina was thinking, "for an imbecile like Annibale, why not?" And she recalled that meeting on the path on Pedrelli's estate, where nothing was said. She was uncombed, hot, and astounded – that furtive embrace in the summerhouse interrupted. He was the apostle, the saint, the absent one, with his suspicion finally raised to a certainty as he came up to her. He had stopped for a moment in front of her with his clear animal eyes saddened, as if he were going to attack her. "Boor!" Clementina was thinking. "Boor!" Under the hunting hat those staring, vacillating eyes... She was so close to him that she could feel the aggressive bewilderment of his breath. There was a fleeting moment of pain, of madness, and of the smell of dead leaves.

Then Annibale's large head was lowered as if in shame or an impotent sigh, and he walked away, breaking some of the smaller branches in the wood, making the noise she and her friend of the moment had heard in the summerhouse. And she had run off in the midst of the rifle shots and the barking of the dogs.

It was an historic moment, which had tied them to the one tangible complicity of their whole life together and which had justified Annibale's rebellions and forced Clementina to accept them, bringing into the picture not so much her humiliated arrogance – just imagine, Clementina was never humilated for anything and boasted of her sins as if they were prizes, punctilious with the one as with the other – but her nobility.

Her defeat would have consisted in her ascribing any importance to certain foolishnesses and in giving Annibale the satisfaction of her forbidding them. Let him do it! Let him relieve himself with anyone he pleased! Knowing him as she did, she was well aware that he would not go far – on the contrary, clean as he was in mind and body, he would get sick of whoring around as soon as he boiled off the excess, and he would be quiet for a long time. It was a relief measure which did him good, all in all, and which did Clementina good too, since it brought back her beast with his head low, docile and governable. The important thing was not to lose control; and it was all taken care of by the expenditure of just a little money thrown away for an apartment or a ridiculous attempt to clean up a whore. Basically it was a work of charity: a small price for that light-headedness which would have cost Clementina a lot more, for that incident in which, with their eyes almost touching, their misunderstandings, their ambiguities, and their accusations had exploded with an intensity never reached when they talked, and she was afraid that he would get fed up, and that there would be a break.

"He's getting tired now," repeated Clementina to herself. "It's time for him to catch a fever, because at his age it takes less and less!" And her contempt made her feel younger and she stamped her feet, shouting "Sara! Ernestina!" There was the slamming of doors and the clatter of feet and Clementina was lifted bodily up and helped out of the room. The gray windows no longer reflected the flashing of eyeglasses on the embroidered chair and Califfa's ride, gay and foolish on the

179

bridle path heavy with rain, went on with no spectator, as if a little boy's game had broken up.

II

It had therefore been an ironic act of prudence on the part of an old lady who had never let anyone get the better of her, playing it decisively one moment and cautiously the next. But that bet with herself on how and when it would all be over had become more of a pretext than a conviction. The days had become weeks and the weeks had become a month. Morning after morning Califfa would appear around the bend of the bridal path, punctual as the clock on the tower; if she missed one morning and Clementina deluded herself on that account, it was a brief delusion, because after that respite Califfa's laugh and the sound of the horse's hoofs sounding along the foggy path would again float into the silence of her room.

From irony Clementina had descended into contempt, as she demeaned herself for nothing at all (an idiotic annoyance, as if she didn't have too much to annoy her already!), pushing the chair in front of her to see the balcony approach, then the extent of the park, and finally the red clay of the bridle path.

She stared down there, hoping, and raising herself a little from her armchair. But then she fell back, hurt by the sound of Califfa's voice muffled in the early morning mist. "But this is getting ridiculous! Well, let it be ridiculous!" she exclaimed. "Now it's not just a temporary adventure!" And her brain was still buzzing with the problem at lunch, when, sitting next to Giampiero and facing Annibale, she studied her husband as she ate. "Are you still at it, you stupid boor? If it weren't for me, you'd still smell like a stable, you third-rate Don Juan!"

She stared at Annibale, not as she once had to criticize his every mistake in table manners, but to find a key to him in his most innocent moves.

He hasn't taken his medicine today, she was thinking.

180

Today he's had three glasses of wine, three of them, and he's eaten a banana… so much poison for him. Why did he eat the banana, if he never did before?

Annibale was pretending that he did not see her staring at him. He didn't raise his eyes from the plate even when Clementina's unspoken thought led her to open reproof. "That's enough, Annibale! Why do you drink wine if it's bad for you?"

With an imperceptible sigh, Annibale put the top on the bottle and pushed it away from him.

"And the medicine, do I have to take your medicine for you?"

Immediately, and without giving her the satisfaction of looking at her, Annibale opened the tube and bolted the pills, perhaps a few more than had been prescribed.

Clementina, still unsatisfied, was rolling her eyes at Annibale, while Giampiero, who intervened with his priestly little voice in these painful conversations only when his mother spoke too loudly, said, "Mamma, please… the servants can hear everything!"

"Let 'em hear!" After all, she was the only one they listened to, and that was part of the house rules.

But one day Clementina went a step further in these veiled allusions. Seeing Annibale fussing around on his plate and almost falling asleep in his chair, she began the attack, saying: "And some people should leave the late hours to the boys, get some sleep, and take care of themselves, especially when the carcass is what it is – "

Annibale did not let her finish. He opened his eyes wide, threw his spoon and napkin on the table, and got up shouting: "Stop! Just shut up, for God's sake!" Clementina and Giampiero, with their forks in their hands, got up, astonished. "But, Dad…" murmured Giampiero. And before he slammed the door, Annibale said: "And you shut up too, you boob!"

Mother and son stayed there staring, open-mouthed, and then without a word Clementina went out of the dining salon up to her bedroom. Furious, with her anger clearly marked in every line of her face, she managed by herself in the corridor, with surprising agility. And she saw clearly that this had been the straw that broke the camel's back. She called up Martinolli right off and made an appointment for confession that afternoon.

"A confession on a Thursday," thought the Bishop as he hung up. "What a nuisance!" Because it was well known that Clementina confessed only on Saturday and the few exceptions always had to do with emergencies, which meant nuisances having nothing to do with the purity of the spirit. Quite the contrary. "Yes, it's a nuisance," Martinolli muttered. "But I'm not going to get involved this time. I'm going to stay out of it. The undersigned won't fall for this one, my friends!"

III

But there he was in his bare feet at that ungodly hour – in the hall of his house, trembling with the cold in spite of the heavy sweaters he had on under his tunic, while the priest who acted as his secretary bent over his feet, trying to get a pair of hunting boots on him. So promising a Sunday morning robbed from him, now that he had to face the prospect of going on a tramp through the woods and the mud, and only because he needed to speak to Doberdò in peace and had to take advantage of the only available moment. Blast the rich and their caprices!

In Doberdò's office one could talk only about work, and woe to anyone who ever brought up any other subject. He was hard to reach in the evenings since he had stopped frequenting the club, and for this reason there was only Sunday morning left, when he went hunting. It wasn't really hunting, but just a bow to what had once been his passion. Doberdò would limit himself to taking the pure air in the woods, as the doctor had ordered, giving up those long walks. And he took along a rifle, just to justify his getting up at that awful hour, with the moon and the stars still in the sky.

He would reach his estate, and after a few paces up and down in the hope of catching some woodcock early, he would sit on the bench in front of the hut, conceding a bit of conversation to whoever had accepted the invitation to follow him. And curious situations often arose because Gazza, Martinolli, Farinacci, and the other vassals would be there, too, inspired by the same calculation that they could speak to him alone and in peace. Doberdò was seated on the bench like Christ among the Apostles, and the apostles were giving each other dirty looks, holding their secrets back in their craws, impeded by their mutual presence from saying anything.

But this time Martinolli was prepared beforehand – better, Clementina had prepared him, saying: "Don't worry, I'll take care of that," and ending a long, agitated confession, she had concluded: "In other words, you're the one to do it. Personally I have never given certain satisfactions to my husband and I don't intend to now. Just imagine if I were to make a scene about certain things! The main thing is that it would be counterproductive. He'd enjoy it all the more. I know him, the pig!"

"But, Countess, I must remind you that we are in the house of God!"

"Yes, a pig! A pig which sticks its snout anywhere! If only he'd picked a decent woman…"

"Countess, I understand your resentment, and I think you're right to feel it, but please don't put me in a position –"

"In short, I think I have explained it enough. Make him realize that it's fun if it doesn't last, and tell him that it's a question of his health and that it's our duty not to let him make an ass of himself and become the laughing stock of the town. And if it goes on even a little bit longer, Excellency, it will be worse than any laughingstock…"

The Monsignor, with a sigh which Clementina took to be only the bitterness of the pastor for his lost sheep, had accepted. "All right, I'll try, even though he's a difficult man, as you know full well…"

With one last push, he got his foot into the second boot, got up from the chair, and stamped his feet. Then he wrapped up his neck in the scarf, motioning the young priest to follow him. The young priest was the Monsignor's shadow in operations like that. He followed him at a respectful distance so as not to disturb his thoughts or his conversations, ready at any moment to rush up to him like a waiter whenever there was need of his servile assistance.

They went out into the moonlight along the empty street. Black and silent and with their heads hanging low, they looked like death itself. The car was parked behind the church. The priest sat down in the driver's seat and off they went. Martinolli arrived at the estate, about twelve miles out of town, when the first light was breaking over the dry fields, and a cold wind that pinched the nose was blowing.

"I hope it doesn't rain," said Doberdò, turning his head. And that was the only thing he said before he went off to battle. They walked for five minutes and by now there was a light halfway between blue and green, a dark cloud about to be overcome by the sun, with the three of them – Doberdò in front with the rifle on his shoulder, Martinolli, who tried in vain to keep up with him, and the young priest bringing up the rear – marching along the frozen crest of a hill.

"As soon as we stop, I'm going to begin," Martinolli was thinking, and the idea that this was the usual quarter of an hour of walking before they got to the bench and the discussion of the thorny problem gave him comfort, just as when he postponed getting out of bed from minute to minute. "But how can I begin? Confound these confidential missions anyway!" Martinolli, who was already sweating, took his handkerchief out of his pocket and wiped his face. " 'Now listen to me, Mr. Doberdò,' I'll say to him. No, that's too official-sounding, I need something witty – maybe some pun, a light word. He never laughs at anything when I talk to him… Let's see. 'My friend…' Yes! 'My friend' is the thing to say in a calm confidential tone to make him understand that even a priest, even a Monsignor, is someone who doesn't do it just because he doesn't want to… But there are certain things he understands, definitely!"

Unfriendly, hostile, Doberdò's back continued to bounce up and down in front of him: "Or I'll tell him, 'My son…' That way, I'll take the bull by the horns. I'll give him a lecture as a Monsignor should, from on high, without any friendly confidences! But the trouble is that this atmosphere isn't the right one for that... out here in the country, with that smell of manure around us!"

The sun was shining on the fields. The quarter of an hour went by, but instead of turning left toward the hunting lodge, Doberdò set out to the right to continue farther into the woods. Martinolli thought, "What's going on now?" He lengthened his step and caught up with Doberdò: "Excuse me, but where are we going?"

"This morning we're really going to walk! We'll walk until about noon and get up a really good sweat, then take a hot shower and come back." Doberdò turned to him and his eyes were burning with gay cruelty. "What's the matter? Don't you feel up to it?"

"I?!" exclaimed the Monsignor with a grimace. "Of course."

"You know," Doberdò said with a laugh, "you priests are too tied down with saying your prayers and dreaming of intrigues! This is bad for your intestines and your bladder and the functioning of the muscles. It gives you what my doctor calls venous something or other..."

"You're always joking," Martinolli interrupted unctuously, and he was thinking: "I'm on the right track, but I'll have to learn to act like a saint next time. Now I've got to bring it up on the way and I have to find the right time to do it. Holy Mary, what a task I have!"

They went down a dusty path and struck out into a field of millet; the sun was already quite high. Then the path got muddy and they slowed down. "Now's my chance!" thought Martinolli, and he ran forward, but when he was about to catch up with Doberdò, and when he had hardly had time to say "Mr. Doberdò..." because the official way was the only one which came spontaneously to him, the path narrowed suddenly and Martinolli was obliged once again to fall behind Doberdò's back.

"Confound it!" he sighed, as he got more into the mud.

"What was that?" asked Doberdò, who knew perfectly well

why the Monsignor was so vexed. He had read it in his face as soon as he saw him and was amusing himself by drawing in the bridle in this way, anticipating and making more subtle the vengeance he had planned for the end of the morning.

"Oh, nothing, Mr. Doberdò, nothing," answered Martinolli, panting lightly. "We're in good shape this morning, eh?" ("But where does he get all that energy? What sort of a heart condition is he supposed to have?")

"It's the fresh air, my friend – it's good for you. Can't you feel it?" ("I'll tear him to pieces, I will!")

"So…," answered Martinolli, who already could feel his legs giving out and his back bathed in sweat, and he couldn't understand why he had to walk like that and in such a rush.

The sun was beating down on the three heads bouncing about in the field. Taking advantage of the privacy of the canebrake, the Monsignor unbuttoned his cassock and, fumbling about, balancing on that row of beaten earth, he took off a sweater and threw it to the young priest. Then there were some more fields, and Doberdò continued to lead the way, as if someone were following them, and he was as fresh as a daisy.

"He isn't even breathing hard," Martinolli was thinking. "And he can hardly climb a flight of stairs, but here he's not even breathing hard. Oh, this is just wonderful…"

Meanwhile Doberdò really did feel a new youthful vigor, since his heart was quiet as a sleeping dog with no barking. ("I'll tear him to pieces," he was repeating to himself.)

"But I've just got to talk to him!… That's enough, now I'll call him, I'll talk to him and get it over with!" A narrow valley opened up in front of them, white with thorny flowers, and Doberdò suddenly stopped, taking off his hat and looking around as if he were listening for something.

"Finally!" Martinolli exulted to himself. "Finally!" And, signaling the young priest to keep his distance, he took a deep breath in preparation for another encounter. But this time he didn't even get to open his mouth because Doberdò seized the rifle, turned his back, took aim, and fired. There was a parting of the branches in a tree and a thump; and

Martinolli, after he got over his surprise, lowered his head and put his hands on his hips. "It's no use…" he murmured.

When Doberdò came back waving the bleeding woodcock, he found the Monsignor muttering to himself. He glanced at him with a moment of ironic satisfaction. He did not say anything either. This time he limited himself to thinking: "Imagine spending his life on that nonsense, poor bastard! But if he wants a fight, he'll get it, and so will they!"

They set out walking through the countryside, and Martinolli, for the rest of the walk more exhausted than resigned to the situation, made no further attempts. Eleven o'clock went by and then it was noon. They came out of the woods like lost soldiers with their shoes sodden with mud as heavy as lead, and Martinolli was being helped along by the young priest, counting his steps, his head down.

But when they came to the azure walls of the hunting lodge, visible from the middle of a field of poppies, he raised his head, bathed in sweat, troubled and full of dignity, and his conscience began its dialogue once again, partly because of his scruples and partly because as he came out of the shade of the woods into the light of the road, Clementina Doberdò's face, that pallid expanse, that sound of velvet on the other side of the grating of the confessional, began to disturb the quiet of his reflections.

In front of the lodge, Doberdò put down the rifle and the game, thinking: "Now that I've wrung his neck, let's hear what the hell he has to say. But first I'll strip him naked, naked as a jaybird…"

"Aren't you taking a shower?" asked Doberdò, moving toward the showers. "A nice hot shower – I've had 'em install the showers here just for that, because a hot shower after a long walk makes you feel a new man again."

Martinolli turned to look at the priest, who lowered his eyes so that he would have nothing to do, even by a look, with his superior's decision.

"Well, really… ," Martinolli objected.

"Oh, come on! You're such a modern priest. I have an extra bathrobe for you."

"It wouldn't be in order, Mr. Doberdò," said Martinolli. "As a matter of fact, it's against the rules... against the *mortificatio carnis*. But the idea of a hot shower, of a cloud of warm water on his sweaty body, together with the possibility of finally beginning his lecture to Doberdò, led Martinolli to follow him. The young priest waited outside, seated on the bench.

"Isn't it marvelous, Monsignor?" shouted Doberdò, soaping himself amid the steam which came out of the shower stalls. "This is really living!"

Martinolli, on the other side of the wall, hesitated for a moment before answering. "Now!" he said to himself. "This is just the right time. But talk decisively, because if you don't, it won't do any good... After all, it's a priest who's talking to him, a priest before a friend... and he has no reason to be angry with a priest..." "Mr. Doberdò, listen," he began, getting up his nerve naked under the jet of water, like a figure of Christ about to be baptized, "do you know the parable –"

"I can't hear you," shouted Doberdò, who had turned up his shower just to make it more difficult. "Speak more loudly!"

Martinolli's head was pounding. "I was asking if you'd heard the parable –"

"What parable?"

Martinolli lost track of his thought for a minute, and then found himself again. The water falling on him suggested a more apt metaphor. "Saint Francis said water is beautiful because it's pure!" he shouted. "Beautiful because it's chaste!"

"Good for him!" answered Doberdò.

"What do you mean?"

"I said good for Saint Francis, because this water is filthy dirty and I'm having a hell of a time with it. That ass of a plumber! I'm glad I still owe him some money because I can just refuse to pay him!"

Martinolli's voice faded away alone in the stall. Rolling his head, he sat on the bench, keeping his hands modestly over his crotch, with his eyes fixed straight ahead to avoid temptations. His mind wandered only a moment because the hot water suddenly gave out and an icy stream poured over his back. "Just in time, eh, Father?" said Doberdò, who, among other things, never knew what to call the prelate. "Just a moment before and I'd still have had the soap on... Oh, I forgot the towel. Here!" and the towel flew over the wall, landing on the Monsignor's shoulders.

Immobile, stock-still as if in a trance, as if it were someone else breaking the silence. Martinolli started off so decidedly that he surprised even himself: "Listen to me, Mr. Doberdò, to the priest and not the friend. A friend could come up to you, put a hand on your shoulder and tell you: just think about it a little, Mr. Doberdò, if you keep up that way, you risk making an ass of yourself, you risk harming yourself physically, morally, and socially." Doberdò stopped grunting and stood there with the towel wrapped around his hips. And Martinolli continued in his Olympian vein, as if he were praying: "But the priest cannot. The priest cannot put a hand on your shoulder. All he can do is suffer for you and be moved at your plight, saying: go away from sin and temptation... flee from the ruin not of yout body, but of your spirit! Flee!" But Martinolli's moving voice suddenly cracked because Doberdò interrupted him with a laugh:

"My dear friend, or my dear priest, if you prefer – are you going to deliver a sermon right here and now, with both of us stark naked in the shower?"

"God does not look at certain things – "

"Well, if you are alluding to that girl – and I understood that before you even opened your mouth. If that's what – "

"Exactly!" affirmed the Monsignor.

"Well, I'll have you know that the whole thing's a lot cleaner than you could even suppose. And if you weren't a priest talking to me, but a friend, I maybe could try to convince you that what I'm doing is good and that I'm not going to flee from anything!"

"You mean that you're going to remain in your state of mortal sin? It's a disgrace... and furthermore, you haven't been to confession for more than a month!"

"My dear Monsignor, it's not good for us to talk about this. There are some things priests cannot and will not understand. I could tell you that I love that girl, that at least with her I don't have to be on my guard all the time, that I'm beginning to understand certain things and to look at life with new eyes. Monsignor, it's healthier, cleaner, more generous, and even more Christian… and she was the one who led me to it, she, the girl you despise!"

"I don't despise her, I'm sorry for her!" and Martinolli shivered, his skin trembled, a little because of the cold and perhaps a little because he had gone just a bit too far.

"You haven't any right to feel sorry for her! Let's feel sorry for each other! Me, you, Gazza, Pedrelli, that scoundrel Mastrangelo, and all the rest of them! A *mafia* that buzzes around its interests like a top, and none of them can love anyone."

"No, Mr. Doberdò, no! It isn't love you feel, but – "

"But what!?" shouted Doberdò.

"A sinful, senile adventure," stammered Martinolli, almost whispering the word "senile."

"You can call it anything you like. But I'm staying with that girl! I'm going to stay with her, and I don't care about anything! This is the time to leave off all that hypocrisy and false shame and tell you right off, and whoever it was that spoke to you –"

"No one did, Mr. Doberdò!" said Martinolli. "No one. This is my personal doing, a *vox populi,* please believe me!"

"– to tell you and everyone that I don't intend to break it up! And if they throw a monkey wrench into it, if they try to get in my way, look out!" Doberdò began to raise his voice, and as he dried himself his whole body was trembling. "Look, I'm going to live with her all the time, night and day. And we're going to have a son."

"In the name of God, I beg you!" said Martinolli, waving his hands in the air to get his clothes, which were on the top of the wooden partition.

"What do you mean, beg! First they come to meddle in your business and then they run to God like to Mama! Now, you listen to me!"

"But what have I got to do with it?" whimpered Martinolli. "If we digress, if we look at the worldy aspects of it, I have nothing more to do with it!"

But Doberdò, in his mounting anger, did not even listen to him. "A son, a healthy son, by God, a son like a son should be. A Doberdò with the blood of the Doberdòs!"

"O Jesus, what blasphemies!" and the Monsignor, without drying himself, got dressed with his hands trembling on his buttons, while the other man kept yelling: "My blood, and it's not senile! You're senile! My wife's senile! And you're all senile, all of you!"

"O Jesus, what have I done?" and tears of vexation came into his eyes.

"My blood, which has its rights, and you priests have weakened it, you whores of society, yes, whores and you know it, but you joke and laugh at us, and you go into our houses –"

"A little respect, Mr. Doberdò, for a priest, at least that…" and confound those buttons which made him stay there, knotted up with anger and fear under that avalanche of insults and shouts.

"And don't feel sorry for them! Feel sorry for a poor girl who has suffered and who's never done anything wrong to anyone! Who's not robbed like so many of you have, who are on my back like leeches. You've been taking advantage of me and now you want me out of the way!" It wasn't a shout any more, but more like a death rattle.

Finally Martinolli got his cassock buttoned, and, shaking the handle of the door, he summoned up that last bit of courage which precedes a flight. Opening the door, he shouted: "So you won't listen to reason! I'll tell everyone you're declaring war on 'em all!"

"Get the hell out of here!"

"And you know what I say to you?"

"What?" thundered Doberdò.

Martinolli got one final inspiration: "Nothing!" he shouted, slamming the door, and the alarmed young priest saw the Monsignor come out of the lodge with his cassock half unbuttoned, his shoes unlaced, and his face purple.

"Away from here!" shouted Martinolli. "Let's go!" while Doberdò's invective was still coming from the wide-open door: "And you just tell my wife that that's enough from her too! Tell her to stop harassing me, and everyone else!"

Doberdò fell to his knees on the wooden platform with his hands waving in front of the wall, and he stayed there until his headache passed, and his breath came short, like that of a drowning man...

CHAPTER FIFTEEN

He heard the car door slam and the Monsignor's automobile skid on the gravel as it fled toward the city. There was a silence around him and only the sound of the shower – those drops which were gradually petering out pouring onto his bent head, while the blood flowed back into his veins and his mind came out of its fog – gave him the measure of his return to things as they were, as a sound can give a sense of revival.

He got up and dressed, and when he came out of the shower room into the light it was very much like an awakening. He had a clarity of thought and a repose of the senses after that last trauma such as he got when he emerged into the light of day from the tormented shadows of a state of drowsiness. And now he was judging himself, half closing his eyes against the shimmering noonday sun, with that unemotional objectivity which can be attributed to another; it was as if a different man were walking among the broken walls and over the frozen ground. Under that sky which seemed extraordinarily high to him, it was another man who said, with his slow, intense breathing, not "I'm alive!" but "I'm myself!"

"I'm myself and I can do what's right and what I have to!" just as a people can dictate its aims in the heart of a revolt without any possibility of turning back. He was happy because the words which had surged forth in anger now came back to his lips, humble and perceptive. They were words he had long held in his heart without thinking about them and which made him realize that these recent revelations of life, its shocks, and his own now distant fear of death, had not been repetitions of something which had gone before, but part of a long period of waiting to live again, as he should, as he had to.

The hills, silhouetted by the light of that late morning, sunken in the cold shadow of the clouds which were rising against the city, were getting steadily darker. And he was thinking: To go there and live like a sheik with Califfa, to have a son who for all his life would have not only his mother's good looks but also the intoxication he was experiencing at that moment, the tranquillity of spirit, the freedom from shame inspired by petty convention, and the desire to assert himself. And that was not all. He was thinking of a son with the same newfound awareness of the mistakes he would not make any more and the things he would do, the things which allow a man never to feel shame any more.

And he was reflecting on the things in his life which did not belong to him alone. He was thinking of his factories, his workers and their families, and the crowded canvas of men and women whom he had involved in his affairs, creating personal feelings and personal egoisms with their lack of awareness. And he felt their passions and feelings within himself, incensed at his useless career and at the grandeur of his empty name, which had reverberated all those months with the bitter echoes of an immense emptiness.

The light now was steadily giving way to the shadow of the rising clouds. The shadow was running over the fields and the city while he was counting up the things he still had to do – many things, too many things, with an order to be reestablished within himself and outside himself. And he looked like Christ on the point of going back to his people, a Christ Who was thirty-three years old, Who had no more time to wait, Who was only disappointed that he had not gotten up earlier. But he was a Christ Who was not to die on the cross, and he was free of self-pity; because that was enough of pity. Now he understood that life was just an affirmation of that egoism which is based on rights, ours and others', happiness, pleasure, and revenge when they are based on rights.

He had a storm of ideas and a happiness for having begun his Sunday with such consoling violence, while the shadow

194

of the storm was running over him and the first drops were falling on his hunting beret without his noticing. And what could they do to him, the Gazzas and his vassals, or even Clementina, if he continued to be so sure of himself? He was himself and he was alive, conscious of his power, of the decisive importance of a yes or no from him. A Doberdò who was strong for having finally realized what he should be like and for having tired of his own weakness. He was made strong by love, by a name, by a face which he saw the following morning as he began his busy Monday in a photograph which he drew from his pocket.

II

He passed the sleeve of his jacket over the glass, before he put the picture on his desk between the blotter and his memo pad, turning it around in the light so that the shining black of those eyes overcame the reflections in the glass. From then on Califfa's picture would stare at anyone coming into the room, with her ardent but uncertain eyes in which the world and life were revealed. And Annibale, between her picture and the other of his father at the opposite angle of his desk, leaned back in his leather armchair. The far-off years fueled the flames of his rediscovered ardor, extended the boundaries of his imagination and revitalized his blood, his mind, and his hands.

Annibale Doberdò was a boy between his love for his father and the love of his first love, a man with the hot blood of a boy, as Gazza came in, announced by a bare wink of the light, one so short that the secretaries looked at each other open-mouthed. With astonishment which made sweat drip down his forehead and along his nose imprisoned by his glasses, Gazza was face to face with him, staring at him, judging him, disarming him.

Another die was cast, Gazza thought, and he sat down stammering a *good morning*. Doberdò had not even raised his eyes and he continued to play with a pencil between his

195

fingers. Gazza took a bundle of newspapers, selected the *Corriere della Sera,* and opened it. But Doberdò interrupted him:

"Listen, my dear friend, today I don't want to talk about politics. There's always time for politics!"

"But, Mr. Doberdò, there's an editorial on foreign policy which is particularly interesting. I would even say – "

"Forget about foreign policy, please. Just listen to me! How long have we known each other?"

Gazza was as alert as a tomcat prowling in the night. "I don't understand why you're asking me, Mr. Doberdò, but it's been many years. It's as if we'd always known each other... it seems to me!"

"You're right. It's just as if we'd always known each other, and never have we once looked each other in the eye the way we are now, to tell ourselves the truth frankly."

Doberdò's face, for Gazza, was the face of an enemy. And it was as if they were looking at each other from two opposing trenches with that huge desk between them. Gazza, looking at Doberdò's bronzed skin reddened under the eyes, with its little wrinkles of old age, was experiencing the same discomfort, the same fear that anything at all might happen, which he had felt many years before in Albania when he had been taken prisoner and first found himself face to face with a rebel. Now he had Califfa and Doberdò's father smiling at him from the desk and he had the same fear of exposing himself. This time there was no escape for Gazza in the soldier's code of honor. "Excuse me, but I still don't understand," he said.

"For so many years," Doberdò went on, "without ever having spoken to one another the way each of us would have wanted... You, without ever admitting your boredom, or your ironic contempt for your boss – "

"But what are you talking about? This is absurd!" Gazza interrupted him.

"Let me talk!... And I with the sadness I feel at having to play your game and sit there talking with you about things you don't believe in!"

Gazza got up from his chair. The room was yellow and then green in his eyes and his head was spinning.

"Stay in your chair, please!" Doberdò said to him. "Part of your job is to sit quietly and listen to me. I pay you for that too!"

"Mr. Doberdò, I won't tolerate – "

"What!" shouted Doberdò, and the secretaries in the other room looked at each other again. "You've spent your life tolerating things, you're a professional tolerator, with a tolerance equal to half a million lire a month! And now you won't put up with it!"

"Mr. Doberdò," sobbed Gazza, going back to his chair, and he spun around like a drowning man in an unexpected wave.

"We've put up with each other," Doberdò went on. "But why? What for? We've put up with each other with hate, weariness, contempt, and boredom! And neither of us has had the guts to say *go to hell!* Why?"

"Mr. Doberdò," Gazza was able to stammer, "Mr. Doberdò – to attack me like that all of a sudden on a fine morning, you know it's not fair..."

"So that my offices are filled up with this influence peddling, because there are a thousand things which aren't going right, to cover up things we shouldn't cover up, to prevent even religion from becoming a lot of nonsense!" Doberdò was at ease as he relieved himself of those thoughts; it was not like the day before with Martinolli. He looked straight in front of himself as he talked beyond Gazza. "Sorry, I'm not really angry at you personally, but you just irritate me the way everyone else does. I'm just mad at myself for having listened to you, for pretending to take you so seriously!"

"That's enough, Mr. Doberdò, please! You have no right to insult me this way. I have some self-respect too!"

"Your dignity consists in listening to me, and dirty politics... And now listen! You can do your dirty politics later!"

Gazza got up again and, standing straight in front of Doberdò, gathered together his dispersed forces. "I think you're just getting something off your chest, Mr. Doberdò, just that. And that's no reason for someone who has nothing to get off his chest to put his cards on the table."

"I'm perfectly calm, dear Gazza, and you're wrong. And if

you have some cards to show me, show them to me, finally, for God's sake!"

Gazza hesitated. "I say you can't beat me the way you beat the others, like – like Pedrelli, like Mastrangelo, or Farinacci! After all I've done for you, Mr. Doberdò…"

"And what difference does it make? You're all afraid – you to discover what you aren't, Pedrelli to find out what he is, and Mastrangelo what he's tried to be!"

"That's just playing on words, if you'll allow me!"

"Playing on words or not, dear Gazza, from now on I want to change things around here. That's all I wanted to say!"

Gazza took a step toward the door. "Change? In what way?"

"Just that I want to do things my way, just my way! I say enough of this favoritism in which you're such an expert, enough of your little *mafia*! I don't want any more useless people around me! Chair-warmers! Boot-lickers! Pimps! Change in the sense that I'm going to clean things up and I'll consider only how good a man is, not how pliable!"

With his face twisted and his eyes wet with tears, Gazza got to the door. "Mr. Doberdò! Mr. Doberdò, this is – "

"And the change is that I'm going to do whatever I feel like! And if there's a scandal, that's just fine! I'll throw the scandal in all your faces!"

"You're mad!" Gazza finally was able to shout, slamming the door, while the stockbroker, who had sweated and trembled up to that moment, had not the strength to take a step when the red light went on, inviting him into Doberdò's office. He stood there with his legs trembling, looking in horror at Gazza, who was running down the steps shouting: "This is unheard of! Simply unheard of!"

And the new Doberdò who had dared to treat him like that, a Doberdò who now at the first appearance of the broker's bald head, when he stammered "Excuse me, Mr. Doberdò, shall we postpone it?" turned three-quarters around in his chair and said peremptorily: "And as for you, smile, for goodness sake! Smile because I want happy people around me, not mourners following a hearse like you! You look as if there's a death in your family every day! Smile, wipe that expression off your face, or I'll fire you!" A Doberdò like that was a Doberdò who demanded a lot.

Gazza went into a cafe, put a token into a public telephone, and dialed a number, and it was as if someone were tickling him, his arm was so agitated. The blood had gone to his head, and when the telephone was answered, a fit of frightened silence took over. He leaned his hand on the wall before begging in a quaking voice: "I'd like to speak to the Countess, and please hurry!"

"You did well to call me," said Clementina. "If you hadn't, I would have called you. Is four o'clock all right with you? Four o'clock at my house; don Martinolli will be there too."

"He simply blew up, Countess," sobbed Gazza. "He just blew up in my face, after everything I did for him, and you know, after all the dedication I put in, all the years I devoted to building up his name –"

"Calm down, now."

"Insulting me like that…"

"I apologize for him and I'll expect you at four. We'll take care of everything, you'll see. We'll know how to handle him; it was just a temper tantrum!"

"I still have hours to wait," thought Gazza as he looked at his watch, and he could hardly contain himself, because he wanted Clementina there right then, in front of him, listening to him unburdening himself, and not only with words, but with certain support from Chief Mazzullo, to make Doberdò beg pardon on his knees and kiss his feet.

Gazza went off to his house, to the camomile tea his wife would prepare for him. Martinolli's church clock struck one and the sirens of the factories sounded over the city.

III

And Doberdò's office emptied out. Even his secretary, who usually waited for him to go before she went home, had gone. But Doberdò had invited her to precede him, and after that exciting morning she had not dared to observe the usual routine of false courtesy.

Doberdò was happy to be alone with great numbers of clouds in the sky visible from his window. He looked around him as if to seek one last suggestion about the remaining decisions to be taken that day, on that battlefield which he had seen revealed in front of him and which involved him in new problems. After Gazza and the broker had come his son's tutor and the doctor.

He had been explicit with the tutor: "Flunk him! Throw him out, if that's the right thing to do. And if he has snot on his nose, just tell him so in words of one syllable! Don't beat him like my son, beat him like all the others, that's your job!"

"But I thought..." stammered the tutor, fearing to lose the extra income which for some years had been allowing him seaside vacations.

"If that's what you're worried about, forget it. You'll be paid. Not as compensation, but as a present, if you don't do your job! But what I want is for my son not to have any special treatment. That's bad for him!"

And as for the doctor, he did not even want to see him. He had postponed it, telling him to come by the next day, or the day after, as he liked. He did not need doctors any more, did Annibale Doberdò. He was in perfect health. He had never felt so well, and he had never felt so much like moving about. He was a man in perfect shape who was excellently prepared for the new tasks which awaited him, with a sanity which derived from his newly found common sense – the most aggressive and optimistic sanity.

And all this gave him a sense of well-being, the same as the day before, which continued and thus convinced him that it was no longer a passing state of mind, but a permanent condition. Maybe it took many years and too many mistakes, he thought, before he could come to deserve something really worthwhile.

In the silence around him, after so many words, having put away the uniform of his own and everyone else's executioner, he stretched out his legs under the table, leaned back in his chair, and looked in the telephone book for the number of a restaurant in the center of town. He asked about the quality of the wine, and ordered a complete dinner. And he left instructions to deliver everything to Califfa's house, and then he telephoned her too, to tell her that he wanted a party that night.

It was a call carried out in a low voice, as if someone could have listened to him in the silence of that great building, with the photograph in front of him which meant so much. Yes, he was born again, and nothing more prevented his being the boy with the red skin brought back to where he had started, after a long mistaken journey.

And that was what he was like and that was what he was planning to do. The mistakes remained by the side of the road where he had passed. He leaned back in his chair again, to look through the window at the city basking lazily in the sun of the early afternoon...

IV

It was already night and from the river a thin winter moon, rising into the clear cold atmosphere, cast a reflection on the still waters on which also were playing the reflections of the façades of the old houses on the opposite shore, when Doberdò, getting out of the car with his arms loaded with packages and bottles, looked at what seemed to him to be other, hostile bundles visible between the buildings across the river and at the little squares veiled in the night. Dismissing his chauffeur, Doberdò leaned on the back seat and bent his head in a sudden fit of exhaustion which came like a dash of cold water on the expectation which had kept him warm all day, and now that he saw Califfa's window lighted on the balcony, he felt faint.

He held on tightly to the packages in his arms, and that was enough for him to regain his bearings and see the deserted street and the dark of the river where the muffled water sounded forth. Its nostalgic presence was clearly brought to Doberdò in that night, with no other voice or sound, in which he was thoroughly caught up. Then he crossed the street and went up to the warm room, and shook the sleep out of his tired limbs and blood. Califfa had never seen him like that before. He looked twenty years younger and his erect head was trying not to lose its arrogant touch, with his shining eyes and rosy cheeks. He was dying to talk and to walk around, to touch her, as if that evening were the first time, or as if he had come back from a long trip.

Califfa said it was strange, because they had seen each other only the night before, and Doberdò answered her: "Let me be, if I feel like it, if I feel better, Califfa…"

They must have heard us from the street. We were laughing, and I was gayer than he was and we were both very loud. And we were so loud that someone from upstairs telephoned to complain. And what did he do then, with all that wine in him, which made him nasty – and he'd always been such a gentleman? As if he were waiting for a reason to tell that man what he wanted to say to me, he told him right off to go back to bed and not to make any more noise. And he said he was going to buy that building and so they'd better shut up! And he was serious. He put down the telephone and turned the record player up. And he tells me he really will buy the building and leave it to me in his will. And so I'll be an owner myself, he says, and he'll come live with me, away from all the troubles in his own house, away from all those things that'll kill him if they keep up.

And then, even though it took a long time, he finally understood that you should accept certain changes in your life if you're lucky enough to have them. Didn't I think like that too? Wasn't I the one to teach him that sometimes there's nothing to be done about it because that's the way it is? I was so surprised I couldn't think of a thing to say. And what could I have said? It's the wine, I told him, it's the wine and then anyway I am what I am. After all, couldn't he see me, a poor girl, and just imagine whether I deserved that? Me… and then with him so important and all… He wouldn't let me finish.

What did I mean, a poor little girl? He tells me I shouldn't cover myself with humility, and that was enough of this poor-little-girl business, that now I had all I wanted and he was with me. It was time for a change and time I learned to give myself more importance even when we're together. If not, he might think I hadn't understood a thing and still didn't understand, and if that's the way it was, goodbye... In other words, he made my head spin with all that talk. And I was like a dope as I let him kiss me and hold me close and repeat that he thinks of me as a lady and maybe even his wife. Yes, why not, what's wrong with that? Poor man, it made my heart melt to see him with those shiny eyes. He was so anxious to please me. And maybe he was telling the truth, about his loving me; maybe he was really crazy enough to come live there with me in that little apartment, to ruin himself once and for all by living up to his feelings...

But Califfa doesn't want to talk about that night ever again, because there are times when words help me even less than usual. They just get me mad, and they take away from the few nice memories I have left. That's what happens to me when I think how happy we were that night, and I feel it pulling me here, as if there was a hand squeezing me, even if I've thought about it a lot and even if I'm still thinking about it until I'm almost crazy, until I feel my head bursting open and I have to say that's enough! enough! – enough of everything, even all this talk! That was the last happy night of my life and it was like a miracle. And that's enough of that!

Califfa recalled Doberdò in his shirt sleeves as he was when he got up. His head, shining with sweat, was turning around under the light of the lamp, acquiring familiarity with those rooms which were to be the witness of their daily life from then on. He was half closing his eyes, shrewd and infantile at the same time, as he always was when he wanted to gather to himself the exact flavor of his happiness, and he was talking to Califfa about furniture and about how they would go shopping for it, and how they would arrange it, a bureau here, a table there, and a double bed in the biggest room. "Califfa, what are you thinking? But can you see all the problems we'll have, like two newlyweds?" And he laughed again.

And when he had finished eating, he pushed the plate from him, just a little more slowly in his euphoria, as if it had cost him a light struggle to get up from the chair and go to the window to open it. The night air came over him; he took a deep breath of it and for a moment he remained with his head on his chest like one who is coming from the water and needs air, while Califfa came up to him. Then he turned his gaze to the point where the dark of the night made the lights on the hills tremble in the veil of distance, and he pointed out to Califfa the place where he was born, by the farthest visible bend of the river.

He would have liked to see the hills every morning, and the fields, and the road so fragrant in spring and summer. There wasn't any fragrance at all where he was living, he said, and you couldn't see any trees. How could you with those high walls which kept out the sun, and those plants, which were as constipated as the people around him?

Then he took me back in from the balcony. And he began holding my arms to make me understand that it wasn't all there. He said to me: "That's not enough Califfa, that's not enough!" He tried to tell me, as if I didn't already understand, and he told me that it wasn't only the effect of that evening, or a passing fancy. So if I wanted another proof that he was serious about certain things and that I was talking to a man who really wanted to remake his life, no matter what, he'd give it to me that evening, all I had to do was say the word. And he was inviting me not to take any precautions that time; and if a son were to come, hurrah, because he wanted a son from me, he wanted one and claimed one – a son like the one we could make together, healthy, rich, with plenty of potential, by God, so that the others would take their hats off when they saw him, and treat him like a gentleman with all the rights of one!

They threw themselves on the bed and Califfa was so eager as she took off her dress, and as she hugged him and sought him, that she thought she was ready to have his son, a child as handsome as a god. And she was thinking of him in the great flood of thoughts which accompanied her pleasure, and how he would be born and live. And for this reason she tried to enjoy it in every fiber of her being and to be completely happy, because this was how she thought she could make her son handsomer, stronger and freer. And she would call him Attilio, as she had her first son who died, and she would fight against everyone, so that he would not have to be ashamed of her, or the way she had had him. In this gritting of her teeth, there was her desperate desire to scratch with her fingernails as if she were fighting for her life. And meanwhile she was praying: "O God, just let him come, let me feel the warmth of his body, please God!" She had always been ashamed to pray, but not at that moment.

And her prayer was part of her swift course to a new life, and for that reason Califfa, like any satisfied woman, wanted it to end only when she was again on that bed. And she found him a real man that night, something he had never been before, and this had nothing to do with his ego as a lover, but with his hope for that son. And when they came apart, they became aware of the cold which was coming in from the open window, and of the late hour.

Califfa went to close the window and Doberdò's shadow moved about as he sought calm in his sleep, in the dark around the bed, but still with enough energy to say almost angrily to her: "And this time it'll have to be a Doberdò, by God, a real Doberdò, even if he's as red as I was!"

With her forehead on the windowpane, Califfa had stopped to look at the night and the sky whitened by a veil of distant stars, and the houses with their usual lighted windows in the area she came from. She cried again, but she did not turn around, so that he would not see her tears.

And she recalled her mother, her dead son, and even Guido, all the people with whom she had not been able to be happy. She would have to be happy for them too, her success in life would make up for their failures, and it seemed to her that they were the ones who wanted her in that new existence. For this reason, she thought that even in the dreariest of days to come she could not help but feel that consolation which makes up for everything. She saw them as if they were all alive again, with their own ways of looking at her and of pitying her with a glance, even when she was wrong. She wept for the pity they had been able to give her, perhaps because, for too short a time, they had loved her.

"And if he isn't conceived this time, he'll be conceived tomorrow, in a month, but he will be conceived, by God!" Doberdò repeated, and she continued to look at that great sky above her house, that witness-bearing sky.

V

It was far into the night when Annibale Doberdò left Califfa's house and stopped at the entry stairway to observe the city between the black lines of the plane trees, with the lights of his factories guarding it. The shining profile of the roofs marked the boundary between the city and the sky; and Doberdò took a deep breath of that air which had a smell in it of coming snow, and of the dead land. He pulled his overcoat about him. The chauffeur had fallen asleep in the Mercedes and Doberdò, who had called him more than an hour ago, apologized as he got in, while the other man raised his head and composed himself.

But Doberdò did not want to go home right away.

"Would you mind if we went for a drive?" he said "Just for a quarter of an hour, to get a little fresh air..."

The chauffeur, who for years had not been used to such courtesy, looked at Doberdò in the rear-view mirror as he set off for the country. "If you like, sir. It is a nice night."

His legs wide apart, his arms stretched out on the back seat, in the breeze which blew his scarf into his face, Doberdò was experiencing the languor of the adolescent who unconsciously enjoys being half asleep. And in that ride through the sweet and humid nocturnal city he was still enjoying the victory of a man who has done it once again and succeeded in the field in which he is most interested.

Doberdò felt the peace and elation of a successful lover, and now he had everything. He looked at his hands on the plush upholstery, his body wrapped up in the overcoat, and he had some esteem for himself, and pride for what he recalled, for the whispered words, and for the kisses – which weren't pretexts any more, but expressions of desire. There was a weak but bitter fever nesting far off in his heart, present as was that pale moon shining on the fields from which arose nocturnal humors.

He wanted to speak, to let himself go. And how different this was from the other times when he went back, disturbed, wanting only to sleep, to cancel his bitterness as soon as possible with slumber, as he came from Califfa's house, humiliated at what he had not been able to give her, an accomplice in a silly farce.

But not this time. Holding his head high and enjoying the air which was coming at him, stripping his nerves naked, clearing the ashes away from his embers, he wanted his nighttime ride to go on forever. The Mercedes proceeded between high walls, through the silence of the factories, and Doberdò indicated with a signal which street, now passing in front of his offices, now going to the suburbs where the houses were fewer and farther between and where the lights on the roads over the hills could be seen.

And he was noticing that his chauffeur had gotten thinner and older; and only now was he seeing that there was much less hair around that absorbed and immobile face reflected in the windshield. Only now did he notice those dry hands trembling on the steering wheel. These were signs of the years passed in mute association, distant, without a glance at each other or one word outside the routine. He, his chauffeur, the most faithful of them all and the one he had most ignored.

"How old are you?" he asked almost involuntarily, and a little painfully. His voice filled the car and changed the silence into cordial expectation.

"Sixty, Mr. Doberdò."

"And your children?"

The chauffeur hesitated. He turned to stare at Doberdò, the shimmering form of his face and that shadow at his shoulders. "The oldest one's just out of high school, sir. I'd like to send him to college. If he can't get to college, it would be such a waste, because he's intelligent and loves to study, but me – I mean, how can I help him? Do you remember him, sir?"

Yes, Doberdò remembered his chauffeur's son, and so many other things. It was as if his mind were bubbling over with a violent synthesis of emotion and memories. Perhaps because if he turned his head to one side he could see the countryside where he grew up, white with frost, and on the other side a new profile of the city, its great shadow flanked by the chimneys of his factories. Above him a bank of clouds was passing rapidly by, briefly connecting those fields which had seen him as a boy and that stricken ship cut adrift which was the city he dominated.

"Come see me tomorrow," said Doberdò. "Let's see what we can do for this genius."

The chauffeur could see him putting his legs in a more comfortable position, rearranging his head as if he wanted to sleep. "Thank you, sir," he said.

"For what?" murmured Doberdò before closing his eyes, finally placated, and he murmured other words, which the chauffeur didn't understand, before he heard "... because the important thing is not to feel all alone... the important thing is to see that you aren't alone..."

Doberdò saw Califfa saying those words, before he saw nothing more. He remembered Califfa as he had left her at the top of the stairs, her hands on the railing, smiling at him.

The chauffeur thought Doberdò was a worthy man, much more than people said, and he loved him at that moment, while the car was leaving the fields behind, in the lazy dust which was rising up among the naked pines, on its way to the city.

In front of Doberdò's house, the chauffeur opened the door: "Mr. Doberdò..." he said. "Mr. Doberdò!" and he touched Doberdò on the shoulder to awaken him. But that huge head, fit for a Cardinal, did not move; it stayed where it was, leaning back on the blue plush with the mouth open. And only the jeweled hand slid along the back, to strike inert, lifeless, on the seat...

EPILOGUE

The crowd invaded the street and it was as if the city had acquired another atmosphere, a feverish stupor which had paralyzed it but also made it more aware of what was going on, in that quiet flow of people from the bridges to the Doberdò mansion, in that fluctuating mixture of the rich and the poor, the mourners and the disenchanted. The people came from the tenements, from the polite bourgeois streets, from the suburbs and from the country, and meanwhile Palazzo Doberdò, with all the windows closed and the curtains drawn in front of the balconies an with an air of solemn abandonment, appeared larger and more aggressive, an aggressive heart of cement and marble which had stopped, within the city, like that of its master, and to which the crowd bore witness, flowing in ever different streams, like the fast spurt of lifeless blood.

And above, the white light of the coming sunset hushed the city, and below there was only the rustling of steps to be heard, coming in waves around the bends in the deserted streets when the cortege moved forward after a long pause in front of the door; and, quarter by quarter, the city began to strip from itself that part which was too vital, and that name which was so well known that those who had not gone down into the street filled the windows and the balconies, immobile in that strange light which comes at dawn or dusk, which made emotions deeper. It was as if the expectation also belonged to that countryside veiled in fog, where the chimneys were smoking and the houses in the country had already lit their lights, and the passage of the hearse which was squeaking along the ill-laid stones bore witness to something much greater than man, as happens before every natural catastrophe.

Or at least this was what everyone thought. Certainly that funeral cortege left a mark on the emotion-stricken faces as it passed by, a last heavy stroke of power and death. And many, seeing that coffin inside the glass, felt the same sensation of enduring power they had received from Doberdò. It was as if they were taking away a dying man, who could still attract people to himself with the fatal light of his eyes, just as he was about to expire.

Califfa was the only one who did not see all this. She was not present, because she was hiding in a corner behind the closed shutters of the balcony window. She would have liked to shout, throw open the windows, rush down into the street like a madwoman, for the last gasp of her pain which by now was almost spent. But she had not even the courage to show herself, seeing only between the slats of the shutters the waving veils and the jackets of that funeral procession which had proclaimed itself slow and inevitable *ad nauseam*. But to shame and modesty was also added the absurd egotism of sadness when all hope has gone, and it seemed to her that the image of Annibale Doberdò, whom the great city was carrying to its edge, was more hers in the suffocating shadow of the room.

More hers for the things which surrounded her and which existed mostly as a function of his life, until the last evening: Annibale's pajamas on the chair, the pillow on the left side of the bed which she had not touched and which, as she looked, reminded her again of his heavy head whose mark was still there. Over these things were passing the continuous sounds of the steps, the shadow of the cortege, the murmur of voices, while Annibale's words came back to her, the words he had told her the day they fled into the country.

"The important thing is to be alive, Califfa, alive!" But that hearse was taking him away, more and more into the distance, to the country road which she had come to know so well, with a bevy of flags behind, then Gazza, Farinacci,

Mastrangelo, Pedrelli, and especially Martinolli, stuck on to the back of the hearse in front of all the others. And when the procession passed under Califfa's window, it was as if he swayed. Martinolli interrupted the pious cadence of his feet and turned his glance instinctively to that balcony crowded with dried-up flowers, so that the head of the line of march wavered slightly but perceptibly, something entirely out of place in a procession of that kind. But it continued immediately in a more orderly manner.

Gazza and Martinolli were the ones to pronounce the funeral oration. Gazza came forward, in the light fog, into the clearing in the crowd, more bent than usual around the shoulders, and when he turned, he stared at Clementina.

And he succeeded in pushing visible tears onto his cheeks. A few tears stayed on his glasses so that he had to take them off and polish them with a handkerchief, interrupting his speech. It was a shrewdly staged interruption, the trick of a born actor, and he had the whole crowd hanging on his words before his grand finale.

"And so we will keep him ever present in our hearts!" concluded Gazza, who went back to his place with bowed head, while Martinolli came forward in his turn, wrapped in that melancholy disinterest for the affairs of men and for this life with which, on certain solemn occasions, he was able to confer an air of imposing wisdom on his body, making it seem an unavoidable weight carried along only reluctantly.

"Never," he said, "have we heard anything from him that was not full of charity and comfort. Never have we seen a gesture of his that was not one of help to those in need, one of trust and hope... We who have had the great privilege of being near him in life, of being direct witnesses to his profound faith as a practicing Christian, as a man of the Church as well as an industrialist, we who have loved him and been loved by him, who have had the benefit of his example... we now know that from the position of the elect he looks down upon us, his favorite brothers, united here to give him a last greeting. He died in the grace of God, and his life, his success, and his fortune have left us a heritage which we must keep alive, and I say to you here on what is to be his tomb that this is his true spiritual testament. And that is to work, to struggle, so that the success of his humane qualities will be the expression of the dignity of man and therefore a barrier against misunderstanding and discord which would contaminate us, against the danger of false ideas, political lies, the deception of iniquities created just for that purpose. Let us pay homage to him" – and Martinolli's voice cracked with emotion, sounding at a higher pitch – "let us pay homage to him in this final moment, to him who has always heeded the advice of wise counselors against lies and silly sentimentality, an example of both humility and grandeur of the spirit, one for whom true justice, that which is inspired by the will of God, and just actions among men have always triumphed, in his factories as in his heart, in his heart as in his family relationships. Thanks be to Thee, o Lord," shouted Martinolli, kneeling in the gravel beside his little monument, immediately followed by the others, "for having given us such an example of Thy grandeur in Thy subject whom we have loved like a brother, and who now, we are certain, sits in glory at Thy right hand!"

The gravel scratched under the bended knees; the crowd descended onto the tufts of grass and the Bishop's words of prayer lost themselves over the extended heads bent in final tribute in the foggy night which by then had fallen. "Give us other brothers like him, we pray, who can defend us from evil! Amen!"

II

But Califfa went alone to see him. She knew that the best and most honest way of paying her respect to him was to do as she did. She sat by him, and fixing in her mind the kindly face in the photograph on the tomb, she talked to him under her breath, smiling, free from the conventions even about death, as if nothing had happened. It was as if they were still together in the room and Doberdò had come up to see her after a day's work.

They were close in that moment even if he was dead and she alive, because she understood what he meant by the phrase: "The important thing is to be alive, Califfa, alive!" And they were neither divided nor alone that afternoon, amid all those funeral wreaths which were already beginning to rot. She held tight onto that dry earth in her fists, as if she had his hand in hers, his round hand like a country priest's... And she let her smooth white knee be exposed, because he had liked to stare at it when she wasn't looking and she pretended not to notice. Her bare knee was laughing at death, as she had laughed at life with him, although with love, not contempt.

She did not shed a single tear for Annibale Doberdò because it was better that way. But as she left his tomb, so large, strong, and rich, it brought to mind what he had been like in life. There was a good deal of brown earth around, and as she looked at it, it seemed to her to have his spirit. And she remembered the first words he had said to her after they met: "Califfa? But what sort of name is that?" and she had thought back to herself in pigtails, when her name, Irene, sounding strange to her then after what was already a long period of disuse, was beginning to change into something else. She was already mysterious and seductive, promising so much with those great eyes and that impetuous little body, where one could see what legs and breasts were going to develop. Irene, as a little girl, with all those boys following her, led them with crude tenderness through the tenement districts and became the sheik or caliph of that little band of street Arabs, so they called her Califfa. But in the laughter with which the others had dubbed her Califfa was contained the bitterness of those who knew what a beast beauty can be, in those neighborhoods where shadows are only a natural pitiful sign of mercy which prevent the exposure of life's hardships to the light of day.

And, in fact, life was hard all around her at this moment, whether on the poor side of the river or in the circles of the rich. So she went toward the gate, proceeded along the city wall, and resisted the temptation to look back along the street which led to town. Even in winter it was so wide out there in the middle of the country that it had its own joyousness in light.

Only Gazza came to see her at the apartment which was to be hers no longer. He discovered her packing her bags, putting into her suitcase those four rags with which she had come, not touching any of the rest, not even an ashtray.

Seeing the suitcase open on the bed, Gazza bent his head. All he was able to say was that she had already seen much of life, so that she could accept the worst it could present her without there being much need of words. Then he asked her: "And what will you do now? Where will you go?"

Califfa continued to pack her bags without answering him.

Then Gazza pointed his professorial glasses at her: "You know," he continued, "we cannot conceal from ourselves the fact that he has left us a heavy legacy, I would say even an incredible one, an unbearable one. But I want you to know that we have faith and that our shoulders will be strong, capable of bearing this new burden, in his name."

There was a photograph of Doberdò on the bureau. When Califfa took it and put it into her suitcase, Gazza averted his gaze. There was also the new shiny record player nearby, her favorite of all his gifts to her. She passed her fingers over it, but left it where it was.

"Well, don't you have anything to say to me at all?" insisted Gazza.

Califfa looked at him. He was sitting on the edge of the bed, always with that air of a spy about him, as if he were about to unmask himself and beg pardon. She did not understand him. She had never succeeded in understanding him.

"Why are you telling me these things?" she said to him. "What difference does it make what I think about them?"

Gazza bent his head and said softly: "Life is hell, Mrs. Corsini, life is hell."

He stopped. He seemed quite moved.

"And did you come here to tell me that?" she answered. "I've learned that, and how, and you know it. You've found out about everything, haven't you?"

"Yes," said Gazza.

But Califfa did not feel any rancor for him. There was something in that room so bare of her usual things, something which was preventing her from hating him any more, even if she could detect the smell of his clothes and his skin so well.

"I never did like you, Mrs. Corsini," Gazza said suddenly. "I felt an antipathy which I have learned to feel over so many years, a professional antipathy…"

"Don't take it so hard," Califfa answered. "You'll have much worse things you'll have to confess."

He didn't answer. But he said: "Do you know why I've come here tonight?"

"No, but I can guess!"

"Just to say this to you. That I disliked you as soon as I laid eyes on you, that I wanted to get back at you for that time on the banks of the Po, that I hoped he'd throw you out the way he did the others. But he loved you… very much."

"Since you've said you don't like me, what's the good of saying it again?"

He stared at her once more. "You don't understand me. I've come to tell you these things in another way, to confess them to you, with that pity we feel for each other."

The room had grown dark. Lights were coming on along the avenue outside.

"You don't believe me, do you?" he continued. "You're quite right not to believe me, but that's the way it is. This has never happened to me before, but I want to apologize. And I'm not trying to get your sympathy. Because I'm apologizing just because I can't do anything else – with the same coldness, I might say even with the same cynicism with which I would or could insult you."

The suitcase was packed on the bed, near him. All that remained for Califfa to do was to look over the room for the last time, give the keys to the superintendent, and go.

215

Gazza got up, took the suitcase, and went off to the door. Califfa looked at the bed and the curtained windows, which were closed and locked.

It was a night in February, biting cold, but she did not feel chilly; and far from disappointment or regret in going down those stairs, she felt a desire to finish the steps in a hurry, to leave the building behind her. Gazza had telephoned for a taxi. While they waited for it down in the street, he said a few more things to her:

"When you think of me and other people you came to know in these circles, try not to detest us too much. We didn't make the world, and if it's true that life is hell, it's only fair that there be devils in it." He smiled, throwing his scarf over his mouth, and concluded: "Because if a saint is to be born, we'll get some of the credit, because we're in the picture too."

The taxi still did not come. Califfa was looking at her suitcase, tied up with a piece of rope. Then she turned her head to look at her darkened window. The geranium plants were on the balcony along with the straw chairs. In front of her was the frontier of the lights in her part of town – like a far-off country to which she was about to return after a long absence, with the necessity of giving up certain attitudes, a certain way of looking at life, with a sense of distance, of things to be found again, and of persons among whom she would live again.

The lights of the taxi appeared around the street. Gazza bestirred himself. He moved his hands as if to say still another thing before they parted company. He turned to her, opened his mouth, and looked at her. But only when the taxi stopped in front of them and the driver had taken the suitcase was he able to say hurriedly, in the authoritative tone with which she had heard him bring up many other kinds of requests: "I'd like us to part company with a handshake!"

The car started off, and he said, "A handshake!" almost running, "A handshake, Mrs. Corsini…" and he waved his hand in front of the window. And Califfa put her hand out. They were able to touch the tips of each other's fingers.

Gazza stayed down there, and up above, in the window,

were her beautiful curtains and it hurt her to have to leave
them there…

IV

Califfa went back to Viola's house, put down her suitcase, and
didn't even look around. They greeted each other with a kiss on
the cheeks, but there weren't any dramatic scenes or useless tears.
It was as if they had left each other the night before, not as if it
had been many months ago. It had been many months, and an
adventure whose traces Viola noted in Califfa's involuntary
elegance, a different bearing on her part, and another way of
moving. The change was especially strong in her hair, which fell
more gracefully around her face than before, in the perfection of
her makeup, and the cut of her clothes.

And it was therefore with timidity and with proud but sad
affection that Viola led Califfa to her bed. Under the window
the bed had remained intact, with the double pillow which
Califfa liked so much. And for this reason what had at first
been only the desire to commemorate their association could
now appear to Viola herself as a presentiment.

The sheets with the embroidery, the most beautiful ones
which Viola had had from her mother in the hope of a
wedding which was stubbornly denied by the facts; the
slippers in their place, and above the bed the window through
which the cherry tree was shining with frost; the red curtain
which divided that corner of the room from the rest of it, from
the double bed where the children were already snoring with
those sighs which betrayed hopes and the first obscure
uncertainties assimilated in the day like air and sunlight –
everything was the same. Everything was exactly as it had been
before, even the water stain above the bed, just as when Califfa
had gone away.

And this rediscovery of the same order could help her, and
delude her. Because now Califfa had to take off her dress in a
hurry, because she was no longer in the luxury apartment
building on the avenue and the drafts were playing up and

down her naked skin. She could see the white of her skin in the little mirror near the head of the bed, and she could get into the bed, pulling the covers around her, falling asleep and waking up the next morning as if nothing had happened.

And even the fields, the ones visible through the window as Califfa turned her head to lean her cheek on the pillow, were the same frozen fields she had seen when she had left on the way to her new illusions.

The fiction would therefore have been perfect if it had not been for that money in her purse on top of her clothes which she put on a chair by her side, for the lack of a bureau. There was a nice pile of banknotes which swelled the purse. It was what she had saved, not stolen, money that she had taken away, day by day, from the serenity which should have been full and was not. Just as she had never allowed her face to surrender to an expression of total unwariness, so she had left in her soul a tender pettiness which was an atavistic defense.

And all that money, under that roof, could not delude anyone. It was a foreign organism and it was both handsome and monstrous. And on the first night of her return, during her troubled sleep, full of lights and shadows, and chills and fevers succeeding one another across her forehead, Califfa stretched out an arm from the bed and groped about with her hand in search of the chair and the purse. Because the confirmation of the absurd illusion which her sleepy state had been able to give her depended on what her fingers would find.

But her fingers stopped on that swollen purse, as if on the belly of a well-fed child. And then her hand slipped back, because the whiteness on the trees and on the fields was a forgotten bitter whiteness; it was the color of the new winter, which gathered her to itself in poverty.

V

Califfa kept some of the money from the envelope she gave to Viola the following day to keep in a corner of that armoire whose key Viola kept in her bosom. She took just

218

what she thought she needed to build at least a new balcony for that barn of a house which was so crooked up on the top that from a distance it looked as if it was going to roll down the hill, a miserable hiding place vulnerable to the first strong gust of wind.

"I want a big balcony," said Califfa to Cernusco, who knew about that sort of thing, "so we can sit there in the summer and enjoy the fresh air and the view of the city." And Califfa did it all for Viola, to see her eyes get bluer when she was moved, and to be able to say, if only to herself, that her stay in that house was not entirely at the expense of someone else's misery.

The walls rose higher and stronger, and from the balcony, flaming between the hanging sheets, could be seen the huge bouquets of flowers which Viola picked in the neighboring fields, because Viola loved the red of flowers so much, a red which meant life to her. It was the ardor of her inexhaustible senses; it was revolt, pride, and embittered poverty. So that the house was transformed and no one could recognize it the day after they took down the scaffolding.

Nor was it recognized by the railway men of the Apennine Express, the one which went along the Sarzana line. They knew that another run was over, and that they would have to slow down when they saw the light of Viola's house at the top of the fast hill, with Viola sitting in front and her children around her.

"Viola! Viola!" shouted the men when they saw that lantern adorning the balcony, waving from the little window. But Viola was impassive, lost in looking at the city in the luminous veil of the evening, looking down as if she were mistress of it all, with that smell of fresh paint around her.

Califfa was next to her.

"We still have a lot of life before us, don't you think?" asked Viola, if only to justify the contentment she felt in the eyes of her friend.

Califfa did not answer right away. She looked at the poor houses piled up in front of her, where misery breathed with arrogant breath. "Yes…" she said.

"We have so much to do before we die," continued Viola, "so much to say."

Califfa looked at Viola and understood the hope she was trying to transmit from the way she pronounced those words, with her hands aligned on the railing of the balcony, and her head down, removed from the illuminated background of the city, no longer as mistress of the affair, but in a way both self-confident and modest. Then Viola suddenly turned. "Because we're not useless yet," she said. "Because we still have a reason to go on, don't we, Califfa?"

They looked at each other. Viola was mirrored in Califfa. They were so united in their survival, in their unsuccessful search for faith in life and in their failures, that their comfortable situation made them smile.

"The important thing, Viola, is to be alive, alive!" said Califfa, and she understood what Annibale Doberdò had meant when he had said that; that there was a truth beyond her and Viola, which required them to be witnesses to the misery which surrounded and oppressed them, to these little sprouts of children, sown in the night, to that absence of pity, to those lights which illuminated the emptiness of the reality around their consciences.

There was the truth of being present in evil and pain, as parts of the same battered and violated body, present as others were at the frontier of hell, so that the world could change and come forth from its errors. And there was the truth of feeling united so that the new equilibrium could find a reason for its appearance, without any importance being given to the humiliations of love on the part of a poor worn-out woman whose name was Viola, or the illusions, presumptions and immense solitude of another woman whose name was Califfa.

That evening they knew that they were to wait in a unique way for revelations greater than what they would be able to offer to their feelings as lone women. They felt a different kind of love, that which is not carried out in a bed or in a rented room, which does not need a face or a name, but which requires a less violent dedication and a profounder one. It was connected, for example, with those glances which

220

wandered down over the houses of their lives and revealed their brothers below coming out of doors, bringing their chairs with them, to take a little fresh air under that high brown sky.

And for this reason, travelers coming from Emilia to the north can observe, in the air glittering with coal dust rising from the embankment, the balcony where Califfa's head of hair is to be seen above the rail. And farther on, from the curve which dominates the city, she appears bent over Viola's children seated around her.

Discover the culture and arts of Italy

ITALIAN CINEMA

Stefano Masi – Enrico Lancia
SOPHIA LOREN
(soon available)

Stefano Masi
ROBERTO BENIGNI
80 pages • US$ 17.99/£ 7.99

Fabrizio Borin
FEDERICO FELLINI
A Sentimental Journey into the Illusion and Reality of a Genius
192 pages • US$ 29.95/£ 19.95

Oreste De Fornari
SERGIO LEONE
The Great Italian Dream of Legendary America
184 pages • US$ 39.95/£ 24.95

Claudio G. Fava
ALBERTO SORDI
An American in Rome
190 pages • US$ 29.95/£ 19.95

Matilde Hochkofler
MARCELLO MASTROIANNI
The Fun of Cinema
192 pages • US$ 29.95/£ 19.95

Riccardo Ferrucci and Patrizia Turini
PAOLO AND VITTORIO TAVIANI
Poetry of the Italian Landscape
184 pages • US$ 29.95/£ 19.95

Stefano Masi and Enrico Lancia
ITALIAN MOVIE GODDESSES
Over 80 of the Greatest Women of Italian Cinema
226 pages • US$ 29.95/£ 19.95

Jean A. Gili
ITALIAN FILMMAKERS
Self Portraits: A Selection of Interviews
192 pages • US$ 24.95/£ 15.95

ITALIAN DANCE AND OPERA

Roberta Albano, Nadia Scafidi and Rita Zambon
DANCE IN ITALY
From the 18th Century to the Present Day
La Scala of Milan – San Carlo of Naples – La Fenice of Venice
192 pages • US$ 32.50/£ 19.95

Enrico Stinchelli
GREATES STARS OF THE OPERA
The Lives and Voices of Two Hundred Golden Years
224 pages • US$ 32.50/£ 19.95

COOKING ITALIAN WAY

Maria Chiara Martinelli
AL DENTE
All the Secrets of Italy's Genuine Home-Style Cooking
208 pages • US$ 29.95/£ 18.95 (P/b US$ 19.95/£ 12.95)

Paolo Scotto
WINE AND CHEESE OF ITALY
160 pages • US$ 29.95/£ 14.95

ITALIAN (AND AMERICAN...) CATS!

Grazia Valci
OBEY YOUR CAT
(soon available)

Grazia Valci
WHAT DID THE CAT SAY?
Your Complete "Cat Talk"
Dictionary and Phrasebook
120 pages • US$ 12.95/£ 7.99